Coming Down

Carrie Elks

Coming Down by Carrie Elks

Copyright © 2014 Carrie Elks
Published by Carrie Elks
All rights reserved
190914
ISBN: 1500714135

Cover Design: Okay Creations
Interior Image: Clipartof.com
Editor: Emily Nemchick

This book is a work of fiction and any resemblance to persons, living or dead, or places, events or locales is purely coincidental. The characters are fictitious products of the author's imagination.

For Ella and Oliver

To Jodie
Thank you for reading!
love
Carie Elks x

Nine Years Earlier

The night air smells of freshly cut grass and rain. I move through it, my hips undulating to the sound of music that stopped playing an hour ago. Blood fills my veins like thick black treacle, making me feel weightless, dizzy. High.

The party is over, the rain has seen to that. When the downpour started, everyone ran inside, heading for dorm rooms or calling cabs. I stayed where I was, inclining my face to the sky, letting the rain cool my flesh. It washed away my makeup and the stench of alcohol. It felt so good.

My clothes are stuck to my body. My hair is plastered to my head, but still I dance. The ecstasy I took earlier hasn't worn off yet. I feel strong and invincible, as if I'm some kind of goddess.

I see shoes first—blue Nike Airs sticking out from under a copse of trees. A plume of smoke spirals above the leaves. A few steps closer and I smell it: smoky and sweet. That's when I see *him*.

His eyes are heavy as he stares at me. Dark blue depths I want to dive inside. He gazes at me without recognition, has no idea who I am. I know him, though. He's one of the beautiful set; an artist.

"You're wet." He's still staring at me.

Unlike the rest of my body, my throat is dry. I swallow hard. "It's raining."

"Your observational skills astound me." There's an Irish lilt to his voice that thrills. I try to imagine what it would sound like whispered in my ear. The thought makes me shiver.

"Are you cold?"

I shake my head and say "Yes" at the same time. I'm so mixed up by the drugs and his proximity it's hard to think straight.

"Come here." He opens up his arms. I hesitate for a moment before I step into them, feeling like the fly walking into the spider's parlour. A moment later, all rational thought disappears as his strong arms wrap around my waist, pulling me against his chest. He presses his face to my wet hair and takes a deep breath. "You smell like rain."

Silence surrounds us as I look up at him. His pupils are dull and unfocused. He's much higher than I am. Soaring.

"You smell like weed."

"You want some?"

Taking the joint from him, I raise it to my mouth. Though I try to pull away as I inhale, his arms tighten around me. I feel as if I'm made of gas. Melting around him. Into him.

"What's your name?"

"Beth."

"Are you a student here?"

His question makes me roll my eyes. I've been following him and his friends around like a devoted puppy for the best part of my first year. Not that he's ever noticed. He's always too busy: painting, smoking, looking beautiful. He's good at all these things. I know, I've studied him as if he's my favourite subject.

"Art History," I say.

"One of the thinkers." He gives me a smile. It's wicked and dirty and makes me want to lick his lips. "Do you paint?"

"No."

"Shame. Do you model?"

I blush at this one. "No."

"You should. Come and model for me. I want to paint you." His words slur but his voice is still seductive and lyrical. Somewhere, far beneath my high, I know he's spinning me a line.

I bite, nonetheless.

"I'm not pretty enough."

"Yes you are."

"Or interesting enough."

He pulls me closer, his erection digging into my hip. "Yes you are."

My heart starts to hammer against my chest. This is Niall Joseph holding me. I made Niall Joseph get hard. I don't think about the drugs or the rain or the fact he's ignored me all year. I'm too worked up for that.

"I want to kiss you." He murmurs it softly. Then he presses his lips to my forehead. My skin feels hot and fevered. This time, the rain does nothing to cool it down.

"Okay." I'm almost breathless. He drags his mouth down to my jaw, peppering my skin with kisses.

"You fucking taste like rain, too."

By the time his lips reach the corner of my mouth I'm almost trembling with anticipation. My whole body is buzzing with desire. I have to grab hold of his shoulders to steady myself.

Then he presses his mouth to mine and everything else disappears.

Now

1

It's seven in the morning and the sunlight breaking through our bedroom window is tinted a pale pinky-orange. I sit on the edge of our king-sized bed watching my husband pull on his suit, painting on a smile that only pretends to be mine. The ceiling lamp glows yellow, and the light reflects from his grey-blond hair, casting a pale halo around his head.

You only have to glance quickly around our bedroom to sense his masculine influence—dark wooden floors that look beautiful but freeze my feet off on winter mornings, stark eau-de-nil painted walls. Bleached wooden shutters frame the sash windows he's had lovingly restored.

Though he's shuffled things around to fit me in, essentially this is still his room, his house. Not that I brought anything with me that would be worth changing things for. He took me on—penniless and low—as if I was another doer-upper. Polished me until I was shiny and bright.

"I'll try to get home by six." Simon threads his silver cufflinks through the slits of his blue Oxford shirt. "I promised Elise we would get to the gallery early."

Elise is his only daughter. I should think of her as my step-daughter, I suppose, but at twenty-seven she is only two years younger than me. It's hard to feel anything other than ambivalence to her when she stares at me down a perfectly formed nose whenever I walk through the door. Even then, she's always polite, always measured, and she hides her dislike of me as much as she can. Simon and his ex-wife brought her up well.

"You forgot your tie." I stand up and chase after him. Wrapping the blue silk around his neck, I knot it neatly, patting it with my extended fingers.

Simon says nothing, simply stares at me through his chocolate-brown eyes. Making me wonder if he's waiting for me to kiss him. I do it anyway, pressing my lips softly against his cheek. It plumps up when I feel him smile against my mouth.

"You should wear that dress I bought you last month. The one with the silver straps."

I nod, not bothering to remind him the straps are actually golden. I know he doesn't really care. He simply likes it when I dress up, regardless of what colour I wear. I like it when he's happy. It makes life easier, both his and mine, and I'm all for that.

When he leaves, carrying a briefcase full of papers he spent all last evening reading, I run to the shower and let the hot water wash away the final remnants of the night. Then I pull on my old jeans and a well-used t-shirt and head for the Tube. It's always rammed at this time of day. I squeeze my way through the wall of bodies and onto a train, breathing in when I'm pushed against a young girl dressed in school uniform. I flash her an apologetic smile. She rolls her eyes and looks away.

This is the language of the underground. Humans were never meant to live in such close proximity. We haven't learned how to communicate when we are constantly bombarded by sensation and emotion. We fear what we don't know, and we loathe it when it's pressed against our bodies.

Or at least I do.

It's almost nine o'clock when I walk into the clinic and up the stairs. Lara, one of the counsellors, looks up from her desk and gives me a quick wave. She's holding a phone in her other hand, rapidly talking into the mouthpiece. I smile back at her. Lara is one of my closest friends here. We met when I first started at the clinic. If I ever feel up or down, she's the first person I want to talk to.

Lara covers the phone and mouths at me, "Daisy MacArthur."

She doesn't have to say any more. Daisy has been a client on and off for the past two years. She's relapsed three times since she first walked through the door. Each time is worse than the last.

My stomach drops. "What about Allegra?" I ask.

Lara shrugs, making me feel worse. Allegra is only eight years old. She's been in and out of care since she was a baby. The reason Daisy even came into the clinic in the first place was to try and regain her parental rights—and it worked. She's an addict, but there's no doubt she loves her daughter.

I love her daughter, too. Maybe too much. Allegra has lived such a hard life in her short years, I can't help but feel protective of her.

Lara finally puts down the phone. "Have you got space for another kid at after-school club?"

For the past four years I've been running an afternoon club for the children of addicts, while their parents attend group therapy. We have a different theme each day. Music on Mondays, craft on Tuesdays, movies on Wednesdays. Thursdays is art. Allegra loves it. She has an innate ability to draw, and we encourage her to express her feelings on paper.

"Sure." I nod. "It's just me today, though." Until now, an art student from St. Martin's has been teaching the class. Now she's graduated I'm searching for her replacement. It isn't easy, though. We can't afford to pay them anything, and not everybody can work with traumatised, sometimes violent children. It takes a special sort of person.

"No luck at the college?" Lara shoots me a sympathetic look.

"Nope. I'm going to have to go cap in hand to Elise." I make a face. Lara reflects it right back at me, making me laugh. She knows Simon and Elise well. Everybody at the clinic does. He's one of our biggest benefactors. That's how I met him; at our annual fundraising gala four years ago.

"Well, before you grovel, let's get a cup of tea."

Later that afternoon a minibus arrives, bringing children to our after-school club. I've set up the classroom with paints and brushes. The tables are covered with large sketchpads. All the equipment has been donated from various sources. I'm the one who goes out begging. Lara calls it my "Oliver" act. I'm always asking for more.

The kids pour into the room, babbling incessantly. They squabble over where they sit, elbowing each other out of the way. It's all good-natured. Allegra is the last to walk in. She drags her trainers along the tiled floor, making them squeak. Her jet-black hair is falling out of her messy ponytail. I try to bite down the urge to hug her; she doesn't like being singled out.

Instead, I smile softly and give her hair a quick tug. "Hi."

"Hello." Her smile is almost genuine. I tug her hair again, and this time she laughs. It's like the sun coming out from behind a cloud. Her eyes dart around the room, making sure nobody is listening. "Is she here?"

I nod. "She came in this afternoon."

An expression of relief passes over her face.

Daisy was sent to the clinic as soon as she was released from hospital, having patched up the head wound she'd got when

11

she passed out on the pavement. Now, she's all ours. One step forward and two steps back. It's a fateful dance.

Allegra lingers by my side. "Am I going home tonight?"

My heart aches at her casual way of asking. She's been moved from place to place so often she doesn't really see how wrong it is—group homes, foster care, us. Even if her mum's a messed-up addict, Daisy's the only constant in Allegra's life.

"I think so. I'll ask Lara once you're all settled in. This time wasn't as bad as the last." I can't believe I'm discussing her mum's heroin bender. The poor child has seen things nobody should have to. She's old before her time.

"Okay." Allegra walks over to a desk and grabs some overalls. A few minutes later, she's painting. A pretty green landscape is peppered with trees and flowers, below a sky that's a shade too blue. I wonder if it's her happy place.

I used to have a happy place when I was going through counselling. A white sand beach with a deep azure ocean gently lapping at the shore. The colour of *his* eyes. I haven't thought of it for a while. Haven't needed to. I have Simon now. *He's* my happy place. My protector. He loves me, and I'm grateful. I'm aware how bad that sounds. In these days of insta-passion and lust-fuelled desires, our relationship is stubbornly old-fashioned. I've had passion, though, and it almost killed me.

At five o'clock the kids start to leave in dribs and drabs. Eventually, Allegra and I are the only two left. I sit on the corner of her desk and admire her painting. The old art teacher taught her so many techniques while she was with us that it looks advanced for her age. I'm glad I called Elise earlier; Allegra thrives in art class. Hopefully Elise can find us a new artist in residence.

The door clicks and Daisy MacArthur walks in. She looks crap. Her dark hair falls in lank strands across her pasty-white face. The worst thing is her expression of apprehension. I catch her eye and try to smile reassuringly.

Allegra looks up, her eyes wide, her bow lips half open. Then she stands up and runs to her mum, her sobs echoing through the silence of the room. She flings herself against Daisy, almost knocking her over. Daisy catches her and pulls her close, burying her face in Allegra's hair, murmuring, "I'm sorry, baby," over and over. It's like a mantra.

"I thought you were dead." Allegra's voice is a wail. My eyes glisten as I watch them; it's heart-breaking. No child should find their mum unconscious outside their flat, covered in blood and barely breathing.

"It's okay. I'm here, I'm here," Daisy whispers into her hair. "I'm so sorry."

I feel like a dirty voyeur; I can hardly bring myself to watch. My throat is constricted, my chest tight, because I know this is never going to get better. Daisy is always going to be an addict and Allegra is always going to be the daughter of an addict. No amount of therapy is going to change that.

When I get home I can't stop thinking about them. The addiction, the fear, the never-ending cycle. I came so close to being a Daisy myself. I know from first-hand experience that drugs kill, but it's the way they maim, breaking minds and hearts, that's as hard to take.

Simon arrives home shortly after six. He grabs me around the waist and kisses me hard before heading for the shower, and it shocks me. His grey hair is damp from the rain that's started to fall and it makes my palms wet when I touch his head, trying to work out what's got into him.

Not that I'm complaining. I'll take affection where I can find it. I'm fickle that way.

While he showers, I put on some makeup and scoop my hair away from my face. When I pull on my midnight-blue dress, I look like a different Beth to the one who works at the clinic and gets covered in paint. Elegant and polished. Poised, even.

On the outside, at least.

It's a disguise I've managed to perfect over time, aided by Simon's patient coaching. The first time we met, I was wearing a cheap black dress from Topshop, feeling way out of place among thousand-pound gowns and evening jackets. Maybe that's why I spent most of the night hiding. If he hadn't found me leaning against the back wall while he tried to make a phone call, I dread to think where I'd be now.

Lost. Alone. Like I was for those five years before we met.

Simon looks up and meets my eyes, the skin around his crinkling as he gives me a quick smile. I've seen him look at Elise in the same way. He's fond of both of us, proud to take us into smart restaurants and elite dinner parties. Elise is more polished than I am, though. She has a head start on me, an expert to my novice.

I'm still a work-in-progress, and I probably let Simon down too often. He doesn't ask for much in return for everything he gives me. I have a husband who loves me, who takes care of me, who soothes away the nightmares and makes me feel protected. In return, I try to behave the way he wants me to.

I don't take drugs, I don't smoke, I drink occasionally. I have a job he tolerates as a hobby. As long as it doesn't affect our marriage. I promised him that from the start.

We take care of each other. For the most part it works.

"You have lipstick on your teeth." He sounds amused.

I grimace and stare in the mirror, rubbing the scarlet from my bared teeth with the pad of my finger. "I swear I shouldn't smile or speak when I've got this stuff on."

"You're too pretty not to smile."

So, of course, I do. He has the ability to keep me calm and on an even keel. That first night we met, he spotted me as soon as he finished his call. I was standing by the bins, my fingers wrapped around a full glass of wine, and he approached me as if I was a frightened deer. When he spoke he kept his voice low.

"Are you okay?"
I was suffering from severe social anxiety, and I couldn't speak. Only nod.
"You don't look it," he said.
"I don't like parties. There are so many people. Too much going on." My voice wavered as I spoke. He took another step forward, and I shrank back.
"Are you claustrophobic?"
This time I shook my head. "No, I'm just not good in crowds."
"Why did you come here then?" His question wasn't mean. He sounded confused more than anything.
"I've just started working at the clinic, and I couldn't bear to tell them. I didn't want them to think I was completely crazy." I laughed, but it came out too harsh.
"Would you like me to get you a cab? Or I could drive you home, if you prefer."
My eyes watered at his kindness. This man, who looked old enough to be my father, was being sweeter to me than anybody had in a long time. More so than my own parents, who by that point had pretty much disowned me.
"I can't leave until later. Somebody will notice."
He smiled and it was the first time I realised how handsome he was, in spite of his age.
"How about you come and sit with me? I can hold your hand and talk you through any panic attack. I'll protect you."
That had been the start of it. He did everything he promised; escorted me all night, held my hand when I started to shake. He even managed to coax me onto the dance floor once. When he dropped me home that evening, barely flinching when he saw the run-down squat I was living in, he'd taken my number and promised to call me the next day.
He was a man of his word. He always has been. What he lacks in passion he makes up for in loyalty.

Over the next six months, he courted me assiduously. Spoiled me with flowers and gifts, took me to beautiful restaurants and upmarket art galleries. And though I liked all these things—who wouldn't—it was the way he treated me I liked the most. He made the decisions and looked after me like I was his second daughter.

For the first time in a long while, I felt happy. Safe. Within six months I was spending more time at his house than mine. We were married two years later.

I haven't had a panic attack since.

2

We take a cab to the gallery so Simon can have a drink. As much as he loves driving his Jaguar, he likes a glass of wine more. I hate driving through London, even at night.

"Elise called me this afternoon," Simon says as we make our way through the wet streets of Soho. "She thinks she's found you an artist."

"Really?" My grin is genuine. Elise has never been my biggest fan, but she loves her father, so she tolerates me. I don't mind; I think I'd feel the same in her position. To the outside world I'm no better than a gold digger—a trophy wife.

"Apparently he's just come back from the States. Not a student either; an honest-to-God artist."

My eyes widen. "Is he going to have time to teach at the clinic?"

"Elise says he'll do it. He's not short of cash. Don't look a gift horse in the mouth, Beth."

When the cab stops outside the gallery, Simon gets out first. He opens an umbrella before helping me climb out. His chivalry took some getting used to when we first got together. I was more accustomed to boys, then. Ones who took more than they gave.

In spite of our best intentions, the showing is in full swing when we arrive. A waiter stops in front of us and holds out a tray full of drinks, and Simon takes two glasses, handing me a white wine, while he sips the red.

"Not bad." He takes another mouthful. "Elise did the right thing and ordered the good stuff."

I don't reply, sipping my wine instead. Since he's the one funding the whole party, why the hell wouldn't she order the good stuff?

Simon stops and talks to a group of friends. They're all around his age, mid-fifties or so. I stand dutifully beside him, smiling when he introduces me, ignoring their raised eyebrows and pointed stares. They look at me as if I'm a money-grabbing bitch. I want to tell them I rarely spend his money. I have my own salary, paltry as it is, and my own bank account, too. It's not his money that ever attracted me to him. It was his protection.

I swallow the bile collecting in my throat. The paintings on the gallery walls call to me. I drift over to them, getting as close as I can, admiring the composition, the colour, the brushstrokes. I could lose myself in their beauty for hours. I've always loved art. I'm not a great painter, but I am an admirer. Not quite a connoisseur.

"What do you think?" Elise's nasal, upper-class voice whispers in my ear. I turn to her and smile.

"They're fantastic. So beautiful. It's killing me not to touch them."

"I'm glad you didn't. I've just sold this one for forty thousand."

I don't know why I'm shocked. I've been with Simon for long enough to know the sort of things the over-rich spend their money on. I can't help thinking of what we could do with that kind of money in the clinic.

"I bet the artist's happy."

She smiles. "He is. And so should you be, because I've persuaded him to teach at the clinic."

My breath escapes in a rush. Mister forty thousand is going to teach our class? Our deprived, jaded, undernourished kids? I don't know whether to be pleased or apprehensive.

I laugh lightly, though the smile doesn't quite reach my eyes. "Does he know what he's letting himself in for?"

"Why not ask him yourself?" She walks me to the centre of the room where a large crowd has gathered. A hum of conversation lingers in the air. I hang on the edge, a little embarrassed when Elise pushes her way through, trying to open up the crowd like Moses would the Red Sea.

"There you are, Niall." Her loud voice carries across the room. "I'd like you to meet Bethany. She works at the clinic I was telling you about."

I see his blue eyes first—bright, intense, azure as the ocean. They make my heart stutter. He narrows them when he looks at me. My stomach tightens and twists as if it's being wrung by a mangle.

My past has just walked back into my life, and it's all I can do to breathe.

* * *

The last time I saw Niall Joseph, I pretended I didn't know him. I was being marched away from the university administration building by my father, his fingers squeezing into my wrist, his lips tight and angry. It was early evening, and I'd been given two hours to clear my room out and leave the campus, otherwise I'd be escorted away by security.

We'd almost reached the halls of residence when I noticed a tall figure lolling against the front porch. He had what looked like a cigarette in his hand, but by the time we reached him I realised it wasn't a cigarette at all. The musty aroma and his red eyes were a dead giveaway.

Of course, my eyes were red too, but for an entirely different reason. I'd been crying on and off for the past few days. Had been in floods when I answered the investigator's questions, trying to tell them about my friendship with Digby, and to describe what happened the night he died.

Lying through my teeth that I didn't know where he got the ecstasy from. Of course I knew. We all did. Niall was quite the supplier back then.

Every time I sobbed, my father rolled his eyes. He'd made it patently clear he'd rather be anywhere than there. He was only accompanying me to make sure I didn't make a fool out of myself. Out of our family.

"Are you okay?" Niall pushed himself off the wall and walked toward us. My dad said nothing, but I felt his fingers tighten on my arm. "I've been trying to call you."

"I'm fine." Short, terse. I glanced at my dad from the corner of my eye. He was staring at us, open-mouthed.

Niall put the joint to his mouth and inhaled again. Jesus, did he have a death wish? "You don't look fine. You look crap."

"Do you know this young man, Bethany?" My father's patience finally ran out. I was shaking by the time I looked up at him, scared of pretty much everything that had happened. In the past few days I'd seen one of my closest friends die, been questioned by journalists and policemen, and finally been hauled up in front of the administration. I was spent, done. Nothing more than a quivering wreck. Now Niall—who had given Digby the drugs in the first place—was smoking a joint in front of my dad.

Maybe, if my dad had been somebody else, less concerned with appearances and more worried about his daughter, it would all have been different. Perhaps if I had been stronger, not the broken girl I'd ended up as, I might have been able to answer him properly. Instead of that, I shook my head.

"No, I don't know him at all."

***

"It's a pleasure to meet you." Niall reaches out and shakes my hand. I stare at the way his long fingers curl around my palm, and feel beads of sweat break out on my skin. It takes everything I have not to let him feel my hand tremble, because I don't want him to know just how shocked I am to see him again.

"It's good to meet you, too. Elise tells me you're going to be working with us." I can't look at him. Instead I stare at his feet, noting how shiny his black leather shoes are. They look so different to the trainers I remember him wearing. Always beaten up, splattered with paint.

Like the rest of him.

"I'd like to." His voice is softer than I remember. The Dublin lilt is still there, though. "It's something I feel strongly about."

"Drugs?" Surprised, I look up at him, my eyes wide. I have to take a deep breath when I see him staring straight at me.

He's still beautiful. His hair is a little longer but still as dark as newspaper ink. His face has lost that youthful plumpness, replaced by chiselled cheekbones, shadowed by stubble. But I'd recognise him anywhere. Those full, red lips, that nose with a slight bump on the bridge, the tiny scar next to his right ear that he got playing football when he was a kid. They're all there, a reminder of everything that happened all those years ago. Everything I've tried to forget.

"I want to give something back. I've been given a lot of good things in life. Other people aren't so lucky."

My mind is full of questions I don't know how to ask. How he's been, what he's been doing, but I don't voice any of them, I'm too afraid. Scared of dredging up the past like a river full of silt.

"Well, we'd be really grateful for your help. The kids love art on Thursdays; it's their favourite class." I feel better when I talk about the clinic. More grounded. This is my reality now, not those memories that are trying to resurface. "They're not da Vinci's or anything, but some of them seem to have talent."

"Well, I'm no da Vinci either." I glance around the gallery. "You're pretty good."

He actually blushes. "Thank you."

It's hard not to stare at his red cheeks. Hard to forget how they used to feel as I traced my finger across them. Niall doesn't show the slightest hint he remembers me, and I'm trying not to feel disappointed. This situation is embarrassing enough as it is. I don't need to make it any worse.

"I got you another drink, darling." Simon hands me a white wine. The glass is misted. Small droplets of water run onto my hand as I take it.

"Simon, this is Niall, the artist Elise has found. This is Simon, Elise's father. He owns the gallery."

The two men shake hands, and I can't help compare them. Simon's are pale and pinched. Grey hair curls over his cuffs.

"Pleased to meet you. Elise says you're going to do wonders at the clinic."

An awkwardness descends. We make small talk. I fidget with my wine and glance around the room. Simon and Niall seem so much more comfortable, enough to strike up a conversation without me. It gives me the space I need to calm myself down. I remind myself I'm here as Simon's wife. The old Beth is gone. I don't need to be scared anymore. It's as if my brain knows, but my body doesn't, and for the first time in years I feel that familiar constriction in my chest.

Breathe. Just breathe.

There are too many people in the room. It's as if they're crowding toward me, crushing me. My heart is speeding so fast it's almost painful.

"I need the bathroom." I shove my glass into Simon's free hand and almost run across the gallery floor, stumbling a couple of times when I barrel into a guest. Looking back, I see the two of them staring at me.

My husband and the man I used to know. The one who protects me, and the one who taught me what passion was.

He painted it across my body when I was a blank canvas.

Something long dormant sparks inside me as I remember how good it felt.

Nine Years Earlier

"Hey, Rain Girl!"

I whip my head around and nearly drop the books I've balanced precariously in my arms. The grass is teeming with students. The sun beats down. It's warm enough for girls to be dressed in tiny shorts and skimpy tops. It seems half the boys have taken off their t-shirts, revealing pale skin that's turning pinker by the second. I can't see where the voice is coming from, so I shrug and carry on walking. My last lecture has just finished and I'm heading back toward the halls of residence. Clad in jeans and a long-sleeved top, I'm hot and completely overdressed.

"Over here." Niall rounds his 'r's and for some reason it sounds insanely sexy. I glance to my left and spot him, sitting with a group of friends alongside the lake. He catches my eye and smiles, making my stomach clench.

I want to wave, but I'm holding too many books. Instead I kind of tip my head to the side and give him a toothy, lopsided smile. I silently kick myself for being so lame, because this is Niall Joseph we are talking about. God of Gods, King of Kings and he's talking to me.

He's still smiling. I begin to feel stupid, standing here goofily, so I raise my eyebrows in what I hope comes across as a nonchalant, see you around kind of expression, and start to walk away.

"Wait up." He stands up and half-runs after me. He's holding a spliff between his index and middle fingers. When he comes to a stop in front of me, he raises it to his lips. He exhales and the breeze wafts the smoke over my face.

"You want some?"

I shrug and look down at my arms. He follows my gaze and notices how full my hands are. Switching the spliff around in his fingers, he lifts the blunt end to my lips and I breathe it in. A moment later, I catch his eye and he's still smiling at me and I don't know if it's him or the drugs that's making me lightheaded. He sticks the spliff back in his mouth and then grabs my books, lifting them easily in his arms. Without even asking me if I want to join him, he walks back to his group.

Of course, I follow him.

Awkwardly, I sit down beside him. His friends are a who's who of campus elite, either rich, talented or a mixture of both. It's hard not to feel boring and prosaic in comparison.

Niall puts the spliff back up to my lips, even though my hands are free now. My cheeks heat up when I realise he's still staring at me. He has this intensity that makes me want to shiver even though I'm boiling in my long sleeves and jeans.

"Does she have a name?" The boy sitting on the other side of Niall looks at me. Or I think he does; it's hard to tell when he's wearing Ray-Bans and a cap that cover his eyes.

"She's called Rain Girl." Niall's voice is soft. His lips quirk into a smile and it feels as if it's just for me.

"Weird name." The guy screws up his nose. "And singularly inappropriate for this kind of weather. But I guess it suits you." He reaches across Niall and shakes my hand. "I'm Digby."

Digby?

"Hi."

"I think I'll call you after the Greek goddess of rain... who is... um...."

"There is no Greek goddess of rain, dickhead." That comes from a girl lying down on her stomach, across the way from us.

She has a deep, croaky voice and sounds as if she's been on sixty a day all her life.
"Yes there is. It's Iris."
Throat girl chuckles. "She's the goddess of rainbows, not rain. Zeus is responsible for rain."
"I'm not calling her Zeus."
Thank God for small mercies.
"My name's Beth," I say with a small voice. They all stop talking and look at me. Suddenly I understand how a zoo animal must feel.
"I prefer Iris," Digby says.
"Well, it's better than Zeus," throat girl says.
Niall just leans across to me and places his soft lips on the sensitive skin just below my ear. "You'll always be Rain Girl to me."

Now

3

I meet Daisy at a cafe on a damp Tuesday morning. She's sitting outside at a stainless-steel bistro table under the awning. A half-smoked cigarette is clutched between her fingers. She raises it up to her dry, cracked lips, sucking at the filter, her cheeks hollowing as she inhales. When she breathes out, the smoke combines with the vapour dancing in the air.

"Would you like a coffee?" I stop next to her. She looks up, almost surprised.

"Can I have a Coke instead? I've got a hangover."

When I come back out, she's finished her cigarette. She has her phone in her hand and is leaning over it. Her lank hair hangs over her eyes. I put her Coke and my over-full coffee cup down on the table. It rocks a little, and coffee sloshes over the rim, spilling onto the metal surface, running toward the edge.

"How are you?" I sit down and take a sip of coffee. It's so hot it scalds my lips.

"Okay."

"And Allegra?"

Daisy tears her eyes away from her phone; her whites look yellow and there are dark shadows beneath them. It looks as though she hasn't slept in weeks. "She's okay."

I ignore the defensiveness of her tone. She's known me long enough to understand I'm not judging her. I'm not her counsellor, either; I'm just here as a friend.

"She seemed better yesterday when I saw her," I remark.

She shrugs and opens her can of Coke. It hisses as she pulls the ring, fizz escaping from the small opening. "She's barely talking to me."

"She's been through a lot."

"So have I."

I don't know how to talk to Daisy when she's like this; defensive, abrupt, angry at the world. She's feeling sorry for herself, and when she's in this mood there's no getting through to her. Worry for Allegra gnaws at my stomach. I swallow another mouthful of coffee. It's milky and sweet—exactly how I like it. Even after all these years I try to keep my stimulants mild. The strongest drug I take nowadays is caffeine.

"Darren's back."

My face falls. Darren is her on-again-off-again boyfriend, and more importantly he's a dealer. He's very bad news.

"Have you told Lara?" I know the clinic has to maintain patient confidentiality where possible, but we also have an obligation to make sure Allegra is safe. We're going to have to get social services involved again. That's certain to alienate Daisy and throw her right into Darren's arms. It's a catch-22 situation and I hate it, but there's no other way.

"Nope." She takes another swig of Coke. Her teeth are yellow from the drugs and lack of hygiene. Without thinking, I run my tongue along my own incisors. "And I'm not going to," she adds.

"You know I'm going to have to tell somebody."

Anger flashes behind her eyes. "The fuck you will. You're meant to be my friend."

"I *am* your friend. You know how I feel about Darren. You know how Allegra feels, too. Last time he came around she ended up alone in the house for two days before anybody found her." I can't believe we're doing this again. Darren's a parasite. It's as though he has a sixth sense. Every time Daisy starts to improve, he comes around and lures her back again. He feeds her drugs like they're sweets, and she lets him.

Daisy rolls her eyes. "He's different this time. He's promised me he's giving it up. The dealing and everything. Wants us to give it another go."

I feel like crying. I know the lure of promises, the hope this time it will be different. I've seen it so many times over the past few years. Not once have those promises been kept. "You really believe that?"

She nods, looking down at her hands. "He loves me. And I love him. It's going to work this time."

As I drink the last of my coffee, I wonder how long it will be before everything blows up in her face. When it happens I know I'll be there to help her clear it all up, the same as last time. Not for her sake, but for Allegra's. The kid deserves to have a bit of stability in her life.

By the time I get to the clinic, I'm worried sick about Daisy and Allegra, and need to talk to somebody. To Lara. She's always been my voice of reason, a friend when I had nobody else to lean on. Seeing her most days at the clinic is one of the reasons I'm on an even keel these days.

Unfortunately, she has a client with her, so I go up to the office and call Allegra's social worker. Grace O'Dell is an experienced practitioner; she works with a lot of our clients, and we've managed to build a good relationship with her. She's a no-nonsense type, and when I tell her about Darren I hear her sighing down the phone.

"I can't believe she's being so stupid. Actually, scratch that, yes I can. I'll put her on my list of visits today." I can hear her shuffling papers. "Is there a space for Allegra at after-school club?"

"Of course." We have a maximum of fifteen, but I can squeeze her in. More often than not, at least one kid doesn't turn up. "If I arrange for a pick-up can you let the school know?"

"Yeah, I'll call them now. At least she'll have a little bit of normalcy in her life, poor kid."

"We'll do what we can. I hate the thought that she still has to go home afterward." I want to wrap her up and take her home with me, instead. It's a dangerous thought. I try to quash it before it can take seed.

"You can't be there all the time. Remember what I told you? If you don't turn it off you'll burn out. And that won't do any of them any good. You either, come to that."

"I know." My voice is soft. If I had my way the house would be full of these kids. But social services don't work that way. Nor does Simon. He'd never let me bring them home.

"When are you going to come over to the dark side anyway?" There's a teasing tone in her voice. A smile tries to tug at the corner of my mouth but it comes to nothing.

"The force is too strong."

Grace laughs. "A few years at university, young padawan. Then you can be just like me. Black mask and all."

"I'm too old to be a student." I don't tell her I tried that before. That I left under a cloud, with much more than my tail between my legs.

"You're a baby. Your whole life ahead of you. You'd make a good social worker, once we teach you how to stop getting so attached."

"You couldn't teach me that."

"Try me."

We talk for a few more minutes and I hang up, anxiety still low in my belly. I can't help feeling guilty that I've told on Daisy, knowing it will almost certainly lead to Allegra getting taken away from her again. It doesn't matter how crap her mum is, Allegra will hate me if she finds out. I lower my head until it's resting in my hands, letting out a deep sigh. My whole body aches, as if I've spent the morning doing intense physical exercise. I rub my eyes with the heels of my hands.

"Um, hi."

I look up. My brow furrows when I see Niall standing in the doorway. Is it that time already? Christ, where has the day gone?

I can't get used to seeing him again.

"Hi. You're early."

The corner of his lip quirks up. "I wanted to make sure I was prepared." He glances at me, then gestures at his eyes. "You've got mascara under..."

Oh God. My eye rubbing must have left me looking like a clown. I swipe at the underside with my fingers. When I pull them away, black ink is smudged all over them. "Thanks."

His smile only widens. "You're welcome."

For a minute I want to wipe the smirk right off his mouth. Mr Bloody Perfect. His hair is immaculate, his face tanned. His jaw is lightly covered in stubble. He looks like a male model.

I look a mess.

This doesn't fit in with my plans. I was going to be cool, calm and collected. I mumble under my breath and stand up from the desk. The movement makes me remember my manners. "Would you like a tour of the place while we have some time?"

Niall nods. He's still grinning. His teeth are white and even, the same as mine. Are they real or veneers? My mind is suddenly full of questions. Does he still take drugs? Has he managed to stop?

Did he break down like I did?

I remind myself none of this is my business. He's only a colleague, a guy who's agreed to do us a favour. He owes me nothing at all. For some reason, that thought depresses me. I notice that he doesn't once refer to us knowing each other in the past. We're pretending we are strangers, even though we're anything but. It would be funny if it wasn't so sad.

Starting the tour on the ground floor, I show him the treatment rooms that aren't being used, the meeting rooms where we hold after-school club, and the kitchen.

"This is the most important place." I fling my arms around the small room. "We have everything you could possibly want; coffee, tea, biscuits... sympathy. Lots and lots of sympathy."

"This place is amazing. How long have you been working here?"

"Almost five years." We walk up the stairs, toward the admin office. I wave at the staff. They seem more interested in ogling Niall than acknowledging me, not that I can blame them. He's wearing old, paint-splattered jeans, worn to nothing at the knees and frayed at the hems. They hug his hips in a disturbing way. "And thank you. We all work pretty hard to make it that way."

"I can see that." His voice is soft. "It's very impressive."

For some reason that kicks me right in the gut. He still looks like the Niall who consumed my every thought all those years ago. But, like me, he seems to have grown up. I like it more than I should—like *him* more than I should.

"We should probably get things ready in the art room." I suddenly wish the kids were here already. They're the ultimate ice-breaker; I'd feel much less awkward if they were around. Even my body feels weird. My arms hang limply at my sides, and I don't know what to do with my hands. I end up balling them into fists, as though it will give me strength.

"Sounds good," he says. "Show me the way."

* * *

Two Saturdays later Lara and I drive to Battersea in her scratched-up Mini. It's early enough for the streets to be fairly clear. She cranks up her tinny car radio and we sing along to the Arctic Monkeys, trying not to remark on the fact that nearly all of their lyrics seem to be about drugs, drinking or both. They remind me of when I was a student. Everything does at the moment.

"So where shall we take her?" Lara drums the pads of her fingers against the steering wheel. We're sat at a zebra crossing, waiting for an old lady to make her way across it. She's pushing a trolley, and peeping out of the top is the cutest little Scottie dog.

"We should go to the park," I say. "It's a beautiful day and she probably needs to work off some energy."

Allegra has been in a group home for five days; ever since Daisy had a fight with Darren and ended up in accident and emergency with a broken cheekbone. She swears it looks more painful than it actually is, but every time I look at her all I can think of is how hard he must have hit her to break such a thick bone.

Allegra saw the whole thing.

"We could go to Battersea Park."

"Maybe." I've a hankering for hills. There aren't enough in London. I miss the way you can climb high and look down and feel so insignificant. I want to feel insignificant, at least to myself. "How about we go to Parliament Hill?"

"Hampstead's miles away."

"I'll chip in for the petrol." I'm kidding. I'll pay for it all. "I bet Allegra has never been there. We can buy some food from Marks and Spencer's and have a picnic." I start to get excited.

"And maybe we can get her a pad and some pencils and she can draw or something."

Lara looks at me from the corner of her eye. "Are you okay? You seem all over the place at the moment."

It's so typical she notices when nobody else does. I can zip on a persona like an old winter coat for everybody else, but Lara's too perceptive. I lean forward and turn the radio down. "I don't know," I admit.

"Is everything all right with Simon?"

I blink a couple of times. "Yeah, why do you ask?"

She shrugs. "You haven't mentioned him much."

"He's been busy at work. If he was ten years younger he'd probably be pulling all-nighters."

We both laugh. The image of Simon staying up all night with only Red Bull for company is incongruous. "In fact, I was going to ask you if I can come to Alex's gig next Friday. Simon's going to be away and I don't fancy staying home alone."

Alex is Lara's husband. He's a printer by trade, but he has a band he jams around with and sometimes they play gigs at their local pub. They're totally laid back and unpretentious. I like Alex a lot, not least because he let me live with him and Lara for a year when I had nowhere else to go. I've missed seeing him. Our circles are so different nowadays. He's chilled out and cool, while I'm old before my time.

"Of course, we'd love that." Lara has a huge grin on her face and I try not to let her see how bad it makes me feel. I can't remember the last time I went out with her anywhere. Most of my time is taken up with Simon, either going out to dinner with clients, or hosting them at our place. It isn't that Simon doesn't get on with Lara and Alex, they just don't have a whole lot in common. It's hard work for all of us when we get together. "You could stay over at ours. Maybe we can hit the markets on Saturday morning."

A smile twitches at my lips. I can't remember the last time I went to the markets, either. I used to love browsing around stalls when I was younger, picking up vintage pieces and mixing them in with the rest of my wardrobe. "Let's do it." I sound resolute and it makes us both a bit giddy.

I'm still smiling when we get to Carter House. When Allegra walks down the stairs she's wearing an old pair of jeans and a sweater that's a couple of sizes too small. Her face lights up as soon as she sees us. She runs into my arms, almost winding me, and I bury my face in her hair. It holds a faint aroma of smoke, and I wonder if she's even washed it since she got here.

When I let her go, she smiles shyly at Lara. They don't get to interact at the clinic. Lara is usually busy with the adults.

"Hi, pumpkin." Lara reaches out and messes her hair. Allegra's cheeks turn a rosy pink. Lara doesn't seem to notice, and decides to tease us both. "Indiana Beth here thinks we should go on an adventure."

Allegra's eyes widen. "What sort of adventure?"

"Oh, I don't know, maybe hunt some sharks or kill some witches, or fight some pirates for their treasure," Lara says.

I grin. "I'm thinking we could stake a few vampires and then have a picnic."

Allegra screws up her forehead, pretending to consider the options. "Are they bad vampires?"

"Probably. Though if you want to be sure we could always ask them first."

She grabs hold of my hand and practically pulls me out of the door. Lara lingers back to sign the paperwork. "What kind of picnic are we having, anyway?"

It turns out to be the kind of picnic where we buy way too much food, and then watch as the birds swoop down, trying to grab the crusts from our fingers. We sit on a tartan wool blanket at the top of the hill, and look down over London. The air is clear and we can see all the way to the city and beyond,

the familiar skyline of Canary Wharf shimmering in the distance.
Days like these remind me why I love living in London so much.
Allegra picks up another sausage roll and pulls the pastry off, stuffing it into her mouth. She discards the pale pink meat, throwing it down on the paper plate in front of her. Outside of its pastry shell, the sausage looks limp and wrinkled.
"Beth?"
I turn to look at her. "Yes?"
"Why do people take drugs?"
I'm quiet for a minute. Her question seems to have knocked the air from my lungs. I glance across at Lara, who catches my eye and shrugs. Message received; this one's all mine.
"It's an addiction, Allegra. At first it makes them feel good, and then they get so used to it they just can't stop."
"Why can't they stop?"
"Because it feels so nice at first."
She picks a daisy up from the grass beside the blanket and starts to pull off the petals, one by one. "But it's bad for you. How can it feel nice?"
I take a deep breath in. The air smells of salt and vinegar crisps, mixed with freshly cut grass—a typical English springtime day. "Things can feel nice and still be bad for you. Like too much chocolate, or staying up late when you should be asleep. But drugs are worse because they can make you poorly, and stop you from functioning properly."
I don't want to tell her they can kill. I know that more than anyone. But she's eight years old and her mum's an addict; I'm not sure I'm ready for her to add up the sums right yet.
"The problem is, once you're addicted, it's really hard to stop. That's why we have the clinic, to try and help people."
"People like my mum?"
"Yes."

She chews on her bottom lip. "So why is she still taking drugs? Why aren't you helping her?"

"We're trying." My voice catches in my throat. "But it can take a long time. And sometimes people have setbacks and get worse again."

Allegra leans into me, and I bring my hand around and stroke her hair. "Will my mum ever get better?"

I pull her closer. "I don't know, Allegra. I hope so."

She curls her arms around me. "So do I."

4

"Are you sure you don't want to come? Drew won't mind one extra if I call him." Simon zips up his case and looks at me expectantly. "I'll let you hold my gun."

"What an offer."

He's being sweeter than usual. I know he's been looking forward to his boys' weekend away for a long time. They're off to shoot some grouse or something like that; I haven't really been paying attention.

"You go and enjoy yourself. Lara's invited me to stay for the weekend."

"I'll be leaving after lunch on Sunday." He lifts his case from the bed, and reaches to embrace me. When he pulls back, there's a soft smile on his face. "Try not to get into any trouble."

"How much trouble can I get into over one weekend?"

"Quite a lot." He looks wistful. For a moment, I wonder if he really trusts me. Since we've been married, I've done nothing to cause either of us any trouble. I left *that* girl behind years ago, although sometimes—especially recently—I miss her. Simon simply smiles and places a quick peck on my cheek. When I stand at the door and watch him climb into his sports car, I wonder why my stomach is churning. Maybe I'll miss him more than I realise.

After Simon has left, I take a quick shower and pull on some clothes. A few minutes after eight, I leave the house, heading for the Tube station at the end of our road. The platform is full of people, some dressed like me for a casual night out, others still in their work gear, heading home after a long day. It's a microcosm of the bigger city: people and nationalities of every description, all pushed together into each other's personal space.

The George and Dragon stands on the edge of a leafy green square, the Victorian edifice decaying and crumbled. The painted pub sign—depicting the moment when George finally goes in for the kill—is swaying softly in the evening breeze. As soon as I push open the heavy wooden door, I'm hit by the warm, musty air and the noise of a dozen conversations. Scanning the room, I seek out Lara, trying not to look too out of place.

The George is a spit-and-sawdust kind of pub. It hasn't succumbed to the gentrification of the surrounding area, although the clientele is an interesting mix of old timers and trendy young things. The older ones sit in the public bar, studiously avoiding the lounge, which is where I'm standing now, looking at the stage in the corner that's already set up for the band. A drum kit, guitars and microphone are all patiently waiting for their masters to return.

It's been so long since I've been somewhere like this. Giving up gritty pubs has been a side effect of my marriage—as much as making sure I always shave my legs and never pass wind when Simon's around. Yet I find that I've missed it. A rush of nervous anticipation fills my veins as I push through the crowds of drinkers.

I spot them at a table in the far corner. Alex is sitting next to Lara, his tattooed arm casually slung across the back of her chair, his other hand wrapped around a pint glass full of water. I have a soft spot for Alex. He and Lara welcomed me into their lives at a time when I was at my lowest ebb. Back then, they'd talk with me into the night, before gently covering me with a soft cotton blanket when I cried myself to sleep. They're good people, and I'm a bit annoyed at myself that I've neglected them. I lived with them for over a year after I managed to escape a squat. It was probably the best year of my life.

Until I met Simon, I remind myself.

It's Alex who sees me first. A huge grin splits his cheeky face and he stands up and walks toward me, enveloping me in a bear hug as soon as we are within touching distance. I cuddle him back, feeling a mixture of relief and exhilaration. It really has been too long.

"Where've you been, doll face? I've missed you," he says.

"I've missed you too." I'm almost laughing. I'd forgotten just how cockney Alex sounds. He's a real geezer, and he likes to play on it as much as possible. "I'm sorry, I feel really bad I haven't seen you in ages."

I can feel him shrug. "No worries, you've been busy. Different worlds. I get it."

When I pull back I feel regretful, because he's right in so many ways. Simon wouldn't be seen dead in a place like this. But I feel at home; excited, nervy and young.

And I like it.

"Hey, you changed your hair." I reach up to touch his black, gelled quiff. It's stiff as a board. The sides and back of his hair are cut short against his scalp. "It looks great."

"So do you." Alex steps back and holds me at arm's length. He's scrutinising me, but in a way that doesn't feel sexual or pervy. I know this stance; he's making sure I'm okay. "You cleaned up nicely. Not bad for an Essex girl."

He's always teased me about where I come from. I love the way we slip back into our old routine, as if I hadn't disappeared off the face of his earth for a year. I guess us both seeing Lara every day, even if we haven't seen each other, has kept the connection going.

"When do you play?"

Alex glances at his watch. He has ink scrolling all the way up his arm. I spot a couple of new ones. If he turned it over, I'd see Lara's name tattooed on his wrist. How she ever stopped swooning over that gesture, I'll never know. "In about an hour. Do you want a drink?"

I smile. "I'll have a beer, please." I can't remember the last time I had a beer. It feels bad, almost illicit. A kid rifling through their parents' cocktail cabinet.

"You go and sit down, I'll bring it over." He inclines his head at the table where Lara and the others are sitting. I start to walk over, the smile still playing at my lips, but then I stop dead in my tracks. Leaning on the table a few seats across from Lara, staring up at me through narrowed eyes, is none other than Niall Joseph.

My pulse instantly speeds. My throat constricts until it is painful to suck air through it, and I find myself breathing faster to compensate. All the while I'm frozen to the spot, wondering what the hell he's doing here, and why on earth he's staring at me like that. Then Lara turns to look at me, smiling broadly, and I shake my head a little, trying to get some sense into my brain and some movement to my limbs.

Of course she would invite Niall to the pub. He's a new colleague, recently arrived in town, and the perfect project for her and Alex to take on. If he's anything like he used to be—arty and charismatic—they'll have both fallen in love with him.

It's so easy to do.

Somehow I manage to propel myself across the room. I lean down and hug Lara, trying not to feel resentful, reminding myself she has no idea that Niall is the guy who twisted my world until I ended up a wet dishrag. Of course she knows what happened—she's one of the few I've confided in—but I don't think I ever actually said his name. So why should I feel angry at her for inviting him?

I haven't felt this mixed up in a very long time.

"Here, have this." Niall stands up and offers me his seat. For some reason his chivalry grates.

"It's fine; I'll go and grab a stool." I look feebly around. The pub is full to bursting. There isn't a spare seat to be seen.

He won't take no for an answer, standing up and lifting my bag from my hands. It's big and heavy—containing clothes and toiletries for my night at Lara's. He places it down next to his now-vacant seat. I swallow the irritation and sit down, squeezing myself onto the edge of the chair.

"I can share." I point down at the half of the seat that's empty, offering it to him.

He shakes his head. "I'm happy to stand."

"Oh come on, my bum's not that big." As soon as I say it, Lara shouts out a laugh. Niall grins and shakes his head again, but this time more in amusement than denial. He gracefully sits next to me, reaching his left arm along the back of the chair, stretching out his right leg to brace himself against the floor. He's sitting close. So close our hips are touching, and our thighs are pressed together. I can smell his aftershave and the faint tang of beer that wafts from his lips. The heat of his body radiates through the thin material of his t-shirt.

It makes my own body do strange things. My heart is still racing and my mouth has dried up. The hairs on my forearms stand on end. I've shared seats before—I'm small so I'm always the first to have to squash up—but this is different.

I try to take control. "How are you?"

"I'm good. You?" He moves his arm, and his fingers accidentally brush against the back of my neck. "Sorry."

"It's okay." Because it is. I can do this. I'm older, married. No longer that girl who fell head over heels for the beautiful art student. "There's not a lot of room here."

Alex passes me a bottle of Peroni, and I notice his brow rise up when he spots me sitting so close to Niall. I reach out to take it with my left hand, my right being held captive by Niall's body, albeit unintentionally. As I curl my fingers around the bottle, I feel him shift next to me.

"You got married. Nice ring." It isn't a question, but it answers a lot of mine. The way he says it, the intonation in his voice, tells me he remembers me. Though it's hard to believe anybody can forget what happened that summer. I know I can't.

"I've been married for two years."

"Where's your husband?" He's doing that narrow-eyed stare thing again. It pulls at his forehead, wrinkling into a frown. Horizontal lines furrow in his skin.

I feel myself start to blush. I hate that I'm almost embarrassed to tell him about Simon. To admit I married an older man. "He's away." I'm not saying he's gone grouse shooting. I'm not. Maybe I should be proud about who he is, who we both are, but the clash between my past and present is making everything awkward.

"That's a shame."

I nod. "It is."

"Is he nice?"

I start to laugh, because this one is easy. "Clearly. Otherwise I wouldn't have married him. Anyway, you met him at the gallery."

Niall scrunches his face up in an effort to recall. I watch him for a moment, taking in the sharp jaw and heavy brow. If it's possible, he's only grown more glorious with age.

He's still silent, and I take pity on him. "Simon's Elise Gordon's dad. He owns her gallery." I try to ignore the way his thick brows rise up. I feel as though he's judging me. I start to babble to fill in the awkwardness. "We met at a fundraiser for the clinic. You'd like him, I think." What a crock of shit. I don't even know this guy sitting next to me. Not anymore. What right do I have to say whether he'd like my husband or not?

"Does he make you happy?"

It's the strangest question. Said softly, in a way that caresses my skin. His accent hasn't diminished in the years since I last saw him. I can recall the way he used to whisper in my ear. The memory makes me want to sigh.

"He takes care of me." It's not a lie. Simon is fond of me. He looks after me. I am content.

"I'm glad."

I turn to look at Niall. His deep blue eyes stare right into mine. Our faces are only inches apart and I can feel the warmth of his breath on my skin. Maybe I'm reading all kinds of things into his expression that probably aren't there: accusations, recriminations, apologies. Each one of them makes me yearn for things I cannot have. He's close, too close. It's as if he's taking me over, nucleus by nucleus, and as with years before, my thoughts are filled with him.

Then our silent conversation is interrupted by the first strum of a guitar as it reverberates from the speakers, and I find myself breathing a sigh of relief. The excitement flowing through my veins feels more potent than any drug I've taken, and it's laying me bare.

* * *

As the evening goes on I get progressively drunker, finding solace in the bottom of a beer bottle and each popping of a new cap. Lara watches me with worried eyes and I flash her the occasional reassuring smile, trying to let her know that my inebriation has nothing to do with substance abuse and everything to do with avoidance.

By the time Alex's band launches into the second half of their set, I'm dancing in my seat, relieved Niall has moved into one of the now-vacant stools across the table, giving me space to breathe, to move, to be. My skin still tingles with the memory of his closeness, and it's giving me an artificial high.

Being near him makes me feel as though I'm nineteen again. I love and I hate it.

"You okay?" Lara pulls her chair close to mine. "You're not acting like yourself."

"I'm good. Great." I flash her another smile. It doesn't wipe away the worried expression on her face.

"You don't usually drink this much. Not recently, anyway."

"I don't usually have to sit next to Niall Joseph." I regret the words as soon as they escape from my lips. Lara angles her head to the left, scrutinising me through sober eyes. I fidget beneath her gaze.

"What's going on, Beth?"

I glance across at Niall. He's talking to a friend of Alex's. He looks so comfortable, so easy-going. He has this aura about him that draws you in. Luckily, he's far enough away from me to talk about him without him overhearing.

"I'm fucked," I admit, resting my head in my palms.

"What's going on between you two?"

"Nothing." I laugh harshly. "Not now."

Her eyes widen. "When? Did something happen at the clinic?"

I shake my head. I'm not trying to be enigmatic, I'm just finding it hard to get the right words. "Before. At university."

Lara knows my history. She knows me. "Niall? He's the one who..." Her voice trails off. She doesn't need to say anything else, we both know the rest of her sentence. I nod my head vigorously. She lifts up her glass and downs the remains of her Coke. "Oh shit."

I follow suit and finish my fourth bottle of Peroni. The beer's grown warm where it's been standing for a while, but I swallow it anyway. I like the buzzed feeling it gives me; it's so much better than panic and nervousness.

"Why didn't you say something before?" Lara hisses. "You should have told me."

"I thought I could handle it."

"But you can't. Not on your own. That whole situation, the memories, the feelings. Oh, Beth..." She trails off again as Alex walks over and kisses her, biting her lip as if she's afraid to say anything. From the way the rest of the guys are laughing with Niall, they have no clue what's happening here. I'd like to keep it that way.

"Later." I promise. The way she looks at me tells me she's going to hold me to that.

The party carries on into the night. We're thrown out of the bar at one in the morning, and find ourselves walking back to Lara and Alex's flat. Even in the early hours the city seems alive, the streets pumped with energy and expectation. Alex and Lara have gone ahead in the van carrying the band's instruments, leaving me with a few of their friends... and Niall Joseph. He's wearing a slate-grey hoodie, zipped to the neck, along with faded jeans and Nike Airs. It seems strange to look at him and know that I was once in love with this guy, that I spent hours beneath him and on top of him and beside him. Sometimes we were so high we couldn't work out which body part belonged to whom.

"How did you end up working at the clinic?" he asks.

"I started as a volunteer. Then I was lucky enough to be offered a job. It doesn't pay much but I love it." I shrug. I can't even be bothered to pretend I don't know him anymore. I'm too drunk for that.

"I guess you don't need the money—with a rich husband and all." His word sting. I look up at him in confusion. He's staring down at me with those narrow eyes again.

"I didn't marry him for his money," I reply.

"So why did you?"

The others have moved farther ahead. We are lagging behind. I find myself shrinking away from him. "Because Simon takes care of me. He'll never hurt me, he loves me." I don't need to add anything else; the implication is there. He's everything that Niall wasn't. Back when I needed him the most.

When he needed me.

"You've just told me why he married you. Not why you married him." His voice is almost too soft. I have to strain to hear it. "That summer, God, Beth. Everything changed. I hoped you'd gone off on an adventure, followed your passions. Not once did I think you'd just go and settle."

I whip my head around. "You don't know anything about me and Simon. *Nothing.*" My voice is thick with fury. "Somebody died, Niall. I don't know about you, but I didn't get over it that easily." I'm finding it hard to breathe. Memories of those summer days, nine long years ago, assault my thoughts. The aching, the longing, the stupid choices I made. The shock, the fear and the ambulance. All of it was our fault. I lost everything that summer. Including myself. "I noticed you never called me. You just disappeared."

"I didn't disappear. They sent me away, just like they did to you. It fucked me up, all of it; I couldn't even think properly. I wanted to call you, to talk to you, to check you were okay. But after you pretended you didn't know me…"

I feel sick. Nausea starts to clutch at my stomach with a vice-like grip. "I didn't know what to do. My dad was so angry. Everything was fucked up. And you just showed up with a bloody joint in your mouth." We've stopped walking altogether. Standing in the middle of a lamp-lit London street, we stare at each other accusingly. I wrap my arms around my waist as if to ward him off.

"You broke my heart when you said you didn't know me. I spent the first few weeks in a drunken fucking stupor." Niall averts his gaze. His expression changes. Suddenly, he looks like a young boy; lost, afraid, alone. "And then I ended up in hospital, too. Whenever I think of that time, about Digby, it messes me up all over again."

Tears sting at my eyelids. My throat is so tight I can barely get the words out, but somehow I manage. "Me, too."

Nine Years Earlier

It's dark in here—shady and damp, loud and alive. Sweat hangs in the air like mist. We dance wildly, our hair whipping across our faces in wet, ropy tendrils, beads of perspiration peppering our foreheads and upper lips. Bodies press in on me from all sides as we raise our hands in the air, laughing and screaming and dancing to the hypnotic beats.

I love them. I love everybody in here. I can't understand how wars ever happen, how hatred exists, because these people are perfect, beautiful, amazing. I don't know most of them, but when we catch each other's eyes we grin with bared teeth and a surge of emotion rushes through me. My heart is so full I think it might burst.

I feel arms encircle my waist, a hard body pressing against my back. I melt into him, reaching behind me, pushing my fingers into short, wet hair. I can smell him so clearly. His soft, musky skin is mixed with the faint aroma of aftershave. He runs his hands up from my waist, brushing fingers up my sternum, then cups my breasts, pressing his thumbs into my already hard nipples. When I arch my back in gasped response, I can feel his erection digging into the side of my hip. He starts to kiss the sensitive skin of my neck, and I think I'm about to explode.

I love him.

That's all I can think of as he grinds himself into me, and I twist my head until my lips meet his. They're soft and gentle and move slowly against my mouth until I'm practically begging him to slide his tongue inside. He takes his time, breathing into me, tasting my skin, murmuring words against my lips that I can't understand.

Suddenly, he spins me round until our bodies are meshed together, pushed into one mass by the people surrounding us on all sides. He laces his fingers through my damp hair, angling my head until it fits his like a glove. Then we kiss and we touch and we roll for long minutes or hours or days until we are both breathless and needy. We both know we should leave or we'll have sex right here, in this club, and he curls his hands around mine and pulls me through the crowd. It's similar to walking through thick mud; we're fighting against the tide and more than a few times we have to stop and make out again. Each time we do I feel my heart race a little faster as Niall's fingers push into places that throb and undulate and beg him for more. Every time we kiss, colours explode in my mind, and I feel them burn me from my scalp to the tips of my toes.

Somehow we make it back to his room. He switches on the lights and I blink rapidly, the brightness hurting my brain. I stumble across the floor, my path impeded by a myriad of half-painted canvasses propped against walls and chests of drawers and even the bedstead. The riot of colours assault my senses and make me want to cry.

Then he's touching me again. Pulling me onto his half-made bed, kicking the crumpled covers down until there's only us and the mattress and peace and love. He spends hours undressing me, kissing and licking each newly exposed inch of skin. When his eyes meet mine I can see the concentration behind his glassy expression, as if he's determined not to miss a single piece of my body. His lips are slow, smooth, gentle, and they feel like heaven.

When we're both naked, he presses his body against mine. It feels as though we are liquid flesh, melting into each other, and the concept of us seems a foreign thing. We are we, me, him, Niall and Beth, one person, one body, one heart, one breath.

As he pushes inside I can feel every inch of him sliding into me. I cling to him tightly, my mouth pressed against his, kissing him, feeling him, taking him. When he grinds against me, his cries rough and breathless, I know it's going to feel better than any drug.

Then we're coming and coming, with liquid bodies and aching muscles. His breath is mine as our mouths move together, and the pleasure is so intense it almost hurts. Then, as the fireworks exploding inside my closed eyes fade into the shadows, I feel his lips pressed to my cheek, soft and gentle. Warm moans wafting against my skin.

"Beth."

The way he says it makes my eyes sting. Reverent. Amazed.

We are all arms and legs, tangled together; bound by crazy, sticky-sweet love. And a hundred tiny jolts pulse through me as he pulls out, my body still buzzing with pleasure. We fall asleep, a mess of hot flesh and deep sighs, our bodies drenched with sweat. When we wake in the morning, the pale light of dawn piercing through the half-shut curtains, we are still twisted together as one.

Even as we come down, I can feel everything has changed. I'm no longer the girl I used to be.

Because now, I'm *his* girl.

Now

5

I spend the next morning bent over the toilet in Lara's cramped, old-fashioned bathroom, vomiting in the bowl as she scoops my damp hair away from my face. She holds it in a ponytail so it won't get splashed. In between heaves I tell her I'm never going to drink again, that beer is the work of the devil, and she's a terrible influence on me.

She just laughs and passes me a damp facecloth. I press it to my skin, feeling it cool my overheated flesh.

By lunchtime I'm almost passing for normal. My head is pretty fuzzy, but at least I can walk without bending over in two. I don't remember hangovers being this bad when I was younger. Even coming down from an E is a walk in the park compared with this nausea.

"I'm too old for this," I moan as Lara bundles me up in a jacket and drags me to the nearest cafe. "I shouldn't have drunk that last glass of Baileys."

"Oh, you remember that, do you?"

I close my eyes, and wish I could shut my nose off, too. The cafe smells of bacon and greasy chips and I feel my stomach churn again. Lara orders us both a full English breakfast and I'm too exhausted even to refuse.

Of course, when it arrives, I gobble up the lot. As always, bacon is the ultimate hangover cure.

"So..." Lara pours us both a second mug of tea. "...Niall Joseph."

I take a sip. It's liquid heaven. "What about him?"

She tips her head to the side and gives me an are-you-kidding-me look. "He's the guy?"

Placing my mug back on the scratched wooden table, I rest my chin on my hands. "Yup."

"How do you feel about seeing him again?"

"Is this a counselling session? Should I be expecting a bill for fifty pounds an hour?" The waitress takes away our plates and I sigh with relief. No matter how good the breakfast tastes, seeing the remains congealing on the white plate is doing nothing for my lingering nausea.

"I'm not your counsellor, I'm your friend. But I do think you should talk to somebody, a professional. You haven't been yourself for weeks."

"I'm not going to fall into depression just because Niall Joseph has waltzed back into my life. I got over that years ago. It means nothing. I worked through all that crap when it happened."

I'm a different person to the girl who could barely bring herself to breathe. Stronger, more together.

"Why did you drink so much last night?"

Her question makes me bristle. "I haven't been on a night out like that in ages. I misjudged. It's a lot easier to be circumspect when you're drinking hundred-pound bottles of wine." I sound flippant, because I want to stop remembering it all. Niall, Digby, that hot, humid night when everything changed. If I don't think about it, I can cope.

Just about.

Lara looks at me and her lips start to twitch. The corners of my mouth rise up in response. A moment later we both collapse into a fit of giggles. I sound like such a loser. Sometimes I think I'm two different people: the Beth who wears jeans and sweaters, who drinks beer and spends her days with addicts, versus the Beth who eats elegant dinners and sips fine wine and listens silently to much older men putting the world to rights. It's becoming increasingly difficult to decide which person I am; which me I prefer.

The thought is still on my mind when Simon finally arrives home on Sunday evening. By that time I'm fully recovered from my hangover and feeling more like my old self. Any thoughts of depression and angst and Niall Joseph are squashed firmly down, and the smile which lights my face when my husband walks through the door is almost genuine.

"How was your weekend?" I pull his coat from his shoulders and place it on a wooden hanger. "You look tired, darling."

"I am. We had a good time. Took a few shots, drank a few whiskies. Turns out that Andrew's had the whole lodge renovated." Simon puts his case at the bottom of the stairs. "How was your weekend?"

We walk into the kitchen and I try to banish the memory of Niall's angry face. Deep breaths. Equilibrium.

"Mostly quiet. I managed to catch up on some paperwork today. I've realised it's only three months until the gala; I really need to get working on that." I'm not as daunted by this as I once was. I've been in charge of the gala for four years now. I pretty much know what I'm doing. Not that it's any easier, though. Even if I don't have that constant feeling of dread as I did that first year.

After a small supper we head upstairs for bed. It's only nine thirty, but we're both exhausted, and have to be up for work in the morning. I take a shower—letting the hot water wash away any remnants of the weekend from my skin—and by the time I've dried my hair, Simon is in bed, his wire-framed reading glasses perched on the bridge of his nose. He's making notes on some briefs he has brought home from work. His chest is bare; his body is well maintained in spite of his age. There is a smattering of grey hair from his neck to his stomach and a tiny paunch that even exercise can't erase. I like the softness of it, even though I know it makes him self-conscious.

When I climb under the covers, he lays the briefs on the bedside table and takes his glasses off. Switching off the bedside lamp, he shuffles down the mattress, turning on his side so he's facing away from me. In the darkness, I feel the familiar gloom wash over me again. I can kid myself all I want to that I'm okay, that the events of Friday haven't affected me, but alone in the dark, I start to feel like that nineteen-year-old girl again—full of emotions and unease. I don't like these raw sensations that seem to be turning me inside out. I prefer the certainty, the almost-numbness I've managed to achieve since marrying Simon.

So I snuggle up to his body, spooning him from behind, curling my arm around his chest. My palm splays against his torso, and he reaches up, placing his hand on top of my own. I push myself against him, letting the tip of my thumb brush against his nipple. A moment later he gently pulls it away.

"I'm really tired." He sounds apologetic. "I need to get some sleep."

I know he doesn't mean for it to come across as a rejection, but that's how I take it, anyway.

"It's okay." My voice is muffled by his back. This is a good thing, because I can feel the tears threatening to escape. I'm almost clinging to him, desperate for the connection, needing to hold on to him as if he's my only port in a storm. Simon's breathing starts to slow, becoming light and rhythmic as he falls gently asleep. A tear rolls slowly down my cheek as I try to stop the longing, the desperation to feel him inside me, the need for him to reclaim me in the basest way possible.

Instead, I cry silently, until nothingness takes over.

* * *

Niall and I don't mention that Friday night again. We're back to being amicable colleagues, working smoothly and easily together. Trying to keep the kids interested and under control takes up all of our emotional energy; there isn't enough left over to get into the angst of our past. It's so much easier to paper over the gaps than try to dig in deeper.

It doesn't stop me from looking at him, while he's preoccupied with something else, and wondering exactly what happened to him that summer. Did he get as low as I did? I find myself wanting to know more about what he's been doing since graduation. I know from Elise's brief, breathless description that he spent some time in the States, but how did he end up there? What made him come back?

All these things run through my mind as I watch him demonstrating a layering technique to Cameron Gibbs, a particularly mouthy twelve-year-old with a penchant for stealing. For some reason Cameron—whose widowed father has a deep and meaningful relationship with prescription drugs—seems to have taken a shine to Niall. He watches intently as Niall's long, paint-stained fingers pick up the brush and feather watercolour paint onto the paper. Niall says something to him that I can't hear, and Cameron's response is equally quiet. Whatever he says, it makes Niall's usually smooth forehead crinkle, his lips pulling down with a frown.

Then he looks up at me and beckons me over. My heart beats a little faster as I walk toward them, trying to swallow the memories down as I remember that action so well. The curled fingers, the come-hither stare. I do exactly what I always did—I obey.

Niall starts to talk as soon as I reach the table. "Cameron says he's never been to an art gallery."

I don't know why he looks so surprised. These are deprived inner-city kids whose parents' priorities include finding drugs, taking drugs, stealing money to afford drugs and very occasionally trying to kick the drug habit. Enriching their children's cultural knowledge doesn't come high on their agendas.

"I don't expect he has." I glance over at Cameron and smile. He grimaces back. In his world, smiles are for wimps.

"What about the rest of the kids?"

Without answering, I glance around the room. Allegra is bent over her paper, splashing colour on with glorious abandon. A couple of the older kids are sitting at the back flicking paint at each other with their brushes. The rest are either chatting or drawing. "I don't expect so, Niall. They probably haven't had the opportunity."

He chews on his lip. "But they live in London. We're surrounded by art galleries and museums."

And also drug dealers and crack dens. I widen my eyes in an attempt to get him to shut up. Cameron watches us interestedly.

"What can I tell you?" I say.

He pauses for a moment, thinking things through. Then his face lights up and a grin slowly forms on his lips. "We can take them."

"What?" I wasn't expecting that.

"You and I. We can take them all on an outing. We can go to the Tate Modern. I know some people there." He looks so young and enthusiastic it makes me smile.

"You want to take fifteen kids on a day trip to a gallery? How are we going to get there?"

He has an answer for everything. "I'll hire a coach. It can pick us up here at four; we can spend a couple of hours in the gallery, and then come back. I'll even stump up for a McDonald's for them all."

I notice Cameron's expression out of the corner of my eye. He looks almost excited. It would be amazing to show them real art, to have Niall talk them through the exhibitions, demonstrating how paint can bring a canvas alive. But these aren't just any kids. They aren't used to having to behave in an art gallery, and the older ones can be almost impossible to control. It'd be like herding cats.

"Can we talk over there?" I gesture to the empty desk in the corner of the room and wrap my fingers around his bicep to lure him over. The warmth of his skin leaches through his shirt, the hardness of his biceps through his flesh. He glances down to where my fingers hold him, then looks right into my eyes.

"Sure."

When we get there I release him. He absentmindedly rubs the spot where I was touching him. "Is there a problem?"

"This isn't going to work. We can't take them to a gallery. They'll end up destroying the place. Cameron will probably try to nick an installation and George will graffiti over some Dali with his spray paint. We're asking for trouble."

"You don't think these kids deserve to see some real paintings?"

He baits and I bite. "Of course I do. They deserve everything and most of them don't get it. But if something goes wrong and it ends up at the door of the clinic we'll all be in trouble."

Niall starts to pull at the paint coating his fingers. I notice it's oil-based, and as we are only using watercolours he must have come here with them like that. I feel curiosity overtake me, and I'm desperate to know what he was doing, what he was painting.

"I'll cover us. Let me speak with the Tate and set something up for next Thursday." He reaches out with jade-stained fingers. "Come on, Beth. Please?"

Next Thursday. I'm meant to be going out with Simon to a party that night, but it won't start until nine. I figure I'll be able to do both—take the kids to the gallery then go to the ball. Niall's so very irresistible, with those pouty lips and ocean-coloured eyes that in spite of my fears, of my misgivings, I find myself nodding in agreement.

My reward is a squeeze of my wrist and an excited grin which practically splits his face in two. Like the Niall-addict I used to be, I take it all in and let him set my pulse on fire.

Feel the burn.

I'm still feeling it when we finish for the day. The kids help clear up in their noisy, haphazard way, washing pots in the Belfast sink and managing to spill dirty grey water onto the floor below. It sprays over the white tiles surrounding the sink area.

When they're gone I clean up again, wiping down the white porcelain. Niall picks up the paintings and hangs them up on the string I've wired across the ceiling for just that purpose, securing them with clothes pegs.

"I'm sorry if I pushed you into a corner."

"What?" An image pops into my head—Niall manhandling me into a wall, pressing his body into mine. I can almost feel the outline of his chest against mine. I shake my head, trying to get it out of my mind.

"Over the gallery. I didn't mean to put you on the spot." His voice is so soft I have to step closer to hear him. "I feel bad for railroading you."

"You didn't railroad me." I am lying through my teeth. I don't want to be the weak one anymore. The girl so easily led astray. "It'll be great; I'm looking forward to it."

His smile is confused. "Okay. Well, thanks for agreeing to it. I owe you one."

I raise my eyebrows and nod. For a moment I find it easy to pretend this could work, that we could be two colleagues taking a group of kids on an outing. No issues, no history. Just good, clean friends.

I'm clearly delusional.

6

Nobody's seen Daisy MacArthur for a while. The last time anyone heard from her was almost two weeks ago, when she cancelled her appointment with Lara. Since then I've tried calling and messaging her with no response. A lump of lead lies at the bottom of my gut when I think of all the things that could have gone wrong.

Every one of them comes back to the same root cause: Darren.

Her lowlife scumbag of a boyfriend drifts in and out of her world like a crisp packet on a breeze. Every time, he wreaks havoc then disappears, leaving Daisy to pick up the pieces of her broken life. It gets harder each time. She thinks they're star-crossed lovers, destined to be together, torn apart by fate. In her mind, he's her Byron, her Romeo. Not Darren Tebbit, local drug dealer and all-round asshole.

Daisy was brought up by a single mother in a council flat not far from here. She watched her mum die a slow, lingering death from lung cancer when Daisy was only twelve. Her next four years were spent in the system, pushed from foster care to group home then back again. No wonder she was seduced by the idea of a white knight riding in to save her.

She's never told me who Allegra's father is—and I've never asked. I figure she'll tell me when she's ready, or if it's something important to her. All I know is she had Allegra at the age of sixteen, the right time to score herself a council flat, paid for by social services. The dad could have been another kid at the home or school. Perhaps a teacher or a care worker. I honestly have no idea. She wasn't the first teenager in the care system to think a baby would solve all her problems.

Even though Simon would kill me if he knew I was here, I arrive at her block of flats at two o'clock on Friday afternoon. The sun is desperately trying to burn through the grey, high-level clouds that've been cloaking the sky for days, lending them a pale lemon hue. It's so much prettier than the dull slate of the concrete tower block.

Built as part of a social movement that flushed through Britain in the 1960s, the tower stands as a memorial to over-optimism. Once there were flower pots and plants hanging from the rails that circle the building. Now there are drying clothes. Walkways wrap around the block—envisaged as 'streets in the sky'—and are best avoided at night. This is where the deals go down, where the gangs fight over territory. This is the Britain we middle-class folk like to forget exists.

I don't take the lift up to the fourth floor. It's out of order, but I'm also scared of getting stuck in there, among the litter and the smell of urine. If I'm truly honest with myself, I don't want to be trapped in there with another resident, either. They scare the hell out of me. Even dressed down in jeans and a thin jacket, wearing nondescript boots with my hair pulled into a messy bun, it's clear I don't belong around here. I don't think it's my clothes or make-up as much as the way my face looks. It's too clear and bright—not marred by a lifetime of poverty and desperation. Coming here makes me realise just how lucky I am, and how far I've come.

By the time I reach the fourth floor I'm breathless. I have to catch some oxygen before I open the door of the stairwell and walk out onto the long wraparound balcony that leads to all the flats. It's not quite so scary here during the day, though I'm still wary as I walk past a group of young lads, leaning against the rails and smoking, their dark eyes following me. I glance at them—enough to take in that despite their cigarettes and their bumfluff beards they should all be at school.

Of course, I'm too chickenshit to say anything.

Daisy lives at 422, about halfway down the block. When I get there, I notice the curtains are drawn. The window glass is so grimy that whatever light the thin fabric lets in must be obscured by dirt. Knocking twice on the door makes a few flecks of peeling red paint fall to the concrete floor. After waiting for a minute I knock again, but there's still no response.

I vacillate over what to do next. Perhaps I should leave a note, or wait until Daisy comes back, but I'm too scared to hang around here for long. I knock one last time and shout her name this time—making sure there's nobody outside who can hear me—but I get nothing.

Then there's a loud creak as the door to the next flat opens. A woman peers around the wooden frame, reaching up to wipe a lock of greasy brown hair out of her face. She stares at me through narrowed eyes.

"You from the council?" she asks suspiciously.

"No." I shake my head quickly.

She raises a drawn-on eyebrow. "The social?"

"I'm a friend of Daisy's. Do you know where she is?"

She's still staring at me. Her eyes slowly scan downward, taking in my clothes, my shoes, the way I stand. "Yeah."

We look at each other, and it takes me a minute to realise she isn't going to follow up. "Where?"

"Who wants to know?"

I take a step toward the woman, then stop as soon as I notice the huge dog standing right behind her. I'm not that great with breeds, but it looks like a wolf crossed with a Doberman. "My name's Beth. I know Daisy and Allegra. I want to make sure she's okay."

"They took her kiddie away."

"I know. But Daisy, is she okay? Have you seen her?" I don't know if it's my persistence, or if my genuine concern shines through, but I notice her expression thaw a little.

"She hasn't been out for days. Not since her boyfriend left."

"Darren's gone?"

"Yeah, and good fucking riddance if you ask me. Coming and going at all hours, bringing bad people back. Fucker."

I try to smile sympathetically, but my stomach lurches. If this woman is describing Darren's friends as 'bad people', they have to be truly awful. "Are you sure she's in there?" I incline my head to Daisy's flat.

The woman shrugs. "I'm not a nosy neighbour or anything, but I haven't seen her leave. And she isn't exactly quiet, if you know what I mean."

Then she's in there. I can tell the woman is *definitely* a nosy neighbour, and she'd know for sure if Daisy had left. I feel panic start to rise in my chest. If Daisy is alone—and has been for days, not answering her phone—then what sort of state is she in?

I pummel on her door, calling out her name. Feeling stupid and alone—except for the neighbour and her dog—I swallow down my panicked tears.

"She won't answer."

"What?"

"She'll think you're from the council."

"But I need to check on her."

Cool as a cucumber, the woman walks out of her doorway and over to where I'm standing. Gently pushing me out of the way, she does something to the lock I can't quite see. A moment later, the door swings open. A waft of warm, dank air hits my nostrils. My gag reflex comes back stronger than ever.

The neighbour goes back to her flat without a word, pulling her dog with her, closing her door with a click. Leaving me alone in Daisy's flat. I start to feel really anxious. What if

Darren hasn't really gone? I've only seen him once, when he met Daisy outside the clinic, but there was an air of malevolence in his stare that scared me stupid. I take a deep breath and walk into the living room, trying to ignore the taste of stale air.

The floor and table are littered with takeaway cartons and beer cans, and there are ashtrays over-spilling with butts of both cigarettes and joints. DVD cases are strewn across the TV stand, and there is a big pile of clothes in the corner.

But no Daisy. Where is she?

I pull my mobile phone out of my bag and clutch it in my sweaty fingers, holding it like a talisman to ward off evil. Then I walk out of the lounge and into the next room. One glance tells me it's empty—from the pink walls and pile of toys I'm guessing this is Allegra's room. I step back out and head for the third door. When I get closer I start to hear something—more than heavy breath, less than moaning. A couple of coughs that sound way too full of liquid.

"Daisy?" I push the door tentatively. My whole body is alive with adrenaline. I'm half a sensible thought away from getting the hell out of here. Just when I think there's going to be no reply, there's another almost-groan.

Right away, I can tell it's her bedroom. Though the curtains are drawn, they're thin enough to let in the light. She's lying curled up on the bed, her hands clutching at her stomach. Her right eye is black and swollen—illuminated with a greeny-yellow sheen where the bruise has matured. Right below it, the side of her cheek is enlarged and puffy, almost certainly broken again. A stench of urine and vomit permeates the air. I have to cover my mouth and nose with my free hand, trying not to be sick.

With the other, I dial 999.

* * *

Simon doesn't get angry very often. I'm used to his softly spoken, gentle way of communicating. Of course, I've seen him in adversarial mode—being a lawyer it's almost obligatory—though with me he's always been a man carefully handling a fragile china doll. But ever since he picked me up from the hospital an hour ago, he's been holding his body like a lion about to pounce.

So many times he's told me that working at the clinic is dangerous. He's asked me to leave before, and I've held out, telling him I'm not in harm's way. Today, we both know that's a lie.

Maybe that's why I'm finding this so hard. Perched on the edge of our leather couch, my fingers clutching the seat cushion, my heart rattles in my chest like an animal in a cage. He paces in front of me, one hand pulling at his white-blond hair, the other balled into a fist.

"What the hell were you thinking?" He stops in front of me. "Jesus Christ, have you no brain cells in that pretty head of yours?"

"I'm so sorry. I..."

He continues as if I haven't spoken, "When we got married you promised this wouldn't affect us. You said you'd give up the clinic before it did."

Did I say that? It does sound like something I might have said. But my heart falls at his words. I don't know if he's being passive aggressive and trying to make me leave the clinic, or if he's simply thinking things through out loud.

I remain silent.

He starts pacing again. It's rhythmic; three steps to the right, stop and turn, four steps to the left, then stop.

"Why didn't you call somebody? Why did you go there alone? If something had happened to you..."

Tears start to pool in my eyes. Even though I swallow hard, they start to overflow, because something *did* happen today. I found my friend lying in a pool of her own vomit and blood, almost dead on her bed. I got to see the bruises and the cuts and the track marks and I can't get it out of my head. Even thinking about the way she smelled when I got close—a horrific mixture of vomit and excrement—makes me want to hurl.

I start to shiver when I think of another death, so many years ago. The way Digby collapsed. How we were responsible. It all comes flooding back, the guilt, the memories, the unshakeable pain.

"Don't turn on the fucking waterworks with me."

My eyes widen as I lift my head up to meet his angry stare. Simon hardly ever swears. I bite my lips in an effort to stifle any sobs. He's starting to scare me, this angry, shouting Simon. It feels as though my blood is fizzing in my veins, all my muscles slackened and useless. Still the tears flow like hot rivulets down my cheeks; cooling at my chin.

"Simon, please."

"Please what? Please can I go and put my life in danger again? For some bloody junkie who couldn't give a damn about herself?"

"Daisy isn't a junkie." I know this is a lie. "She's a friend. Somebody's mother. She counts."

She matters, of course she does. So did Digby. I owe him this.

"You count more."

"I've taken drugs as well, you know." There, I've said it. Brought up my own past before he can. I don't know why I've decided to rehash it now.

"It's not the same. You weren't a junkie, you just experimented." Though his tone is lower, his face is still an angry red. I know that when he's in control of his words he can out-talk me every time. "I don't want you seeing her again."

What? I feel disbelief wash over me, almost stemming the tears. "You can't be serious."

"I'm completely serious. She put you in danger. I don't want you anywhere near her."

"She didn't put me in danger. I did that all by myself." I've walked right into it. His lips twitch at my words.

"Then you need to choose your friends more wisely."

"Since when did you decide to become my dad?"

"When you started to act like a child. You don't seem to be thinking straight, Beth. You went to the worst tower block in London, walked up to the fourth floor and then broke into a junkie's flat. Did you not think it through? What if her boyfriend had been there? What if he'd beaten you up, too? I could have lost you."

Standing up, I throw my arms around him, burying my sobs in his shoulder. His stance is stiff, his muscles unyielding. "I'm sorry. I just wanted to know she was okay."

He pushes me back. His hands grip my shoulders as he looks at me. "This is going to sound harsh but I really don't care if your friend is all right. I do care if you're okay, though. And you're not okay. You haven't been okay for weeks. If the clinic is making you feel like this, if it's going to come between us and affect our relationship, then I want you to give it up."

"It's not the clinic that's made me feel this way."

"Then what is it?"

I open my mouth to say something, but nothing comes out. I know I've been behaving differently—erratically sometimes. My mood has been swinging from high to low, and I know exactly why it is. It's nothing I want to share with Simon, though.

It isn't Niall Joseph's fault he's stirred everything up until I don't know which way is up. Not his fault I've been digging up memories I've long since buried. The past is making me feel raw and open. A wound that refuses to heal.

"I don't know. I've just been feeling down."

"Why didn't you say anything?"

Because I can't stop thinking about another man and it makes me the worst kind of person. "I can deal with it. I promise."

"You don't have to deal with it alone. I'm your husband, let me help you."

I feel like his child again. Rather than accepting his dominance of me, I start to bristle. What once felt like protection now seems more like a prison.

Nine Years Earlier

My eyes feel as though they are glued together, my lips are cracked and dry. I slowly moisten them with my tongue before attempting to open my eyelids, fighting against the sleep that's keeping them closed.

"Don't move." Niall's voice is raspy and low, the aural equivalent of my own come-down state. Of course I do the opposite, sitting up in his unmade bed, seeking him out. He's perched on an old wooden chair, a large sketchpad propped on his knees. Pulling an over-sharpened stub of a pencil across it, his movements are just short of furious. When he looks up and sees I've moved a flash of irritation crosses his face.

"I told you to stay still." Even though his words are harsh, he manages to soften them with a smile.

I reach up my arms and stretch them to the ceiling, letting a yawn escape my lips. "What are you drawing?"

He puts the sketchpad down, locking his gaze on to my exposed chest. My nipples peak as they're bathed with cool air.

"Nothing." He's still staring at me. I cover myself up with my arms, feeling self-conscious. The irritation returns to his face. "Don't hide yourself from me."

"You're being very bossy this morning." I don't tell him that I like it, but I do. There's nothing I don't like about this man. I'm totally infatuated with him.

"And you're being very disobedient." Niall crawls across the mattress until he's looming over me on all fours. Dipping down, he captures a nipple between his lips and scrapes his teeth across it. I arch my back in pleasured response. "What can I do to persuade you to lie still?" he asks.

I gasp as his fingers find me and push inside. "Not that." I prove my point by starting to squirm. He laughs into my chest, and I feel the vibrations on my skin. Then he lifts his head up and kisses me hard, and I forget about everything except the sensation of his body on mine, and the absolute, sheer pleasure of come-down sex.

Later, we lean out of his window and share a joint, looking out at the green, undulating campus, watching the few solitary figures who are braving the early morning rain. Mostly staff; no students would feel the need to be up at this hour. He offers me a toke, exhaling smoke that quickly dissipates into the damp, misty air. "I want you to model for me."

I lift the joint to my lips and breathe it in. "Nude?"

"Of course." He sounds as if he's smirking and I turn to look at him.

Yep, he's smirking.

"How very Rose and Jack of you."

Propping his elbow on the windowsill, Niall stares at me. "Who are they? Friends of yours?"

I start to blush, feeling stupid and suburban and so very ordinary. I can't bring myself to tell him I'm talking about *Titanic*. This is why I feel silly whenever he is around. He paints beautiful pictures and makes love as if it's an art form, and I go around talking about overly melodramatic films. I'm a child trying to catch a butterfly.

It seems like a good time to change the subject. "What time is it?"

"Nearly seven. Why?'

I take another puff. "I have a nine o'clock seminar." I can't miss this one. Lectures are one thing—easy to avoid and then borrow notes from somebody else—but at seminars there's only a few of us. It's obvious when we aren't there.

"Skip it. Stay with me."

I want to, I really do. But somewhere beneath the lust and the intoxication lies obedient Bethany from Essex. Daughter of a city banker. Mostly A-grade student. She stretches her arms and slowly wakes up.

I go to the seminar, but I barely pay attention. Instead, I find myself daydreaming about him.

Now

7

I'm running late again. I almost make it to the Tube station before my phone rings. Stopping mid-pace, I pull it out of my bag, pausing a moment to catch my breath.

"Hello?"

"It's Simon." He has this propensity to think we're still using analogue phones. It's as if he forgets his name comes up on my screen when he calls.

"Hello. Everything okay?" We've been treading on eggshells for the past week. Pretending to be asleep when I know we're not; neither of us mentioning Daisy or the clinic. When I went to visit Allegra last weekend, he didn't bother asking me where I was going. I didn't volunteer the information, either.

"Do you know if my suit came back from the cleaners? I want to wear it tonight." Another thing he does: leaves all things domestic until the last minute. I don't think that's why he's calling this time; we both know his suit came back last Friday. He's trying to remind me we are going out tonight.

"It's there. I should be home after seven. What time are we leaving?" The last thing I want to do after taking ten kids around an art gallery is go out to some dry, work-related dinner party. They're clients of Simon's and it's important to him, though, so I'll pull on a dress and paint my face and make small talk as I always do.

That doesn't mean I have to like it.

"Drinks at eight thirty. Try not to be late."

Thanks, Dad.

"Mmhmm." I hang up, biting my tongue to prevent a pithy response. Even if the train arrives on time, I'll be ten minutes late. I hastily tap out a text and send it to Niall.

When I get to the clinic it's mayhem. The lobby is full of kids, shouting out questions at a harassed-looking Niall. His face lights up when he sees me walk into the room. Smiling, he takes a step forward and reaches for my hand. "You're here."

"Of course I am. And the bus is outside," I say.

A look of relief washes over him. Does he even know what he's let himself in for? We may have limited this expedition to ten children—mostly so we can all fit in one minibus—but that's still a lot of bodies to be following around one very large art gallery.

He gives the impression he hasn't had a lot to do with children. Looks on them as mini-adults. Which is great when you're in the classroom; it makes them feel mature and liked, and that's why they respond to him so well. But when we're out in public, in the middle of a gallery that he has associations with... not quite so good.

"Let's go. Come on, everybody." Niall heads for the door and they all follow him. Cameron Gibbs pushes everybody out of the way and runs toward the bus, calling dibs on the back seat. There are a few stragglers who hang back with me, afraid of the older boys and their over-eagerness.

Allegra folds her hand around mine. "Shall we go?"

"Sure, lead the way."

Predictably, there's a pile-up in the minibus as everybody fights for seats. I end up having to pull Cameron Gibbs off another boy. His hand has already curled into a pretty sizeable fist. I whisper in his ear that I'm watching him, and he rolls his eyes at me.

Cameron has one of those unfortunate faces. A thin, almost mean mouth which, combined with a heavy brow and narrow eyes, serves to make him look like a thug in training. He could be the sweetest kid in the world—which he isn't—and still he'd be the first to get into trouble. Dragged to the headmaster's room after a fight, or up in front of a magistrate after a robbery. A usual suspect waiting to happen.

Now he's growing into his looks. On the cusp of puberty, he's developing an air of menace about him. I'm unsure how much of it is bluster and how much is malevolence, but he's changing in front of my eyes. Whenever he's around there's an edge to the atmosphere. I hate that I can't stop him from growing up this way.

After everybody's sat down, I grab the only seat left—next to Niall. He looks up from his phone and smiles warmly at me.

"You're good at that."

"Shouting at kids?"

"No, you're good at dealing with them. You know what to say and how to say it. I can tell they trust you."

Farther back in the minibus, Cameron is still glowering. While we were having words somebody else stole his seat. He's not happy about it at all.

"Some of them do," I say.

"Are you planning to have kids of your own?" he asks. His blue eyes stare right at me. It's the kind of easy question anybody might ask.

"No." If I left it at that, maybe all would be well. But I'm me, and I find the need to fill in the blanks. I never could stand silence. "Simon doesn't want any more children."

His brows rise up. "That doesn't seem fair if you want some. A bit selfish."

My reply is crisp. Blunt. "He told me he didn't want any before we got married." I agreed to it, too. Back then, children weren't even on my radar. The world still felt like a nightmare place. Bringing children into it would be a selfish act. But now… I'm not sure I feel the same way.

Simon does, though. That's why I could never tell him about my volte-face. I'd be breaking our agreement.

"I'm sorry to hear that." He gives my hand a squeeze. "You'd make a fantastic ma."

The fire in my stomach burns out, replaced by a huge lump in my throat. I try not to choke up, but it's hard when I'm being comforted by the man who's stirred everything up. We're sitting close, his thigh warm against mine, his upper arm pressed into my bicep. Any anger I felt a moment ago has dissipated with his kind words, until all I'm left with is longing. It would be so easy to turn to him, to bury my head in his shoulder and let him hug me until everything else disappeared.

I never did choose easy. Perhaps it's for the best.

Niall and I imploded like a dying star, burning brightly one moment then fading into blackness the next. That sort of excitement, emotional highs and lows, may be something to live for when you're a teenager. Now, though, I should long for comfort, for steadiness, for Simon.

I need to keep reminding myself of that.

We get to the Tate Modern about half an hour later. It's an amazing building. Converted from a decommissioned power station in the 1990s, the brown-brick edifice has a huge chimney rising up from its almost Art-Deco roof. Seated on the edge of the South Bank, it is virtually opposite St Paul's Cathedral, which rises majestically from the north. The kids get all excited when they see the Millennium Bridge over the Thames that connects the two, recognising it from a Harry Potter movie. A couple of them start to run to the steps.

"Oy, get back here." It's amazing how easily the Essex tinge comes back to my voice. "Cameron Gibbs, get down from there now." He's already made it to the top of the stairs, and is mucking about with all the padlocks that lovers have attached to the rails.

Somehow, we manage to herd them all into the building. Niall speaks with the woman at the information desk, and she smiles back at him, handing him a book to fill in. When he comes back, we all follow, heading for the engine room.

The giant turbine hall is in the middle of the building, accessible from stone steps leading down to the recessed floor. Where engines once blasted out energy, now there is space and light. It's the main installation of the gallery. The kids start to run down the stairs and we quickly follow after them. I try not to smile as they look around.

"Where're the paintings?" Cameron Gibbs asks, standing on the bottom step.

"There is no painting. This is an installation," Niall replies. "Sometimes there are sculptures, sometimes images projected on screens."

"So where's the fuckin' art then?" Cameron spits out. He's still annoyed with me.

I catch Niall's eye. Like me, he looks torn between amusement and irritation.

"The people are the installation," he says. "If you go down there, they'll interact with you. The artist has planned it all out."

"I'm not talking to fucking strangers."

I begin to lose my patience. "Language, Cameron." Some of the younger children are staring at him with their mouths open. "We're out in public."

"All I'm saying is," Cameron continues, his voice almost patient, "if this is fucking art, then my street's a bleedin' masterpiece. All you have to do is come over and we'll talk to you for nothing. How much does somebody get paid for something like this anyway? It's like that naked geezer, innit?"

I frown for a moment, before working it out. "You mean *The Emperor's New Clothes*?"

"I mean money for old bloody rope. Seriously, if this is art then I don't want any of it." Cameron turns around and wanders off into the crowd of people. Do the actors know what they've let themselves in for?

"He's some kid." Niall and I walk into the main room. "Not backward at coming forward."

"Were you at his age?"

Niall laughs. "Not really. I was the scourge of the neighbourhood. My ma used to pull her hair out whenever I was brought back by a Garda or one of the neighbours. Luckily, I grew out of it."

"You weren't one for authority at university, either," I point out. "Smoking dope in halls, breaking into buildings at night."

"Ah, but that was all in the name of art. It served a higher purpose."

"What purpose?" He's got me interested now. I remember back to those days with a smile on my face. That doesn't happen very often.

"Mostly getting a girl naked."

What can I say to that? Apart from the fact he didn't need to break into a building to get me naked. I practically tore my clothes off every time we were together.

"Shall we go and round them up? There's only another hour or so." I change the subject quickly.

He smiles easily. "Sure. I thought we'd go around the Abstract Impressionists. Show them some Rothko and Monet." His face lights up, as if an idea has come into his mind. "Hey, you should do the talking; you're the one with the Art History degree."

"I don't have a degree," I point out. "I never finished."

And there it is. Our past seems to seep into everything. There's a reason I didn't finish, one we're both more than aware of. It makes for awkward conversation.

"Well, we can share the burden."

We're about half an hour into the gallery when I decide to do a quick headcount. Trying to get them all to stand still is easier said than done. Eventually, I manage to tap each child gently on the shoulder as I count them off, making my way up to ten.

Except I only get to nine.

Low-level panic starts to twist in my stomach as I do a recount. Still nine. When I meet Niall's eyes he can see something's wrong.

"Who's missing?" I don't know if I'm asking him, myself or the children. "There's only nine of you." I glance over at Allegra, who's standing next to Niall. Thank God she's okay.

The kids start murmuring but none of them are talking to me. "Come on, which one of you knows something?"

Twelve-year-old Maisie Weeks catches my eye. "Cameron walked off about ten minutes ago."

I swallow hard. "He walked off?"

She shrugs. "Yeah, he said this was boring and he was going to find something better to do."

I catch Niall's eye. "We're in the middle of London. He could be anywhere." I know I sound shrill. Sheer panic has raised my voice by an octave.

He puts a calming hand on my shoulder. "The likelihood is he's either still in here or on the bridge. Let's go down to the information stand and see if they've seen him. They might have CCTV."

So we all troop back to the entrance. This time I walk at the back of the group, afraid to lose anybody else. Niall leads the way; Allegra still stuck beside him for some reason. I can see her chatting away to him, which is really unusual. After her experiences with her mum's boyfriend she doesn't usually take well to men.

All is quiet when we get to the information booth. I make the kids stand in twos while Niall and Allegra go up to the woman standing there. He talks rapidly to the lady behind the desk, then nods as she answers. Then she picks up a telephone and makes a call. How did we manage to lose one of them so easily? There's a huge river practically outside the building, and I'm trying to ignore the thought of him falling in.

My heart hammers against my chest when Niall walks back over. It speeds up when I see the expression on his face.

"Bad news, I'm afraid."

"Oh, God. Is he hurt?"

"Hardly. He's been caught nicking stuff from the shop. They've called the police."

Oh shit. Suddenly, this seems so much worse than just playing about on the bridge. This is serious. "Can I see him?"

"I'll ask."

A few minutes later I'm being led down to the security office. I've left Niall behind with the kids, with strict instructions to get them in the bus, and stop for McDonald's as he promised. They won't give him any problems—they were all downbeat and morose when I left them. Cameron's put a dampener on everybody's day.

The head of security—a man whose uniform seems practically painted on his plump body—takes me aside and explains Cameron was caught stealing a £50 ornament. He'd pushed it down inside his hoodie before he was caught. It's all on camera. The guard tells me it's their policy to press charges, and I nod sagely, wondering if it's worth begging on Cameron's behalf.

Then I see him sitting in the office, his feet up on his chair and his arms crossed over his chest. He's got this aura of bravado, wears it like a suit of armour, and I wonder if being taken to the station is the worst thing that can possibly happen. I'm not a therapist, and I'm definitely not a child psychologist, but Cameron's on a track that can only lead to a life I don't want for him. So I take the seat the manager offers and we wait almost an hour for the police to arrive.

8

Cameron stares at the wall with dry eyes, his thin lips pulled tightly across gritted teeth. Following his gaze, I search for the thing that's dragging his attention away from the sergeant sitting opposite him, but the only thing there is the pockmarked, steel-coloured wall. The paint is thick, shiny and dull, dull, dull.

If Dulux made it they'd probably call it 'Suicide Grey'.

He's scared, I know he is. Beneath the cockiness and swagger that form a tight shell around his body there's a frightened little kid. I know it from the occasional look he gives me, and from the way his eyes soften and liquefy when they tell him his rights. It's that little kid that keeps me here, sitting beside him as a responsible adult, trying to get him to answer the questions.

"We've got CCTV evidence," Sergeant Collier says. "Shows you stuffing that paperweight in your pocket like it's a Mars bar. Are you still denying it?"

Cameron shrugs and I want to shake him. His lack of cooperation is infuriating. Not only to the policeman, whose narrow eyes show the impatience of a man who is tired of being lied to. I, too, want him to hurry up, to admit to the crime and let them get on with it. Simon was expecting me home an hour ago. I've not had the chance to call him or send him a message. I'm going to be in big trouble when I finally do.

"Cameron, maybe you should answer his questions."

He folds his arms tightly across his pigeon chest and flashes his bleached blue gaze across the room. "Have you found my dad yet?"

They sent a policeman to locate Mr Gibbs two hours ago. We waited for an hour before Cameron finally crumbled and agreed to be questioned in my presence. He refused to have a duty solicitor present; claimed all they were good for was getting him found guilty and locked up. How a thirteen-year-old knows anything about duty solicitors, I've no idea. I suppose he's been around a lot of crime.

"Nope." Sergeant Collier has a self-satisfied smirk. I can understand why Cameron took an instant dislike to him. I'm not that keen, either.

"I want to wait for him."

"You agreed to questioning," Collier points out. "If we can't find your dad we'll have to keep you here overnight."

A flash of unease passes over Cameron's face. Blink and you'd miss it. "Whatever."

"Wait a minute." I lean forward, resting my forearms on the plastic-coated table. "Let's not be hasty."

Collier looks at me. "I'm not hasty."

Oh, joy. Now I've alienated him as well. "Can I have a word with Cameron? In private." The leaflet they gave me when I agreed to accompany Cameron told me I can request to be alone with him. Collier wasn't there when I got it, though. For a moment he just glares at me. Steely eyes. Unbending gaze. He gives me the jitters. "Please?"

"I suppose so."

"Don't do us any favours," Cameron mutters, and I want to hit him. My knuckles tingle. He's driving me crazy. His one-way route to self-destruction seems to have picked up a hitchhiker, and unfortunately it's me.

"Can you rein it in for a minute?" I hiss. Cameron looks shocked at my vehemence, but wisely says nothing. Perhaps he's not such an idiot, after all.

"You can have ten minutes, I'll get a cuppa." Collier pauses the recording and leaves the room, pulling the door shut behind him. I stare at the closed door for a minute, as though I'm waiting for him to come back. What I'm actually doing is counting to ten. Trying to calm myself down.

It's not working.

Eventually, I turn to look at Cameron. "What the hell are you doing?"

He rocks slowly on his chair—back and forth. Each time he tips I think he's going to fall over, but he doesn't. It's as if he has an innate sense of balance, tuned to a hair trigger.

"He's pissing me off."

"Don't swear." It's an automatic reaction.

Cameron giggles. Not a laugh, it's too high pitched for that. "You're worried about my language?"

I push off the table and stand up. "No, Cameron, I'm not worried about your language. I'm worried about your future. You've been caught red-handed stealing from a shop. The police have CCTV evidence and witnesses, yet still you're being bolshie and uncooperative."

"Mickey always tells me to keep my mouth shut if the pigs pull me in."

There are so many shades of wrong with his words I don't know where to start. Sighing, I take the easiest route. "Who's Mickey?"

"My cousin." He rocks forward, then adds, "He's sixteen." As if that explains everything.

"And what makes your sixteen-year-old cousin the expert on being arrested?" Do I really want to know?

Cameron shrugs. "Been busted a few times. Dealing, thieving. GBH."

Lovely.

"Beating somebody up is a bit different to a first offense," I point out. "If you cooperate, the likelihood is you'll only get a reprimand."

And maybe I'll get out of here before Simon throws all my stuff out on the street.

"I don't care."

I come to a stop in front of him, resting against the table. "Well, you should care. This isn't funny, Cameron, this is your life you're pissing up the wall—"

"Language."

"Shut up and listen for a minute. This is your first time in this police station. The first time you've been arrested. If you don't buck up your ideas it won't be your last. Do you really want to end up like Mickey, or any of those other thugs constantly being hounded by the police?"

His face falls. "I'm not sure I get the choice." And in that voice there's something I want to cling to: a lack of certainty, a wavering fear.

"You do. You get the choice. And I want you to make the right one."

His brow pulls down, as if he's trying to listen to a foreign tongue.

"Because it doesn't have to be like this, Cameron. You don't have to be that guy who just drifts. The one who ends up serving time in a shitty jail and comes out to kids who don't know him and a girl who can't stand the sight of you." I bite my lip, trying not to get too emotional. "We all have to make decisions. What road to take, which route to choose. Make the right one."

His eyes meet mine. "I don't know what to do." It sounds like a plea.

I soften. "Let me speak with the sergeant. Tell him you want to talk. We'll see what he can offer?" Taking a deep breath, I reach out to touch his shoulder. "Okay?"

"Okay."

I'm not stupid. I know it's not a breakthrough. It might not be anything at all, but I let a little bit of hope bloom in my heart. Maybe, in the end, he will still end up like his jailbird cousin Mickey, or his slacker, absentee dad, but I truly hope he doesn't.

* * *

It takes another hour for the on-call social worker to pick Cameron up. By this point we are both drained—emotionally as well as physically—and he barely rolls his eyes when he sees it's Ryan Clark. The unfortunate-looking guy has the nickname 'superboy' because he looks about twelve and is anything but a superhero. Still, Cameron goes quietly with Ryan, only stopping to flash me a cheeky wink before he follows him out of the door.

Then there was one.

It's past ten by the time I emerge from the police station and out into the cool evening air. I'm immediately shrouded by a misting of rain. It hangs in the atmosphere and coats my hair, tiny beads clinging to my eyelashes. When I blink, I can feel the cool wetness against my cheek.

The road outside is bathed with an amber glow, the streetlamps illuminating the city as far as the eye can see. It's never truly dark here in London, not even in the dead of night. Streets and alleys which were once contaminated by thick, cloying smog are now polluted by light.

At first I don't notice him. It's not until Niall steps out of his car and walks toward me, his fingers running through his hair like a nervous comb, that I finally realise he's here. When he comes to a stop in front of me I feel my heart clench for a second. In the half-light he looks more glorious than ever. I stare up at him, his eyes dark in spite of the lamps, and it all comes crashing down on me. The stress of the police station, the misery of knowing Cameron could self-destruct; my fears about Simon's reaction.

The fact Niall's here, waiting for me, when I feel so exhausted.

I do a stupid thing. I start to cry.

Even as the first tear falls, I am embarrassed. A stolen sob escapes my lips. I feel exposed, as if he can see beneath my skin right to the real me.

I don't even know when it happens. One minute I'm staring up at him, his face blurred through a curtain of tears, the next minute I'm in his arms, my chest tight against his. He buries his face in my hair. It muffles his words, but not enough for them to disappear.

"I'm so fucking sorry."

His jacket is open, and when I wrap my arms around his waist, my hands slip underneath. They rest on his back, just above his waistband. The warmth of his body radiates through his thin shirt. As he holds me I take in deep gulps of the fresh night air, the misty rain coating my lips as I breathe.

There's a part of me that wants to stand here forever. I don't have to think about how angry Simon is going to be, and how scared I am to turn on my phone and see dozens of missed calls. Even better, for a moment I can forget all about Cameron Gibbs and his mixture of fear and bullishness that both infuriates me and tears me apart. Right now, with Niall, I can just *be*. It's a luxury I want to hold on to.

But it isn't mine to have.

"What happened?" He cups his hand around the back of my head, fingers tangling in my damp hair. It feels good. Too good. I take a step back and his arm falls back to his side.

"They gave him a reprimand." I push my wet fringe from my eyes. God only knows how bad I look; pale face, running mascara, red eyes.

"That's good, right? Just a warning?"

I shake my head. "It still goes on his record, that's what they said." That hurts more than anything. Cameron's record was clean, unblemished. What's done cannot be undone.

"But nothing else? No court appearance?"

"No." That's something positive, at least. "And hopefully he's learned a lesson." Catching Niall's eyes, I frown. "What are you doing here, anyway? Are the rest of the kids okay?"

"They're fine. I bought them all dinner; they were happy as sandboys." He runs his hand through his hair, and the rain keeps it swept back off his face. It glistens under the light of the streetlamps. "They all asked when we can go again."

I raise my eyebrows. "How about never?"

"My thoughts exactly." He laughs. It only lasts for a moment before he turns serious again. "I owe you a big apology."

"What for?"

"You told me this would happen. That we couldn't keep control. I should have listened to you."

"I was thinking the kids would run in the gallery and talk too loudly. Not *this*."

A smile threatens at his lips. "You set your sights way too low."

"Maybe next time we can aim for grand larceny."

"Hey, I thought we said there wouldn't be a next time."

Good point, I think. One night in a police station is more than enough; I don't want to go there again. Not that I'll be allowed to, if Simon has anything to do with it. Maybe he's right. I can't seem to do anything right. Daisy is still in hospital, Cameron is still headed for a life of crime, and I appear to be doing everything I can to mess up my marriage.

"I need to call my husband." I don't know why I can't say his name. "He'll be wondering where I am."

"We should get out of the rain," Niall suggests, dipping his head so I can't see his expression. "My car's over there. I can give you a lift home."

"I'll call a taxi."

"Don't be silly." He's already walking toward his car, an old, beat-up Ford Fiesta. I don't know what I was expecting from him, but this rusty, downtrodden vehicle wasn't it.

It's unpretentious. For some reason, that warms me inside.

"Is this yours?"

"Yeah." He presses his key and the locks click open. "Why?"

Because I think of you as a glamorous genius. Because I expected your car to be more rock and roll.

Because I love the way you constantly surprise me.

"No reason."

Inside, it's damp and musty, like a pair of shoes left out in the rain. He's tried to disguise the odour with an air freshener that hangs from the mirror, but the cardboard tree is no match for the more powerful smell. I sit down on the fabric passenger seat, kicking an empty plastic Coke bottle with my feet. The car is full of rubbish—used wrappers, stacks of papers, even a couple of canvasses.

"It's a bit of a mess." He states the obvious.

"It suits you."

Niall gives me a "what's-that-supposed-to-mean?" look and turns on the ignition. Even though the dial is turned right up, the heater pumps out cold air. He leans forward and turns the fan down. "It should warm up in a minute."

My handbag is on my lap. I unzip it and take out my iPhone. I turned it off when we arrived at the station, mostly to preserve a battery that can no longer hold its charge. It takes a moment for the screen to light up. As I stare down at it, a huge rock of fear settles at the bottom of my stomach, curdling the contents until I can almost taste my own nausea.

"You okay?"

No, I'm not okay. I'm scared my husband hates me, and that he's left a message to that effect on my phone. I feel like a kid waiting outside the headmaster's office. The phone trembles in my hand as alerts begin to flash across the top of the screen. Emails from clothes websites I used years ago, tweets I've been mentioned in.

There are also four texts and three voicemails. Like the scaredy-cat I am, I check the tweets first. Someone from the clinic has asked if I'm okay. Some guy I've never heard of before has started to follow me. There's a retweet of a book I recommended.

I read the texts next.

Where are you? Simon's just called me. That one's from Lara.

I've just spoken to Niall Joseph. Cameron Gibbs probably deserves locking up. Give me a call when you get out, okay? Lara, again.

I hope you don't mind, Lara gave me your number. How are you holding up in there? Niall.

I glance over at him. "You texted me?"

"Yeah, I was worried about you. The woman at the station desk wouldn't tell me anything."

I don't know why, but his concern touches me. When he catches my eye I try to give him a smile. It comes out watery and twisted.

Only one text is from Simon. *Call me.*

I will, I tell myself, I'll definitely call him, but first I check my voicemails, wanting to know what mood he's in. Whether I should steel myself for the worst.

"Beth, I thought you'd be home by seven. It's now... um... half past. We need to leave soon, so hurry back, okay?"

The next one sounds angrier. "It's now quarter past eight. I'm going over to Bryan's, you'll have to meet me there. Call me please."

The last one was left ten minutes ago, according to the log. "I've just spoken to Lara, because I was worried sick you were at the bottom of a ditch somewhere. I'm bloody livid. You promised. You said the clinic wouldn't affect our lives, then I hear you're in some police station in South London. Call me when you get out. We need to talk." It sounds ominous.

The message ends and I delete the call. I don't want to listen to it again. All I'll do is try to analyse exactly how pissed off he is. Simon's a man who holds his emotions close—calm, collected, perhaps occasionally calculating. Unlike me, he doesn't wear his heart on his sleeve. Public school and a stint in the army would have beaten it out of him, if his parents hadn't already got there first.

"Are you okay, Beth?"

I glance up at Niall, and realise he's waiting for a response. A glib, feather-light reply lingers on the tip of my tongue, and I'm all ready to tell him I'm fine.

But I'm not.

"Simon's really pissed off with me. I missed an important dinner with some clients." I look down at my phone, watching the screen fade to black. "I don't know why I just told you that. It doesn't matter, not really."

"Of course it matters. Let me drive you home and speak with him, tell him it's all my fault."

I try to imagine *that* scenario. Niall standing at the door and explaining to Simon why he's driven me home. I picture Simon's thin lips and folded arms as he listens to Niall. Then to my fumbled explanations as to why Niall waited for three hours in the rain just to drive me home.

That's not going to happen.

"It's fine. He'll get over it."

"You don't look fine. You look upset and scared." Niall reaches across and squeezes my hand. "You look like you need a friend."

That's exactly what I need. Somebody to talk to, someone who won't tell me what a let-down I am. I never imagined that Niall Joseph would volunteer for the job. Squeezing his hand back, I look down at my legs, following the criss-cross weave of the dark-wash denim jeans that cover my thighs.

"That sounds good."

His hand is still holding mine. "Let me take you home first, though. You look exhausted. Things will be better after a good night's sleep."

I lean my head on the itchy backrest. The rain patters on the metal roof, like a gentle drum. Our warm breath has steamed up the windows, turning them opaque and white. As a child I used to love to draw my name through the fog, watching the water run down the window in thin rivulets. God, I wish I could go back to those days.

"I don't want to go home."

"No?"

"No."

He pauses for a minute, then leans forward and wipes the windscreen with his hand. "Then where do you want to go?"

It's almost eleven at night. Raining and cold. My husband doesn't know where I am. I should go home and throw myself on his mercy.

"Let's go to a pub."

Nine Years Earlier

"Iris! Hey, Iris." I turn to see Digby calling after me. He's wearing a black fedora. His hand rests on top of it to prevent it from flying away as he runs. Most guys would look stupid in his get-up: grey, skinny trousers, red braces and a blue striped shirt. But Digby has an aura of cool that crazy clothes can't crack.

"Hi." I smile shyly. It's still hard to believe these people have finally noticed me, after almost a year of mooning around them.

"Party at mine tonight. We've just had a delivery of the finest white widow. Uncorking time." He grins, revealing a row of almost perfect teeth, marred only by a crooked incisor. "You coming?"

Is he asking me to go to this party? Or is he asking me if I've already been invited? I frown, pondering the etiquette for going to drug parties. I want to go. Badly. Because Niall will be there.

"Um, when is it?"

"Tonight," Digby repeats, patiently.

If I was braver I might roll my eyes. Instead, I try to clarify. "What time?"

He starts to laugh, as if I asked the stupidest question. "You're so sweet. No wonder Niall likes you." His grin twists with amusement. "I hadn't really thought of a time. Just tonight, whenever."

"About eight?" I don't want to be early or late.

"Oh, Iris. You know if Niall hadn't claimed you first, I might just fall in love with you." He's staring at me as if I'm a specimen in a museum. "I'll tell you what, you come over at eight and we can share the first joint of the night. I promise not to stuff my hand down your pants, and you can make me all giggly and happy."

I get there at 7:57 p.m. Lifting my hand, I'm about to rap my knuckles on the door when it's pulled open. Standing just inside the hallway is a very bored-looking girl. She sweeps her blonde hair over her shoulders and stares at me for a moment.

"Is Digby in?" I try to peer around her. All the curtains are closed—in spite of the fact it's still light outside—and everything looks dingy and dark.

"Yeah. Upstairs." She wanders off, leaving me standing on the step, the front door open wide. I hesitate, wondering if I should just go in, or if I should wait for an invitation. It takes a few moments for me to realise she's not coming back.

From the outside, the house is a pretty Victorian semi, in a leafy road about a mile away from campus. On the inside though, it's a different matter. As soon as I step into the hallway I trip over a pile of shoes, narrowly avoiding falling on a bicycle that's propped against the wall. There is a heap of junk mail to the left of the bike, and I gingerly step over it.

The whole hallway stinks. It's a mixture of shoe smells and dust, laced with an edge of testosterone. I could have walked in here blindfolded and told you that men lived here. It's exactly the same as the boys' rooms in my hall of residence. They light joss sticks when they bring girls back, hoping it will disguise the stench.

The stairs are wooden and covered with a faded striped runner that's held down with brass rods. The exposed wood is layered with dust bunnies. When I walk up to the first floor I imagine I'm leaving a cloud of dust behind me, like a truck driving through a desert.

When I get to the landing I'm faced with five doors. I know Niall sometimes stays here, and a couple of their friends live here, too. Digby's parents bought the house for him as an investment. I wonder if they're aware of the state he keeps it in.

"Digby?" I call out quietly, not wanting to bring attention to myself. Then, realising I want to bring attention after all, I say it a little louder. "Digby?"

The door at the end of the hall opens, revealing Digby surrounded by a haze of smoke. His eyes are unfocused, and he's only wearing a pair of shorts and nothing else. His bare chest is hairless and a little doughy; scarcely defined by muscles.

"Iris. You made it." He waves his hand, showing me the joint clutched between his thumb and forefinger. "We may have started without you."

"So I see." I'm still standing at the top of the stairs.

"Come in, come in." He waves at his room with a flourish. "I wanted to have the party downstairs, but Bitchasaurus said I couldn't."

"Bitchasaurus?"

"My bloody sister. She's come to stay for a few days. Thinks she's my mother."

I guess that explains the miserable blonde.

Reluctantly, I walk toward his room and am suddenly relieved when I hear voices coming from inside. When I squeeze past Digby, I see the dark-haired girl from the lake curled up on a beanbag with a glass of wine in her hand. Next to her is an earnest-looking boy with wire-rimmed glasses.

She looks up at me without smiling. "Where's Niall?"

I feel a bit miffed, as if I'm not a person in my own right. "I don't know, isn't he coming?"

Digby starts to giggle. "You did tell him, right?"

I shake my head and my heart falls. That's pretty much the only reason I came. Then it dawns on me that the only reason they asked me is because they wanted me to bring Niall. Which is weird, because he's their friend.

"I don't fucking believe it," throat girl says. "We never bloody see him anymore, and then when we ask you to bring him, you forget."

Digby shrugs. "It's okay. One of you can go and call Niall, while Iris and I finish off this lovely bit of smoke." He pulls me over to his unmade bed, where he sits down and takes a deep drag. When he offers it to me, I snatch it eagerly from his hands, desperate for the calmness I know the drug will bring. I feel so out of place and unsophisticated I almost want to cry.

It's going to be a long night.

Now

9

When we walk into the pub it feels as though we're arriving late for a party. The bar is full, almost heaving, and the noise levels are high, people having to almost shout to make themselves heard. There's an atmosphere of amiable intoxication, that end-of-the week feeling raising everybody's spirits until they've forgotten what a grind their work has been.

We are interlopers. Sober, wet and bedraggled, we push our way to the counter. There's a crowd three deep, and it takes a few minutes for us to reach the front, even longer for us to finally get served. Eventually I wrap my fingers around a much-fought-for glass of Coke and lift it to my lips, taking deep gulps of the cool, sugary drink.

"God, I needed that."

We end up leaning against a wall at the far end of the room, squeezed in between a fireplace and a concrete column. There's just enough space for the two of us.

"You should take off your wet coat." Niall reaches out to touch the collar. "Give yourself a chance to dry out."

"I'm cold, though." I shiver. There must be a hundred people in here, warming up the room with their ambient temperature, but I'm still frozen solid. I wrap my arms around my waist.

"That's why you need to take your coat off. Give your body a chance to warm up. Look, give it to me." He reaches out to take it, and I shrug the jacket from my shoulders. Niall hangs it from the corner of the mantelpiece. "That's better."

"For you, maybe." I shiver again. "I swear the cold reaches through to my bones."

"You want me to warm you up?"

Oh yes. "I'm fine."

"Shame." He says it softly, but I hear it all the same.

A loud shout carries across the air. We both turn to work out where it has come from. A man walks through the door wearing only a cut-off pair of jeans, with a white veil attached to his head. Stuck to it are an assortment of condoms, both packaged and open. I hope to God none of them are used.

"Stag party," I say to Niall. I don't know why I bother stating the obvious, it's not as if the half-naked man has popped into the pub with his in-laws.

"So I see." Niall takes a gulp of his beer. "The poor guy must be colder than you."

"The only difference is, he's got a night at the police station to look forward to. I've done my time."

Niall smirks. "What's with Cameron, anyway? What the hell was he planning to do with an etched paperweight of the Tate Modern?"

"I asked him that but he didn't have an answer. Not one that made sense."

He'd mumbled something about it being worth a few quid. It wasn't quite believable.

"You spend a lot of time with those kids, don't you? Visiting them at weekends, sitting with them at police stations. I'm pretty sure none of that is in your job description."

"I don't have a job description. I do what's needed."

"Why?" He tips his head to one side, staring at me. His eyebrows dip, as if he's thinking hard about something. The tip of his tongue pokes out to moisten his lips. I find myself gawking at them. His bottom lip is fuller than the top by a couple of millimetres. I remember the way it tasted when I used to suck it between my own. Sometimes that seems a heartbeat ago.

"Why what?"

"Why do you work there, get so involved with the kids?"

"I don't know. I fell into it by accident, really. I wanted to help, to do something good, especially as I was unemployed. Then they offered me a job and we created the after-school club and I felt like..." My voice trails off. How did it feel? I know that place changed something inside me. "As if I'd found my way home." I laugh. "I know that sounds stupid and clichéd, but that's how it felt. I know I can help those kids. They've been dealt rotten hands, much worse than most of us. I was a good girl from Southend whose parents thought the world shone out of her arse and still I messed up. What chance do they have?"

Niall looks taken aback. "That's fucking amazing. Really. Those kids are so lucky to have you."

"I'm lucky to have *them*." I'm almost shocked by how true this is. Those kids have given my life meaning, trite as it sounds. They can be infuriating and annoying as hell, but all it takes is one tiny breakthrough. A soft smile from Allegra, a cheeky grin from Cameron. They mean everything. The thought I might have to give it all up, to turn my back on them, makes me want to scream. If Simon insists, I don't know if I'll ever forgive him. Or myself.

"Everybody's lucky," Niall murmurs.

"What about you?" I ask, tilting my head. "Are *you* lucky?"

"I'm very lucky. I've fucked things up so many times, and yet I'm still here."

I know how that feels. For a moment I want to reach out and trace the high line of his cheekbone, feel the softness of his skin against my own. I want to comfort him, not because he needs it, but because *I* do.

"What happened after they sent you away?" I ask. I've been wondering this for a while. I know my own story all too well—but he's still a mystery. His hints about messing things up only make me want to know more.

"From university?"

"Yes."

He takes a long sip of his drink. "I don't really remember the first few weeks. I was too messed up. According to my ma I spent most of it in a drunken stupor. Trying to block everything out. To forget about Digby, about the fact I wasn't going to graduate." He looks at me through sooty lashes. "To forget about you."

I'm momentarily lost for words. We were in different countries by that point, but still there was this connection, this despair.

"You told me you ended up in hospital," I prompt. I've been thinking about that a lot. How we lost Digby and then Niall was in trouble too, and I didn't even know.

"I was on one hell of a bender. My ma and uncle managed to cut off my supplies, so I turned to good old whisky instead. The next thing I knew I was waking up in hospital having had my stomach pumped." He leans on the wall, tracing patterns on his glass. "That was my wake-up call. I ended up travelling with my uncle back to the States and finishing college there. And afterward I stayed on for a while."

"And now you're rich and famous," I say.

"Not as rich as you."

"That's not my money. That's Simon's. I didn't marry him for that." It's important to me that Niall understands I didn't marry for money. I don't know why I want him to think kindly of me, but I do.

"I know." He looks chagrined. I wonder if he's remembering our argument that night after the pub, because I am. "But we've both done okay, considering how we could have ended up."

The strangest urge takes hold of me, stealing my concentration away. All I can think of is pressing my lips to his, feeling their warmth, their softness. Letting them move against mine.

I'm losing it. I have to be. Why on earth would I want to do that?

Even though he can't possibly know what I'm thinking, I feel my cheeks flame.

"Thank you," I say.

"For what?"

"For being here." *For talking to me, for letting me remember how it feels to kiss you.*

"Of course I'm here. We're friends, aren't we?" Is it my imagination or did he just emphasise the friends part? My face grows hotter still as I realise he might think I have a crush on him.

But I don't. I really don't.

* * *

The house is silent when I push open the front door. Usually, Simon leaves the hall light on if he goes to bed before I get home, but tonight he hasn't bothered.

The dark is a judgement. A punishment. It's as if I don't deserve the light. I flick it on anyway, dropping my keys on the sideboard, barely pausing to look at myself in the big, carved wooden mirror that hangs above it. But from that single glance

I see my cheeks are blazing, my eyes rimmed with red. Walking into the kitchen, I make myself a cup of tea just to avoid going upstairs to bed.

I'm putting off the inevitable. I should go up right now and apologise, make it all up to him. Instead I lean against the breakfast bar and idly stir my tea, while trying to make sense of things in my mind.

When I take a sip it burns my bottom lip, and I remember how I imagined kissing Niall. I'm mortified. It's not as if I can shrug the impulse off as friendly. I don't kiss my friends on the lips. Hell, I don't even kiss my parents like that on the rare occasion I go to visit them. There's only one person I kiss on the mouth and I happen to be married to him.

Rinsing my mug in the sink, I lay it carefully on the draining board, turning the handle in so it doesn't catch anything. Then I leave the kitchen, flicking the lights off, and set the burglar alarm to night mode.

It's dark in our bedroom. No bedside lamp or en-suite light left glowing.

Point well made, Simon.

"Hi," I whisper softly into the darkness. There's no response, not even the sound of his regular, heavy breathing. I don't think he's asleep, but it's difficult to tell. In the gloom of the bedroom I can barely see his outline beneath the covers. Silently, I remove my clothes and lay them on the easy chair beside the wardrobe, and grab a pair of cotton pyjamas. I clean my teeth hard enough to scrape the sugary sweetness of the Coke from the enamel, enough for a few spots of blood to appear on the white porcelain of the sink when I spit.

Simon hasn't moved. I lift up the blanket on my side of the bed, and try to crawl stealthily underneath, unsure if I should be relieved he's not talking to me, or upset. I don't think I can sleep under this veil of gloom.

Just as I lie back and let my head sink into the pillow Simon switches on the light. "You're back, then?"

I turn onto my side. Sitting up in bed, he reaches for his glasses. It takes him a long time to unfold them and perch them on the bridge of his nose.

"I'm so sorry." It's the first thing that comes to mind. The only thing.

Simon stares at me. Unemotionally. "Why didn't you return my calls?"

"I didn't have my phone on at the station. It was switched off in my bag."

"And afterward?"

"It was too late." I swallow hard. "I didn't mean to ruin your evening."

"Do you know what the worst part is? I kept telling them, *"She'll be here any minute, this isn't like her,"* and they just kept nodding and smiling indulgently at me. As if I'm some old man being taken for a ride. I could read the disdain in their eyes, and I didn't like the way they were thinking about you. As though you're cuckolding me."

I bite my lip, trying not to blurt out that I was at the pub with Niall. I want to confess, I want to be absolved.

"I'm sorry you had to go through that. I promise I won't let it happen again. I'll send a note apologising, maybe some flowers or something?" Sitting up, I curl my legs beneath me, reaching out to touch his cheek.

"We can't go on like this." He pauses, then pushes his glasses up. "*I* can't go on like this. The worry, the tension. It feels as if I'm constantly wondering where you are, if you're okay. Since you found that girl in her flat..." His voice trails off. "And now this. To have to call around your friends until I find out you were at the police station with some teenaged lout. It just isn't right."

I don't know what to say. I open my mouth a few times, but nothing comes out. He's treating me like I'm his daughter.

"You know what I was expecting? To hear that you were lying in a ditch somewhere, or being rushed to hospital in an ambulance." His face twists before he makes his final confession. "I think I would have preferred that."

A tear rolls down my right cheek. I reach up and wipe it away angrily, not wanting to be accused of using waterworks to soften him again. "I'm sorry." I don't know how many times I can say it.

"I'm not sure it's enough, not anymore. I bloody hate this, worrying about you, not able to sleep until you get home because I'm scared you could be hurt."

"I'm fine, Simon. I promise you I can take care of myself." I try to stroke his arm but he shrugs me off.

"How do you know one of them isn't going to pull a knife on you one day? That some crazy boyfriend isn't going to walk into the clinic with a grudge and a handgun? It isn't the place for you, Beth. It isn't the place for *my wife*."

"But I love the clinic."

"More than you love me?"

I hesitate for a second too long.

"No, of course not." It isn't the same. He's asking me to compare apples and pears. "But they need me. The kids need me."

"I need you, Beth. *I need you*. And I have to know you're safe when you're out of my sight." He takes his glasses off and rubs his eye sockets with balled-up fists. "This has to end."

"What has to end?"

"The clinic. I don't want you to work there anymore."

A flash of anger licks at my belly. "That's not fair. It's everything to me."

Putting his glasses back on, he sits upright, swinging his legs onto the pale wooden floor.

"I thought I was that." Simon stands up, letting the covers fall back onto the bed. "I'll sleep in the spare room tonight."

10

By the time I get up the next morning, Simon's gone. I walk downstairs in my pyjamas, switch on the coffee machine and check my watch. It's seven o'clock; too early for the office, but maybe he has a breakfast meeting. I frown, knowing I'm kidding myself. It's avoidance, plain and simple. He doesn't want to see me, definitely doesn't want to talk. This hurts me more than I thought it would.

The coffee machine shudders and steams, and I grab a mug and some cream. If Simon were here he'd make a joke about how I like my coffee just like my man: sweet and rich. What happened to us? Did we get swallowed up by this thing called life, spat out on the heap like all the other marriages that fail? I didn't marry him for us to become a statistic.

Sitting down on a stool, I grab my iPad, and get to work on clearing up my own mess. First I order an expensive flower arrangement for last night's hosts, with an appropriately worded card expressing my regret. Then I make a reservation for dinner on *Toptable*, choosing Simon's favourite restaurant— a pretty bistro just off Upper Street. Finally I turn to Google, and type in "marriage guidance counsellors". If I make an effort, then maybe he'll forgive me.

But he needs to give a little, too. I can't leave the clinic, they're my second family. The kids I'll never have. As much as they drive me crazy, I need that feeling, crave it, even. It's not as if I'll ever be able to lavish affection on a child of my own, so I choose to do it on them, instead. They need to feel love and I need to give it. It's a relationship that works.

Possibly my only one.

I'm on my way to the clinic when Lara calls. I ask her to hold as I walk out of the dark, dank Tube station stairwell and into the crisp morning air. The rain has dried up since last night, leaving a London that positively basks in its absence. Trees are starting to bud, daffodils are starting to bloom and the sun is trying her best to push through. It's one of those spring days when everything feels a little brighter. People smile a little more, step aside when you are walking toward them. In the gardens across from the clinic, cherry trees wear candy-floss hats, the blossom slowly drifting down in the light breeze.

"Hey." I lift the phone to my ear. "Everything okay?"

"I was going to ask you the same question. What the heck happened last night? I had all manner of men calling me and asking where you were." Lara sounds appropriately intrigued.

"Two. You had two men calling you," I say.

She has this way of making everything sound as if it has more meaning than it has. It may be something to do with her training; perhaps she's looking for a way to prise out the truth without actually asking me. Or maybe I'm just projecting.

"They were very frantic men. Well, Simon was. I don't know that Niall could do frantic if he tried."

Niall *can* do frantic, that much I remember. Frantic and hot and desperate. Long fingers digging into hips, lips pressing down until they almost hurt. He may have matured—hopefully we both have—but I don't believe that fire can be doused completely.

"I'm sorry. Simon calling was totally my fault. I should have let him know where I was." Niall, on the other hand, was not my fault. He knew exactly where I was. He was sitting outside the station, for goodness sake.

"Do you want to talk about it? I've got no clients for the next hour; we could grab a coffee somewhere."

I have a few calls to make, plus some materials to order before the children arrive, but I think I can fit this in. I love talking with Lara; it's something we don't get to do as much anymore. "Yeah, coffee sounds great. I'm just walking up to the clinic now."

"And I'm walking out." A moment later, Lara is standing in front of me, her battered brown handbag slung over her shoulder. We both press the buttons to end our call. "Hey." She reaches out and hugs me tightly.

We head to the cafe around the corner from the clinic. It's mostly empty, in that lull between the breakfast rush and lunchtime patrons. Grabbing a table, we wait for the waitress to bring us over our coffees. They've not long had a proper machine put in. We used to have to put up with tepid instant, barely dissolved granules. Now it's all lattes and mochaccinos. Even the cafe has been gentrified.

I open a sachet of sugar and stir it into my cappuccino, completely ruining the bean design the waitress created with powdered chocolate. "How's things?" I ask.

"I was going to ask you the same question." Lara takes a sip. "And I bet your answer is more interesting."

It isn't, not really. It's boring and tedious and not something I want to talk about. "But I asked first."

She wrinkles her nose, making her freckles all squeeze into each other. "Not good."

"Oh no. Why?"

"They're making redundancies at Alex's work. He might be out of a job by next month. He reckons he's on the hit list; his boss really doesn't like him." Alex works in the print at Wapping. It's a pretty well-paid job, and I know they rely on his money.

"That's awful, poor Alex." I catch her eye. "Poor you, too, it's horrible seeing somebody you love go through that."

"That's the worst bit—he thinks it's wonderful. Gives him carte blanche to pursue his dreams of stardom. I'm not sure how he thinks we're going to pay the rent or put food on the table." She rolls her eyes. "And he knows I want us to try for a baby. There's no way we can afford to do that on just one wage."

I didn't realise they'd got that far in their planning. I feel a bit of heaviness in my chest at the thought of it. Though I love Lara to the ends of the earth, I can't help feeling envious at the concept of a baby. It's something I'll never have, and I thought I'd come to terms with it, but since I've been thinking about the past, it's made me change my mind. Maybe I just wasn't ready for a baby until now. Could it be that my biological clock has finally started ticking?

Am I going to feel like this forever?

"Does Alex not want a baby?" I ask.

"I thought he did. But now I think he's going through a midlife crisis. He says the threat of losing his job has given him a chance to re-evaluate things. He wants to see if he can make a go of music before we try for a family."

She looks pissed off, and I don't blame her. Lara is thirty-one and I know she's been wanting a baby for a while. The problem is, with London rent and rubbish salaries, there's never going to be a good time for them to try. They can't really afford a baby, as much as they want one. While Simon and I can afford it, it's something we'll never have.

"Maybe if you let him try it, he'll realise it's not for him."

"He's so excited, though. He's even got Niall designing the cover sleeve of their new CD. Reckons that's guaranteed sales just for the artwork."

"Niall Joseph?" I clarify. I nearly said "my Niall" but managed to stop myself in time. I need to be more careful.

"Yeah. They really hit it off that night we all went out."

"I didn't realise." I don't know how to feel about that. Part of me is excited there's another connection between us, since I'm friends with Lara and he's friends with Alex. I find myself wondering how I can invite myself over to their place more often. I'm also a bit jealous that they get to spend time with him, and they're all having fun without me. It sounds childish and selfish, but I can't help it.

"Why would you? It's not as if we all run in the same circles. Although I sometimes think Niall is more suited to yours than mine. He is a successful artist, after all. Not a starving one like Alex is going to be."

"You won't starve. I won't let you. I'll hand you coupons for McDonald's or something," I tease. It coaxes a small smile from her, but not enough to plump up her cheeks or crinkle her eyes. "Seriously, Alex will get some redundancy pay, enough for you to get by while he sees if it all works out. Maybe you should agree a time limit on his attempts for stardom. A year or something."

"That's a good idea." She stares off into the distance, as if she's thinking it through. "Maybe we need to sit down and write it all out, like a calendar. If I know we can start trying in a year or so, I might be okay with that."

"It's not as if you have to worry about time running out yet. Plus it gives you some time to get as much drinking done as possible, because you'll have to give all that up when the baby comes." I'm teasing again. Lara's not a heavy drinker. A shandy here, a Spritzer there. She's mostly high on life.

"I'll have to read fifty things to do before you have a baby."

"Don't joke, I bet somebody's written it. Travel to the Taj Mahal, eat kangaroo dung, see if you can turn your husband into a rock star."

She laughs and it sounds genuine. "Thank you." She reaches across the table and squeezes my hand. "For letting me spout off and then cheering me up."

"It's a pleasure." I return her smile.

If only my own problems were as easy to solve.

* * *

Two weeks later, it feels as though everything in my marriage is wrong. I measure my failure in bitter asides and pointed silences; in broken gazes and absences that taste like dust.

Simon's still not talking to me—nothing more than pleasantries and the necessary exchange of information. "I'm going to be late tonight," "Can you get me some more deodorant?" and "What's the capital of Namibia?" were among the more notable interactions we've had this week. The latter was him trying to finish the *Times* crossword, something that seemed infinitely more preferable than having to spend time with me.

The longer it goes on, the worse I feel. It's with that sense of shame that I call up a relationship clinic in St. John's Wood and make an appointment for Simon and myself. When I mention it to him, he doesn't refuse to come. That has to be a good thing. Maybe if we can actually talk things through, we can move on. There has to be a way we can compromise.

Yet, I find myself sitting in the pale green waiting room five minutes after our appointment is due to start, making stupid excuses for why he hasn't turned up. Maybe he's tied up with a client, or his taxi has broken down halfway across London. I play with a dozen different scenarios in my mind, all of them preferable to the one I'm trying my best to ignore.

He's making a point.

I suppose I could call and leave messages on his answerphone, or send texts he never responds to. I could scream and shout and rail at him and let him know he's hurt me all over again. But I don't. Instead, I turn off my own phone and push it deep down in my handbag until it's buried under half-ripped tissues and balled-up pieces of paper and Maltesers that've spilled out of a half-opened packet. Then I zip it up firmly and follow the receptionist's directions to Louise Norton's office, hoping I'll find some sort of salvation there.

Louise is sitting on an easy chair when I walk into her room. She looks up at me with a welcoming smile on her red-painted lips. Her black, bobbed hair falls into her eyes and she smooths it away, standing up as I walk over to greet her.

"Beth? Please come and take a seat. Is Simon on his way?"

This is what a hundred pounds per hour gets you. A friendly face and somebody who has enough time to read your history before you walk into your appointment. I sit down in the soft, comfy chair opposite hers.

"I don't think he's coming. I've tried ringing him but there's no answer." It's stupid, starting out by lying, yet it feels preferable to pitying stares. "I'm so sorry he's not here."

She tips her head to the side and looks at me. "Do you think he'll get here soon?"

"I don't know. I don't think so." This is what gets me most of all. I'm all riled up and ready to talk. I've been fixating on this for days. It's a kick in the gut. All the words I have stored up to say are floating around my mind, making me dizzy.

"Would you like to rearrange? I can ask the receptionist to make another appointment for you?" She's still smiling, and it doesn't look forced at all. I wonder at her ability to seem so open and approachable.

"Actually, can we talk, just you and me?"

For the first time Louise looks surprised. "I offer individual counselling as well as couples' therapy, but I'm afraid I can't mix the two. If you want to talk to me now, you'll need to find another therapist to treat the two of you together." She must notice the way my face falls, because she continues, "Sometimes that can work out for the best. Often I ask couples to go away to get individual therapy before they come back to me. And I can refer you to another relationship counsellor when you're ready."

"That sounds good." It really does. It might be self-indulgent to take an hour to talk through my problems, but Lara's made me a great believer in the power of counselling. It's an opportunity to reveal my darkest fears, my rawest emotions, with someone who holds no stake in my life.

Louise opens the session by telling me a little bit about herself and the type of therapy she offers. She also promises me complete confidentiality. I find myself relaxing in the chair.

"Let's start with why you're here. What made you come?" She's still wearing that open expression; making me feel special, as though she's genuinely interested.

"I guess I want to save my marriage."

"What are you trying to save it from?"

I give a small smile. "I don't know. From failing, I suppose."

"What makes you think it's failing?"

Her question makes me stop and think. Why is it failing? Is it me or is it Simon? Both of us, perhaps? Is it sinking under the weight of expectations we've both put on each other? The silence lingers as I try to find the words.

"We both want different things. Simon wants me to be his wife first, to put him before everything else. And part of me wants that, too. But if that's all I am I think I'd end up disappearing. I want more. I want to help people. I want my job to mean something."

"What sort of work do you do?"

"I help at a substance abuse clinic. I run an outreach club for children of addicts, and I fundraise on the clinic's behalf."

"That sounds like an important role."

That surprises me. I'm not sure anybody has said that before. That I'm important. That what I do counts. "It is to me."

"What makes it so important?"

Another moment of thinking. "It's the fact I'm able to make a difference. These kids don't have a lot, and I can tell by their faces they really get a kick out of the program. Sometimes when they're having a rubbish week, that's about all they have to cling to."

"The kids mean a lot to you?"

"They mean everything." I choke up. "They can be annoying and argumentative but they're kids, that's their job. At the end of the day most of them simply need some attention and love. Even if I only get to give them it for a few hours a week, it has to be better than nothing, doesn't it?" I can feel myself getting emotional again. Hot tears scald my eyes. "I don't want to leave them, not even for Simon." Grabbing a tissue from the box on the coffee table, I dab at my eyes. My skin feels puffy and painful, and the tissue makes it worse.

"What do you think will happen if you don't leave?"

"Simon will leave me instead."

"Is that what he said?"

"Not in so many words. But he told me I had to quit." I screw up my face as I try to think what the consequences of non-compliance would be. I assumed from his ultimatum that it meant we were over if I refused. "I suppose I should have asked him."

"Sometimes people say things in the heat of the moment that they don't really mean. And you won't know unless you talk things through." She leans toward me. "This week's homework is for you to try to explain to Simon why the clinic is so important to you. Try not to get over-emotional, or to back yourself against the wall. Just make sure he understands what the clinic means to you. Nothing more."

While she speaks, I nod in agreement, but deep down I'm wondering if I can actually do that. I'm not even sure we're at a point where we can talk things through without it descending into an argument. Though that would be better than the silent treatment I'm currently getting.

I've always found it hard to defy authority. I hated being told off at school, and would have done anything to avoid being reprimanded by my parents. Simon is merely one in a long line of authority figures I've found myself cowering before.

When we finish, Louise hands me a notebook and asks me to start keeping a note of my moods. I shove it in my bag and stand up, my legs feeling wobbly as I do. Even when I'm back in reception, I'm still shaky. I don't like how the world is becoming such an uncertain place.

Buttoning up my jacket, I wrap my green scarf around my neck, before pulling open the glass-and-metal door that separates the clinic from the street. When I step out into the fresh air, there's a certain comfort as London swallows me whole, dragging me deep into her pumping veins.

Nine Years Earlier

I'm curled up in bed, suffering from a combined white widow and wine hangover, when there's a knock at my door. Grumbling, I turn my head until it's facing the pillow and shout out muffled words.

"I'm asleep."

"Then wake up."

I recognise that voice. That lilt. A little pulse of excitement pushes through my leaden body. "I can't. Your friends have poisoned me."

A low laugh. "Is the door locked?"

I've no idea. Before I can work it out, the handle turns and the door swings open. Through half-shut eyes I see him enter the room, clutching a bag of crisps and a bottle of non-diet Coke.

"You're a bit late for the munchies," I tell him.

Niall sits down at the end of my bed and pushes the hair from his eyes. "I looked for you today after lectures."

"I didn't go." That's pretty obvious. I'm almost certain I have the look of a girl who's been in bed all day.

"So I noticed." He pauses for a moment. "I hear last night was fun."

Finally, I sit up and catch his eye. "I thought you were going to be there. I didn't realise I was supposed to invite you. It was all really confusing."

"It's not your fault. Digby's useless at organising anything. That's what comes of having money your whole life. He needs a secretary."

I smile, remembering the way he looked after me. I'm beginning to have a soft spot for him. "What kind of parent calls their kid Digby anyway?"

Niall starts to laugh. "You think his parents called him Digby? Does he look like the biggest dog in the world to you?"

"Not really. So why's he called Digby?"

"No idea. I assume he had a penchant for digging holes as a kid or something. His real name's James."

There's no stopping the giggle that comes out of my mouth. I stare up at Niall, marvelling that this beautiful, funny boy is spending time with me. If I wasn't feeling so crap, I'd be pulling him down on top of me.

"Here, drink this." He passes me the litre bottle of Coke he's just opened. I lift it to my mouth and take huge gulps. The sticky-sweet liquid pours down my throat. After I've swallowed almost half the bottle, I pass it back to him.

"Now you can get up." He pulls the covers off my bed. I'm still in my jeans and top from last night. "Come on, hurry."

I frown. "Why, what are we doing?" I like the sound of 'we'. Want to say it again.

"We're breaking into the art building. All my supplies are there. It's about time I get to paint you."

117

Now

11

Silence can be so much louder than words. Maybe not in volume, or decibels, or however you choose to quantify it, but in meaning and intent, Simon's muteness is deafening. He hasn't mentioned missing our appointment, or asked me how I got on. Over the past month since then, he's stopped making any attempt at pleasantries or conversation. In fact, he's become active in his avoidance of me. Early meetings, late-night dinners, weekend working. He's finally started to text me with excuses, when all I long for is his voice.

While I feel angry, I also feel guilty. Just a few simple words from me and we'd be able to work our way back to where we started. All I have to do is promise to give up my work and I know he'd thaw. That thought, though, leaves a bad taste in my mouth. He's trying to emotionally blackmail me and it just doesn't seem fair. I've already failed on my first homework assignment for Louise. I'm too afraid to explain why I want to stay at the clinic.

He's made it patently clear it's his way or the highway. He's used to making the decisions while I do as he asks. I'm not living up to my side of our bargain.

On Thursday he disappears to the country for the weekend. I go into the clinic early to seek out Lara, to ask her if she wants to do something on Saturday; anything to avoid four days alone.

"I'd love to, but Alex is whisking me away." She looks a lot happier than she did last week. "We said we'd go to a nice hotel in the country and talk. Try to work things through."

I smile at her as if it's the best news in the world. And it would be, if I didn't have that little bit of envy gnawing at my stomach. "That sounds lovely. You two will work it out, I know it." They will, because they're speaking to each other.

A smile stretches across her face. "It's not cheap, but separating would be more expensive, so we're going for it anyway."

Separation. I wonder if that's where Simon and I are headed. I wish I could see into his mind, work out if he's playing brinkmanship or has simply thrown in the towel. How can I fight for something if he's already given up on it? Even if I want to.

Lara looks at me quizzically. "Are you okay?"

I snap out of my thoughts. "Yes, I'm fine. Why?"

There's no way I'm telling her about Simon and me. She has her own worries. She's been so strong for me in the past, the least I can do is show some support to her now.

"I don't know, you just looked far away. Sad. You'd tell me if there was anything wrong, wouldn't you?"

I force a smile. "Of course I would. Stop projecting on me. You and Alex are going to be fine. You're back on track."

She grins. "D'you know what? I think we are."

At two thirty that afternoon I'm pulling supplies out of the art cupboard when the door swings open. Niall walks in and hangs his jacket over a chair, revealing a baggy, paint-stained t-shirt that barely reaches his waistband

"You didn't have to dress up just for me," I say, deadpan.

He catches my eye and laughs. "What, this old thing?" He pulls at the hem and I get a brief glimpse of skin. I quickly raise my eyes so I'm looking at his face. "Just something I found at the bottom of the wardrobe."

"All crumpled up in a paint pot?" I ask, trying not to look down again. I can picture the red and green streaks that criss-cross the front of the fabric, and the pale, taut stomach that lies underneath.

"Something like that."

"Well, it suits you."

He walks over and takes the pot from my hands. "You, of course, look as beautiful as ever."

His words light a little fire inside me. "Thank you."

We work together, putting the equipment out, making small talk as we go. We both try to take the rise out of each other, and fall into a comforting banter. It's such a contrast to the silence I've been enduring; easy, pleasant.

"Hey, I meant to ask. Have you heard from Cameron?" Niall turns to me when we've finished getting ready. There are a few minutes until the kids arrive. "He hasn't been here lately."

"No, he's laying low."

"Is that a good thing?" He looks at me as if I have all the answers.

I slowly shrug my shoulders. "I don't know. I guess it's normal to lick your wounds when something like that happens. A kid his age doesn't like to show weakness or emotion. The last thing he wants to do is apologise."

"The affliction of a teenage boy. So many emotions but no ability to put them into words." He sounds almost wistful. "Christ, I'm glad I don't have to be a teenager anymore."

"You sound as if you're talking from experience."

His voice thickens. "I am."

The atmosphere turns on a sixpence—from carefree and playful to charged and deep. He stares at me and I gaze right back, guessing at the meaning in his words. I want to ask him what emotions he had then, what regrets he has now. For the first time, I want to tell him about the ones that I still carry. I even open my mouth to say the words, to spill my story out like blossoms on the wind.

Then all thoughts of confession are silenced by the sound of the door opening. Kids pour in, their chatter drowning everything out, and the moment passes. I get caught up with talking to Allegra, while Niall explains what we are going to do all afternoon.

I can't help feeling relieved that my secrets are still safe.

* * *

"I painted this for you." Allegra hands me her picture. This week Niall has them trying Impressionism. The paper is covered with thick paint strokes, each colour blending into the next; blue outer, red inner. I think it's a London bus in the pouring rain.

"That's beautiful. Is it really for me?" My throat constricts as she gives me a small smile. "I'll put it up in my kitchen. Every time I look at it I'll think of you."

"It's to say thank you. For taking care of me." She pulls at her bottom lip with her paint-crusted fingers. "Are you still coming to take me out on Saturday?"

I want to hug her. To pull her close until I squeeze the uncertainty right out of her. Only a kid, and she's already used to being let down.

"Of course I am. Is there anything special you'd like to do?"

"Can you take me to see my mum?"

I shake my head sadly. She asked the same question last week. I even called her social worker to see if we could, but was told there was to be no contact. Allegra is still at risk, and though Daisy has been released from hospital, knowing Darren is still at large makes me agree with them. "How about we go to the cinema?" I suggest. "You can choose the film. We can share a bucket of popcorn." I bump her with my hip, but there's no sign of a smile.

"I miss her." A wobble of her bottom lip. "When will I get to go home?"

"I don't know, sweetheart."

Daisy isn't able to look after herself right now, let alone her daughter. Her bruises may have faded, but she's so anxious and highly strung she can't sit still for more than a few minutes. When we met for coffee two days ago she could barely light her cigarette, her hands were shaking so badly. Darren really did a number on her.

"I don't like it at the home. Can I come and live with you instead?" Allegra grabs my hand and squeezes it tightly. "I'll be really good and I'll do whatever you tell me. I promise I won't make a mess."

Tears sting at my eyes. How do I explain to an eight-year-old that my husband wouldn't let her stay? That my marriage is in crisis and she'd probably be unhappier at my house than at the group home. "Why don't you like it?"

"The other kids are mean. One of them threw my book in the toilet." She takes a shaky breath. "They told me I'll have to live there until I'm eighteen because my mum doesn't love me."

I crouch down until our faces are on the same level, and reach out to hold her. "You know that's not true, right? She loves you so much. She's just not well enough to take care of you at the moment. But she's trying to get better, and she told me she misses you. So much."

"You've seen her?"

I nod, aware of the unfairness of it all. That I can see them both but they can't see each other.

"Will you tell her I love her, too?"

I hug her close, as much to hide my tears as to give her comfort. "Of course I will."

* * *

It's nearly six by the time we finish clearing the room. The kids took Impressionism seriously, mixing a myriad of colours together until they all blended into a muddy brown mess, spilling paint onto the desks and floors. After I put the mop and bucket back in the cupboard and Niall places the last few containers of paint on the shelves, we turn out the lights and walk into the lobby. I'm in no real hurry to go home to an empty house, and Niall seems to be of a similar mind. We lean against the wall and chat as if we have all the time in the world.

"Are you okay?" He rubs his chin. "You seemed a bit upset earlier. Allegra did too."

I don't know whether I'm surprised that he noticed, or shocked that he's said anything. "She misses her mum. And poor Daisy misses her, too. But they're not allowed to see each other. Not until Daisy's back on her feet and able to prove she's responsible."

"Even though she's her ma?"

"She's a drug addict who got beaten up so seriously she was in hospital for over a week. I don't even want to think what could have happened to Allegra if she'd been there."

"Jesus." He looks as though I've just kicked him in the stomach. "That poor kid. She doesn't really stand a chance, does she?"

"No." I stop talking because more tears start to threaten and I'm so sick of feeling like this. As if I'm walking on a knife edge, inching my way along, frightened of falling.

"She's got you on her side, though. That has to count for something." Niall reaches out and lifts my chin up with his fingers until I'm looking right at him. "Don't forget that." He's still holding me, his fingers cupping my face, and it makes my pulse speed.

"I won't."

We're still staring at each other. My skin tingles. Every time he gets this close I have the same reaction. It's not conscious, but the strength of my response still surprises me. I want to reach out and trace his bottom lip, touch the part where soft skin becomes moist mouth. I want to feel his teeth digging into my thumb as I push it inside, before he closes his lips around me.

More than anything, I want him to pull me close, meld his body to mine and kiss me like he used to. As if he had no choice.

But I'm married.

I'm married, I'm married, and I'm married.

If I think it enough times maybe my body will listen.

"Have you got anything nice planned for the weekend?" I change the subject, making my voice breezy and light. When I take half a step back his hand falls from my face.

"My ma is visiting for the weekend. A few days with me then she travels north to visit her sister." His face turns almost comical when he adds, "I've been cleaning all week."

I burst out laughing and it's such a relief. Niall grins as if he's accomplished something.

"Are you scared of her?" I ask.

"My mother? Of course." He looks at me as if I'm stupid. "She's lovely and all, but if I don't clean before she visits she insists on spending the whole weekend clearing out the flat. There's stuff in there I'd rather she didn't see."

This sounds interesting. "What kind of stuff?"

He shifts his feet. "I dunno, just stuff. Paintings and things. I don't like her looking through them."

I raise my eyebrows. "At the nudes?"

"You've got a dirty mind, do you know that?" He shakes his head, but the grin on his lips tells me he's kidding. "What makes you think I've got a flat full of nudes?"

His smile is infectious. It's so easy, this conversation, the gentle teasing. "What else can you be hiding from your mum?"

He leans toward me, his dark hair falling over the side of his face as his head inclines. It brushes against my cheek as he hovers his lips close to my ear. "Maybe I've got a red room of pain."

There's something about the sentence that makes my toes curl up. I'm not sure if it's the physical sensation of his breath on my sensitive skin, or if it's the fact he's saying dirty words in my ear.

Dirty, funny words.

I pull back and raise my eyebrows. "If you can afford a red room of pain in central London, you're obviously making more money than I thought."

"I'm not quite in the Damien Hirst ranks yet. Let's call it an off-pink cupboard of slight discomfort."

"Now *that* I'd like to see."

"Why don't you come to dinner tomorrow night?" He almost stumbles over the words. "You and Simon. I'm sure my mother would love to see I actually have some friends over here."

"You cook?"

"I try. I've been known not to completely bollocks up a steak." He's looking at me quizzically, as if I'm some puzzle he's trying to solve. "It probably won't be up to the standards you and Simon are used to but—"

"Simon's away for the weekend," I blurt out.

"What about you? Are you free?" His voice is soft. "I can cook steaks for three as easily as for four."

Thank God his mum will be there. If bones could sigh, mine would right now. I'm reading into things that aren't there, seeing complications where there is only simplicity. A friend, his mum and a dinner, nothing more.

"Sounds good. What time do you want me?"

12

Niall's flat is on the top floor of a Victorian terrace in Ladbroke Grove. I stand outside, clutching a bottle of chilled white wine, letting anticipation waft over me like a welcome breeze. In the road behind cars idle, honking impatiently, their horns cutting through the almost-balmy evening air. I wait, one hand clutching the bottle, the other in a fist that's too scared to move forward and push a tiny silver button that will let Niall and his mother know I'm here.

Why am I here?

It's only dinner—a meal with a friend and his mum. No different to a night with Lara and Alex, after all. Plus, Simon himself is out somewhere without me, not bothering to call to check in, or even deigning to answer my emails. So I shouldn't feel guilty about this, should I? Yet I hesitate, standing on the concrete steps that lead to the shiny black front door, breathing in the aroma of the sweet peas trailing down from hanging baskets.

There's a part of me that wants to spin on my heel and walk straight down the steps and into a cab. Away from the madness and back to my reality. Except I want doesn't exist anymore, if it ever did. I'm starting to think that my steady marriage and supportive husband are a product of my fevered imagination; a grown-up equivalent of an invisible friend.

A comforting lie.

The shrill sound of a police siren in the distance brings me out of my thoughts, and I realise I've been standing here for too long. Swallowing down the last remnants of fear, I finally press the button for flat three, my finger shaking as I pull it away. In the moment it takes for Niall to answer the urge to run away crescendos, and I'm a hair's breadth from sprinting down the road when his voice crackles through the speakers.

"Hello?"

I lean closer to the intercom. "It's Beth."

"Come on up. Third floor." A buzz followed by a clunk tells me the front door has unlocked. Pushing it open gingerly, I step into an empty hallway that echoes with every click of my heels on the wooden floor. I put my foot on the bottom stair and wish I spent more time at the gym than I do thinking about it.

By the time I get to his floor I'm so worn out I forget that I'm scared. At least until he opens the door. Niall stands beneath the lintel, his hair brushed back off his face, wearing clean, dark jeans and a black shirt with the sleeves rolled up to his elbows.

"Hi." He takes a step forward and his forehead furrows, his brows pulling together as he looks at me. "Are you okay?"

I'm still gasping for air, my heart hammering against my chest. "I'm a bit... unfit."

He bites his lip, trying to stifle a smile. If I had any spare oxygen I'd huff.

"Let me take that from you," he says, grabbing the wine bottle. "Come in, come in."

The first thing I notice is how light and airy his flat is. Though it's almost twilight, the evening sun illuminates the room as if it's still midday. It makes sense, I suppose, that he'd choose to live somewhere with good light. He's an artist, after all.

I'm so busy looking around that it takes me a minute to notice the petite lady who comes to join us, a wine glass in her hand and a smile on her lips.

"Ma, this is Beth. Beth, this is my auld ma." There's a sardonic lilt to his voice.

She hits him on the arm. "Stop it, you little horror, you know my bloody name." When she looks at me she's all sweetness and light. "You can call me Maureen."

"It's a pleasure to meet you, Maureen."

"You, too. It's always lovely to meet one of Niall's friends." Her eyes are the same colour as her son's, a deep blue that reminds me of oceans and seas. "Niall, stop hanging around and get your friend a drink."

She nags him with humour and he takes it in the same way, doffing an imaginary cap at her before he winks at me. When he walks into the small kitchen at the end of his living room, I can't help but admire the way his jeans skim over his behind.

"Shall we sit down?" Niall's mum asks.

I tear my eyes away from her son's arse. "That would be lovely."

I've barely sat down on the battered leather sofa before she starts talking. She's perched on an over-stuffed easy chair opposite me. "Niall tells me you work at a drug clinic. Do you enjoy it there? It sounds hard work."

"It's not so bad. I work with children rather than addicts, so I don't get to see the worst of it."

Niall hands me a glass of wine and sits down next to me. "Is she giving you the third degree?"

"Hush up, you auld spa." There's a grin on her lips and I presume she's insulting him. "It's the only way I can find out what you're up to. It's not as though you ever call me."

He catches my eye. "Once a week. Every Sunday at six or I'm a dead man walking."

"He schedules me in like I'm a trip to the dentist," she tells me. "Is that any way for a boy to treat his mammy?"

There's fondness in their mutual insults, and I can't help but smile. They seem to have the sort of relationship I could only dream of having with my parents. I think I might like Niall's mother as much as I like him.

They eventually stop talking long enough to draw breath, and Niall says he'll start cooking the steaks. He takes me up on my offer to make the salad, and the two of us work away in his kitchen, chopping and seasoning as we chat.

"I'm sorry about my ma, she can be pretty full on."

"She's lovely." I take a sip of wine and lean on his breakfast bar. "You're lucky to have her."

The corners of his eyes crinkle up. "I really am. I don't know what I'd do without her." His voice deepens. "That summer...when everything happened. God, she was a rock. I think I would have given up without her."

I look down, feeling a tug in my stomach so strong it hurts. I should be pleased that he found some support where I had none. A cheerleader instead of the critics I had to endure. But if I'm truthful, there's something galling in knowing he had her while I had months of angry silences and recriminations.

When my father brought me home from college that summer I was an embarrassment to them both. I'd let them down. They'd proudly sent their pretty A-grade daughter off to university only to have her return as a drug-addled failure who'd been at the centre of a national tragedy. I was their dirty little secret that year, hidden away at home.

No matter how hard I try, the pain never heals over completely. There's still a little scab that's so easily picked at.

"Are you okay?" he asks, concern etched in his eyes.

I take a deep breath followed by an even deeper mouthful of wine. "Yeah." It comes out as a sigh. "I just hate remembering what happened. It still hurts, thinking about it."

He reaches for my hand. "I know, believe me, I do. I spent years wishing I'd never given him that tab. That I'd listened to him when he said he felt ill. Sometimes I still dream about him."

There's no need for him to tell me they're nightmares, because I know they are. The same terrible images that flicker through my own dormant mind; the party, the music, the dancing. The feeling that we could rule the world with love and peace. The way we ignored what was happening in front of our zoned-out eyes.

Digby wasn't hot or thirsty. He wasn't just shooting the breeze with us. While we danced our way through the night, high on E and God only knew what else, he was dying. He stumbled through the crowd, maybe clutching his chest, his heart fighting against the effects of MDMA. Losing spectacularly. We were his friends, we let him down. We let him die on a muddy, grass-covered field all alone.

While we danced.

That knowledge is so much worse than the clusterfuck that happened afterward. The investigations and the media frenzy, followed by the unseemly influence of his parents' money. The fact we bore all of the blame for his death in the eyes of the press and the university seemed like karma.

"Beth?" Niall squeezes my hand softly. I squeeze back, swallowing down the bile that's collected in my throat.

"We'd best get on with dinner; we don't want to starve your mum." I start chopping tomatoes, slicing the sharp knife through their rosy skins. But he doesn't move, though; simply stands and stares at me until I'm embarrassed enough to stop.

"You know what you're doing, don't you?"

"Chopping tomatoes?"

"Avoidance. You even have this tone you use when you change the subject. Breezy and chipper, as if it's your job to cheer everybody up."

The impact of his words is so strong it almost hurts. It's as if he can see right through my bullshit and understands who I am underneath. As though he wants to break through the shell I've carefully built around myself; the pretty one I show to the rest of the world.

If he does, I'm scared he's going to find something rotten underneath.

* * *

I think I'm falling in love with Niall's mother. Maureen is a one-woman ball of energy, a force of nature that has no half-life. She spends most of the evening taking good-natured jibes at Niall which he happily endures, and I sit and let their mutual love envelop me like a soft, warm blanket. I've managed to shake off my earlier angst enough to join in her teasing about Niall's general messiness. He protests loudly when I tell her he's been cleaning the flat all week.

When he disappears to the bathroom, she turns in her chair and smiles at me. "How long have you and Niall known each other?" She glances at my left hand, and I know she's looking at my wedding ring.

"He started volunteering at the clinic a couple of months ago, but I knew him before. At university." Her eyes cloud over when I say the words.

"You were there when that poor wee boy died?"

I nod.

"Such a tragedy." She shakes her head slowly. "And everything that happened afterward, too. Did you hear Niall was thrown out?"

I swallow hard and glance at the door to the hallway. Unsure how much I should tell her, or how much Niall would want me to say. But I've seen them interact enough to know she doesn't judge, not unless she's making a joke. If pure love exists, then these two have it in spades.

"I was thrown out, too," I tell her.

Her eyes widen as realisation seems to wash over her. "You're the girl..." she breathes. "The one he left behind."

My voice is thick when I answer her. "That was me."

She looks at my ring once more, before her eyes flicker up to meet mine. "I know Niall looks tough, but he's sensitive underneath it all. He had such a hard time dealing with everything that happened. When I flew into town yesterday, it was like he was really alive again, that he was letting himself be happy for the first time in years." She catches my gaze and I feel like I'm being scrutinised. "My son adored you once, Beth. Don't make him fall in love with you again."

My chest constricts until I can barely breathe. "We're just friends," I manage to whisper.

"His eyes follow you around the room whenever he thinks you aren't looking. When he talks to you there's this gentleness to his voice I haven't heard in years. I'm old but I'm not blind. I can see the way you both look at each other."

I take a big mouthful of wine and consider her words. Remembering the way he waited for hours outside the police station. How he always hangs around after class and helps me clear up.

Oh, God.

"He's worked so hard to get over everything that happened," she says. "Please don't break his heart all over again."

Nine Years Earlier

The campus is dark and mostly deserted. People are either home, in halls, or cozied up in one of the many bars dotted around the university. We pass the occasional runner and a few groups of students walking home from the pub, but for the most part it's just the two of us.

We keep stopping to kiss and touch, which turns the ten-minute walk to the art building into a twenty minute one. My head is still buzzing, but the tab of ecstasy we shared before leaving my room is washing away the worst of my hangover, blanketing me with a sense of sweet euphoria. Whenever he touches my chest it makes me giggle.

When we finally reach the building it's all too easy to break in. He jimmies up a sash window with a metal rod, then pushes it up until we can climb inside. My feet land on the classroom floor, and my heart races, pounding against my ribcage as if it's trying to escape. Suddenly the lyrics from *Bat Out of Hell* start coming out of my mouth, and Niall muffles them with his palm, hushing me as he leads me toward the studios.

"But it's Meatloaf," I try to tell him. "Did you know he changed his name by deed poll? Imagine having to sign your cheques Mr Loaf. He must get really funny looks when he does the weekly shopping."

"You weren't this chatty an hour ago."

I hadn't taken ecstasy an hour ago, either. Now I want to tell him everything. There's so much in my brain that's itching to get out, I barely even know where to start.

This time, he muffles my words with his mouth. Hard, rough kisses that send my pulse soaring. He cups the back of my head with his hand and presses the other against my bum. His tongue is soft, though, almost gentle compared with the rest of him. I let him stroke it against my own.

"You need to be quiet while I paint you, okay?" he says after I break free to take in some air. His words are punctuated by soft pants.

"I don't know if I can."

"At least try and lie still. I can't do the first sketch if you keep moving and speaking." He kisses me again, and this time I feel his hardness digging into my hip. "We should never have taken that bloody E."

"It feels good, though."

Niall pushes me against a table and it rocks precariously on the tiled floor. There's a crash as a pile of books fall to the ground. He laughs and pushes me again, this time until I'm sitting on the edge, my legs wrapped around his hips. He grinds into me, kissing me feverishly until we fall back onto the scratched wooden table top.

"I thought you were going to paint me," I say.

He pulls my t-shirt up over my head. "Later."

Now

13

It doesn't get much busier than Trafalgar Square on a sunny Saturday afternoon. Filled with a mixture of tourists and pigeons, the concrete square seems to vibrate with excitement. Allegra pulls anxiously at my hand, almost running toward one of the huge black lions that guard Nelson's Column.

"Can we climb it, can we, can we?" she chants, her cheeks blooming with anticipation as we reach the iron beast.

"I'll give you a boost." I squat down, linking my fingers to form a cradle. She places her left foot in it and reaches out as I stand up, launching her onto the plinth. My attempts to climb are altogether clumsier. After three tries at hoisting myself up, a middle-aged tourist takes pity and lends a hand, until I finally reach the base of the lion. Allegra has already climbed astride it. Waving me over, she pats the space in front of her, and we sit together, overlooking London.

"This is Aslan," she tells me. "I'm Lucy and you're Susan and we're going to fight the White Witch."

I stroke his metal back. "What a good lion."

"Lucy was sent away from her mum, too," Allegra says. "I wonder why."

"It was wartime. They were evacuated."

"What's that?"

"There were bombs raining down on London; it wasn't safe for kids. They were sent to the countryside to live with strangers."

"In homes?" Her brow pulls down, thread-wrinkles lining her forehead.

"Not group homes like yours. But they had to live with families they didn't know."

Understanding softens her frown. "Like foster parents you mean?"

"Pretty similar, I suppose. Except some families didn't want them at all, and some of the kids had a terrible time. Maybe we should go to the War Museum next Saturday, there's bound to be some exhibitions there."

It's become a regular thing, our weekend trip out. At first we stuck to her local area, to leafy-green parks and Happy Meal lunches, but in the last couple of weeks we've spread our wings. A journey on a bus or the Tube, followed by a visit to a museum or gallery. After lunch we'll go into the National Portrait Gallery and hang around the Holbeins, maybe visit the Van Goghs. Allegra likes to make up stories about the paintings and I love to listen to them.

She's such a funny, wry little girl.

"Shall we climb down and eat our sandwiches?" I ask. In spite of the sunny day, the painted metal of the lion is cool, and it's seeping through my jeans, making my legs shake from the chill. I turn around to look at her and she's smiling happily. The gentle breeze lifts the ends of her hair. The tendrils look like they're dancing.

"What did you buy me?"

"I didn't buy them, I made them." I pat the canvas bag that's slung over my shoulder. "Liver pate or cow's tongue, take your pick."

She sticks out her own tongue and gags until I take pity on her. "Okay, okay. Ham and cheese, I figured that's safe enough."

"I still prefer Happy Meals."

Later, when I take her back to the group home, her little hand tightens around mine until her nails are digging into my palm. The tension wafts off her. It's in the stiffness of her posture and the downward set of her mouth.

"You okay?" I whisper as we walk up the path.

Her bottom lip starts to tremble, but she tries to shrug it off. "I'm okay."

"It's all right if you're sad. I'm sad too. But I'll see you at the clinic on Monday, and we can have another trip out next Saturday." I try to find the right words. The magic ones that will dry up her wet eyes and bring a smile to her lips. I fail miserably. Her little face crumples. The tears welling up in her eyes spill over, making shiny trails down her cheeks. I pull her close, burying my face in her hair.

"I hate it here. I don't want to come back. Take me home with you. Please." The last word is swallowed up by her wail, and in my mind I'm already stealing her away across London, hiding her in our house and contacting a lawyer to gain custody.

"I can't." My voice is thick. "I'll call Grace on Monday, find out how much longer you'll be here." Her face clouds over when I mention her social worker, but she says nothing. Her shoulders slump with resignation and we press the buzzer to the house, waiting for someone to answer.

One way or another, I have to get her out of there for good.

* * *

On Saturday night I'm staring listlessly into the fridge and trying to work out what to cook for dinner. Not that I'm hungry; the memory of Allegra's face acts as an instant appetite suppressor. I'm about to give up on food altogether and run a bath when my phone buzzes. Picking it up, I read the one-word message.

Hi.

It's not the word that brings a smile to my lips, but the person who sent it. I reply right away.

Hi yourself.

I never said I was original. I don't know what else to say to Niall. Even my fingers get tongue tied when he's around.

How was your day?

I hesitate to reply. Do I tell him how shit it was, watching Allegra cry and beg me to take her away? Do we have that kind of friendship yet? I'm not sure, but in the absence of Lara, I feel the need to spill my guts to somebody.

Pretty crap. I'm going to drown my sorrows in a vat of Pinot.

Sounds tempting. Why don't we drown together?

The thought of drowning with him—doing anything with him—is so tempting. My finger hovers over the keypad of my phone as I try to talk myself out of the 'yes' I'm itching to type.

It's been a long day.

Simon wouldn't like it.

Please don't break his heart all over again.

The last excuse almost makes me laugh. Whatever Niall's ma saw last night, it wasn't adoration—pity, maybe, or kindness. I think we're becoming friends, which I like very much, but there's nothing more than that.

Not on his part, anyway.

He offers to come and get me, but I insist on taking a cab to his place, picking up a Chinese takeaway en route. I need that time to pull myself together. There's a ten-ton butterfly doing somersaults in my stomach at the thought of seeing him. It's as though I'm nineteen again, trailing after the popular kids, waiting for them to notice me. Even if I'm older and wiser, my body seems to be ignoring the fact. It's driving me crazy.

When we pull up outside Niall's flat, I juggle the takeaway bag and my purse, handing over a twenty pound note. The driver doesn't bat an eyelid, just pockets the cash and thanks me when I refuse the change.

For the second night in a row, I find myself climbing the steps to Niall's front door and pressing his buzzer to let me in.

I'm almost shocked when the front door opens. I'd been expecting a buzz and a click, not this. By this, I mean Niall running down three flights of stairs to meet me, a huge grin on his face, his cheeks flushed beneath the one-day layer of stubble that takes my breath away.

Why does he have to be so bloody gorgeous?

Niall leans forward and presses his lips to my cheek, grazing the corner of my mouth. I have to fight the urge to move my head an inch and feel the full force of his lips against mine.

"Let me take that." He pulls the takeaway bag from my clutching fingers and holds the front door open. "You look great, by the way. I like your t-shirt."

"This old thing?" I don't even remember where I got it from. It could be a five-pound Primark bargain or a hundred-pound Simon gift. I bat away the urge to check the label.

"It looks good on you." His eyes scan down from my face to my chest, and my cheeks flame as red as his, but for entirely different reasons.

"Is your mum still here?" I squeak.

"I put her on the train to Preston this afternoon." He isn't suffering any of my breathlessness as we make the ascent to his flat. I try to disguise my embarrassingly loud gasps.

"What's in Preston?"

"My aunt. Ma's gone to terrorise her for a few days while I get some respite. I'm still traumatised after she revealed all my secrets to you last night."

My son was in love with you, Beth.

Thank God he doesn't know about that one. If he did, I wouldn't be standing here right now. It isn't true, I remind myself. She was seeing things that weren't there.

"Shut up, she was really nice." I punch him in the bicep and he reaches up to grab my fist. He holds it in his hand for a moment, staring down at our joined fingers.

"Did I hurt you?" I whisper.

His eyes rise up to meet mine. "Never."

He walks into his flat and carries the brown takeaway bag into his kitchen. I follow and watch as he unloads the little plastic boxes, steam escaping as he pulls off the lids. "Shall I serve or do you want to help yourself?"

I'm not at all hungry. "I'll serve myself." He's still staring at me and it's unnerving. My hand shakes as I reach out to grab a spoon. "I wasn't sure what you like so I thought I'd stick to the favourites. You can never go wrong with Chow Mein."

"Unless I have a wheat allergy," he remarks.

I practically snatch the plastic pot from his hands. "Do you get all swollen up? Do you have an EpiPen? Should I call an ambulance?"

He takes the container back and starts to laugh. "I didn't say I had a wheat allergy." He starts to heap noodles onto his plate. "I was just hypothesising."

Now I want to hit him again. "You scared me. I had visions of having to drag your lifeless body down three flights of stairs, screaming out for help. Though I'm not sure which one of us would need the hospital more by that point."

I look up and I'm breathless all over again. He's beautiful. Not just handsome, in that square-jawed, matinee idol kind of way. His face is less ephemeral than that. His straight, even nose, full lips and those bright blue eyes remind me of medieval portraits and dashing knights.

"Hey, I promised you a vat of wine. Will a glass do to start with? They're big ones; I can probably fit half a bottle in there."

Niall and wine. I wonder if it's a good combination.

"A glass will do. I forgot to bring my swimming costume anyway." When he looks confused, I add, "For swimming in the vat."

"Nah, you said drowning. You don't need a swimming costume to drown." He passes me a full glass. "You can do that naked."

Oh.

I take a big gulp, searching for salvation in the bottom of the glass. Although I know even a mouthful of Pinot isn't enough to ward off my demons, because I shouldn't be here. It isn't the same as popping over to Lara and Alex's for dinner and a gossip.

Not even remotely similar.

For one, I haven't had sex with Lara, or Alex. There are no memories of sensual nights, of skin on skin, of slipping and sliding our way to oblivion. Though I love them to bits, they don't make me feel like Niall does. Exposed and raw.

"Do you want to eat here or on the sofa?" I ask. It comes out as one garbled word. His lips twitch at my discomfiture, which only heightens when he reaches out and brushes his hand against my face, cupping my cheek. It burns so hot I imagine there'll be an outline of his fingers etched into my skin even after he pulls away.

But I don't want him to pull away.

A shiver snakes its way down my spine at the same time my breath gets caught in my throat.

"Don't look at me like that." His voice is low. A warning.

"Like what?"

"You know what I'm talking about, Beth." He moves closer, so my left hip is jammed against the breakfast bar while my right is jammed against him. I have to look up to meet his eyes.

When I do I'm lost in them. It's not wine I want to drown in, it's Niall.

"You're the one touching me." I place my hand over his, feeling the warmth of his skin.

"Then touch me back."

My fingers touch his jaw, tentatively at first. I feel the sharp scratch of his almost-beard, the softer give of the skin below. His muscles tense as I brush my thumb along his lips. "Like this?"

"Yes." His voice is strangled. I feel it vibrate against the pad of my thumb a moment before his lips close around it, pulling it inside his soft, warm mouth. My legs buckle from under me. It's such an intimate move; there's no mistaking his intention.

"Beth." He pulls my hand from his face and holds it tightly with his own, leaning in closer still, until his face is a breath away from mine. "You're married."

"Yes."

"And I want to kiss you."

"Yes."

He pauses for a moment, his eyes searching my face as though all the answers are there. "Do you want to be kissed?"

I place my palm on the back of his neck, weaving my fingers into his hair. When I press my lips to the corner of his mouth I feel his warm gasp of air on my skin. With a thumping heart I kiss his jaw, his cheek, the soft spot beneath his ear, and his hands circle my waist, his fingers digging in as if he's trying hard to hold on.

"Kiss me." His words sound like a plea. I continue my route, dragging my lips down his neck, resting them in his collarbone. "On the lips, Beth, please."

I can almost taste his desperation as I move back up. It's as needy as my own. I rock my hips into him and he's as sensitised as I am. I can feel his hard outline through his jeans. I hesitate before I place my lips back at the corner of his mouth, because it feels as though I'm on a precipice. I could turn and walk away right now and somehow salvage some kind of sense out of this whole situation.

But I don't. I couldn't walk away even if I tried. I'm so full of him it hurts. I can feel him, smell the gentle scent of soap wafting from his skin, and hear his harsh breaths as he tries to get some control. He's taking me over and I want it so badly.
"Niall?"
"Yes?"
"Kiss me."

It takes him less than a second to capture my lips, pulling my head toward him until we are crushed together. I moan softly as his tongue slides against mine, sending heat rushing down my body. He alternates between kissing me hard and gently, soft brushes followed by scraping bites. I follow his lead, threading my fingers through his hair, gasping into his mouth when he grinds against me.

Every thought is subsumed by the aching need he creates in me, the desperation to touch, to taste, to feel. We kiss so hard we barely break for breath, preferring suffocation to separation as we move our lips as one.

His hands push beneath my t-shirt, and the sensation of skin on skin makes my spine tingle. He pushes beneath my bra strap, splaying fingers across my shoulder blades.

"I've wanted to do this since I first saw you." He breaks away long enough to breathe. Then he nuzzles his face into my neck, biting softly at my skin. "Christ you taste as good as I remember."

Though he doesn't mean for them to be, his words are like a bucket of ice water being thrown at my face. I pull away, my bra strap pinging against my back as his hands slide from underneath them. Reaching up, I touch my lips. They feel swollen, needy.

"We can't do this." I'm still breathless and sensitised. "I can't do this. I'm married, this is wrong." I should have thought of that before I pressed my lips against him, I know that. There's no question that my judgement's off. "I have to go."

Niall steps back and runs a hand through his thick black hair, trying to undo the damage my own fingers did moments before. "What about dinner?" He motions at our plates, the food cooling and congealed in an MSG-enhanced pile.

"I'm not hungry," I say. "I'm so sorry, Niall, I shouldn't have done that." Tears spring to my eyes. Self-disgust replaces the neediness of before, and I hastily grab my coat and bag.

"Wait." He tries to take my arm, but I pull away. One touch and I'll be done for. His presence overrides any self-control I can muster. "I'll drive you home."

"It's okay, I'll get a cab. You've been drinking anyway." I point at his glass. It's mostly full, forgotten in the heat of desire. "Thank you for the drink, and, um, feel free to finish the food."

I practically sprint out of his door, taking the steps fast, even though I know he could catch up with me easily if he wanted to. He doesn't, but still I run, as if I can leave it all behind—the shame, the embarrassment, my poor sense of judgement. But the thing I want to escape from the most is still with me.

You can't outrun yourself.

14

I spend Sunday morning moving all my things to the spare room, thinking a clean break will be kinder, easier. A stopgap until I can find somewhere affordable. In the afternoon, I move it all back again, re-hanging clothes and re-stuffing drawers. Somehow, I manage to waste an entire day prevaricating, and by the time I replace the final item in my wardrobe the sun is low in the sky, turning the streets pink as it sets.

My indecisiveness has managed to distract me from my phone, which lies on my bedside table in angry silence. Plus, I tell myself, I've had the equivalent of a two-hour gym workout, carrying all that stuff back and forth. I could do with a cardio workout.

The evening drags on. I cook an omelette, pour a glass of wine and stare blankly at *Antiques Roadshow*, trying to stop myself from thinking. Later, I take a bath and have another glass of wine. Before I know it, half the bottle is gone.

Yet I still feel sick. Apprehensive.

It's a day late, but I definitely have sorrows to drown. What the hell was I thinking? I've gone from being a mixed-up woman in therapy to an adulterer. That's how I see it, regardless of whether or not we had sex. We kissed and we touched and I wanted more.

At ten o'clock I climb into bed, pulling the covers over my head, blocking out the thoughts and disappointment with myself. All it does is give me a blank canvass for the memories.

I think about the way Niall's lips felt against mine, the hard ridge in his jeans as he pushed against me.

Kiss me on the lips, Beth, please.

I can almost hear him saying those words. The desperation laced in his voice is reflected deep inside me. These past few months keep repeating in my mind. Simon's coldness, my anxiety. The way Niall's been there to hold me up.

Please don't break his heart all over again.

Is my marriage with Simon even worth saving? It's as if the passion I felt last night has woken something in me. Something I thought I could live without.

Now I'm not sure I can.

I wake up to warm arms wrapped around my body and a face nuzzled into the back of my neck. For one fleeting moment I think it's Niall. Then I reach behind me and feel soft, silky hair, thinner than his, cut closer to the neck. I recoil, wondering why I'm reacting so violently to my husband's embrace.

Because it isn't him, a little voice inside my head tells me.

"Did I wake you?" Simon's voice is soft. "I'm sorry, baby." Whisky wafts from his breath.

"What time is it?" I'm disoriented, not only from waking up, but because of the way he's holding me. We've barely spoken for weeks, let alone touched. It feels wrong.

"Just gone midnight." He's still nuzzling. His lips slide across my neck when he speaks. "I got back about an hour ago, the traffic was fairly light." Another kiss, this time pressed to my spine. "I missed you."

It's hard not to shudder. Should I pretend to go back to sleep; would that be believable? I wasn't ready for this sudden onslaught of affection. I was expecting the usual coldness, hoping for it even. I could have coped with that.

His hand moves up, under my vest, in a grotesque parody of Niall's caresses. Biting my lip, I try not to cry out. When he reaches my breasts I feel myself shake, yet still I say nothing. Perhaps this is penance, a way of paying back for all my transgressions.

Simon must feel my spine stiffen, because he presses his face into my hair, muttering softly, "I'm sorry for being such a bastard. I know it hasn't been easy these past few months, but I'm going to try harder. We can see that counsellor you were talking about." He kneads my breasts with his hands. "God, I've missed this. Missed you."

"We can't see the counsellor. She won't take us as a couple."

His right hand slides down, brushing my stomach, pressing between my thighs. I turn my head into my pillow, trying to hide my disgust. This was what I wanted, wasn't it? For him to talk to me again, for us to work at our marriage. I should be turning over and throwing myself into his arms, peppering kisses over his face the way I did last night with Niall.

Niall. It's wrong to even think of him as my husband pushes his hand beneath the waistband of my shorts. He trails a finger along my thigh and it's all I can do not to clamp them together.

"Are you okay?"

I take a deep breath. "I'm just tired."

"You poor thing." Simon pulls his hand out from my shorts and reaches around my waist to turn me over. Then I'm facing him, staring into his chocolate-brown eyes. He pushes a lock of hair out of my face, and his tenderness makes me want to cry. When he presses his nose to mine I have to close my eyes to block everything out.

"Kiss me," he whispers.

I freeze. Hearing Niall's words coming out of Simon's mouth seems some sort of cruel joke. "I can't."

I can't kiss Niall because I'm married to Simon. I can't kiss Simon because I'm infatuated with Niall.

Infatuation, not love. That's what it is.

Simon lets go of me, rolling onto his back in defeat. Flinging an arm across his face, he takes a deep breath.

"Okay," he says slowly, "I understand. We need to take things slow. But being away this weekend gave me a lot of time to think, and I hate the way I've been treating you. I'm going to make it up to you, I promise." He takes my hand in his, threading our fingers together. And though I eventually fall asleep, it's neither restful nor reviving.

* * *

"You're late." Lara looks up from her lunch: a foil-wrapped ham sandwich and half a cup of tepid coffee. I suspect the latter has been hanging around most of the morning. Brown, sticky stains are dried on the side of her mug. She stuffs the rest of the sandwich in her mouth, yet still manages to talk. "You were supposed to be here at twelve."

"I'm only a couple of minutes late." I step away from the shower of crumbs that fly out from her mouth. "And you're disgusting by the way."

"Just time poor." She balls up the foil and throws it in her bin. "I've a client at one, and from the look of you we'll need more than fifty-five minutes to solve all your problems."

"There's not enough time in the world for that," I mutter, then flop dramatically into the leather chair to the side of her desk. "Aren't you supposed to counsel me without a desk between us?"

"Stop being a layman." She takes a sip of her coffee then makes a face. "And anyway, this isn't a counselling session. It's lunch. Where you get to make me feel better about myself by telling me how crap your rich, privileged life is."

I laugh, I can't help it. She has this knack of seeing the ridiculous in everything. "If you mention first-world problems I'm going to slap you," I warn.

"Hey, I make a living out of first-world problems, I'd never disrespect them." She leans forward, resting her elbows on the desk and clasping her hands together. "So, tell me all about it. I hope there's sexual deviancy involved. I've missed that since I came here."

"Does deviancy include refusing to have sex with your husband?"

"Nope, that's what we like to call marriage."

"Okay, great, you've solved all my problems." I smile cheerily. "Now let's go to work on world peace."

"So the ice king thawed, then?" She ignores my jibe.

"He came home on Sunday, had a few drinks then tried to get it on with me. I guess you could call that a thaw."

"Did he mention the silent treatment?"

"No, he just tried to kiss me. And I kissed Niall Joseph the night before," I blurt out, totally unprompted.

Lara is taken aback. "What?" She leans toward me, her eyes wide. "You did what?"

"I kissed him, or he kissed me." My heart is racing. I'm not sure if it's at the memory or my confession. "We both kissed each other."

"When, where? Oh my God, did you tell Simon?"

"You're judging me," I hiss. "Your face has gone all judgey and it's not meant to do that. Don't you remember your training?"

"I'm not your counsellor. I'm your friend and I'll judge if I want to," she retorts. "But I'm not judging you anyway. I'm surprised, shocked maybe, but not judging." She sits back in her seat. "He came over for dinner last night and didn't mention a thing."

"You had him over for dinner?" I ask. "Without me?" It's hard not to feel aggrieved. Like my two best friends have gone on a day out and forgotten to invite me.

"I'm sorry, I didn't get the memo saying that you two had a snog and now must be treated as an inseparable couple. Is that what you are now?"

I shake my head. "I ran out of his flat and we haven't spoken since." I blush at the memory, burying my face in my hands. "What am I going to do?"

She peels my fingers away until I'm looking at her. I don't point out that she's moved from behind her desk, and there are now no barriers between us. It isn't the time. "How do you feel about him?"

"Which him?"

"Niall. The last thing I heard he was just an annoying relic of your past. Somebody you'd rather forget. How did that all change?"

"We've become friends," I whisper. "He waited outside the police station for me after Cameron's arrest and took me for a drink. And then he invited me for dinner with him and his mum—"

"His mum?" she splutters. "You had dinner with his mum? Christ, this is serious."

"Shut up! We were only friends then. We are still, I think, though I haven't seen him since Saturday night." I frown. "Maybe we aren't even friends anymore."

"So how did you go from having dinner with his mum to a tongue sandwich? You didn't do it in front of her, did you? Because that would be all kinds of weird."

"No. He invited me over on Saturday night."

"Two nights in a row," she interrupts.

"And?"

"I'm just saying. He invites you to meet his mum one night. The next he invites you over for a snog. Didn't you think it was all a bit... much?"

"No," I wail. "I didn't think anything. That's the problem. I should have thought, then maybe I wouldn't be in this mess."

"Sweets, it doesn't have to be a mess, not unless you let it. You just need to decide what it is you want to do. Whether it's Simon you want, or Niall."

She makes it sound so easy. But the things that look simplest on the surface end up being the most complicated underneath. At the end of the day I don't know what the hell it is I do want. The lack of certainty's making me feel sick.

* * *

On Thursday afternoon I'm fluttering around the classroom like a demented butterfly, picking things up, putting them in the wrong place and generally freaking out. A glance at the clock tells me it's just gone two. Only half an hour until I see Niall again. For the first time since Saturday. I'm not ready for it. No solutions have been forthcoming, no decisions have suddenly been made. How can they when I don't even understand what I'm deciding on?

I'm staring blankly into the supply cupboard when I hear the door to the classroom open. The drawn-out creak causes me to turn my head with nervous anticipation, but the person standing in the doorway isn't Niall. Instead, Lara walks in, her mobile clutched in her hand. She stares at the screen for a moment before she looks up at me. "Um, I've just had a text from Niall. He isn't coming today."

"What?" Suddenly, I'm desperate to see him.

"According to him, he's had an emergency." She widens her eyes at the last word. "Apparently he sends his apologies."

Apparently. What on earth does that mean? I shrug, trying to ignore the crushing sensation in my chest that feels way too similar to disappointment. "Nice of him to give me some notice," I grumble. I've got about an hour to think of some way to entertain a group of rowdy kids. I don't like the odds.

"Maybe he's sick," Lara says. "Perhaps a sudden wave of nausea has just engulfed him, chaining him to a porcelain prison."

"He's probably sick of me, I'll give you that."

"It could all just be a coincidence." She doesn't look convinced. "It doesn't mean he's avoiding you."

"If he isn't avoiding me, why did he text *you*? He has my number, he could have used it."

I should be relieved. The moment I've been dreading all week has suddenly been postponed. It's like turning up to an important test and finding out the teacher is off sick, and there are no question papers to be found.

But I'm not. It seems ironic that Simon has suddenly started talking to me at the same time as Niall has decided to ignore me. And wrong that I'm desperate for it to be the other way around. What does that say about my marriage? When I'd rather be talking to the man from my past than my husband?

I'm still stewing over it all when the children arrive. Allegra is first—bright eyed and red cheeked with excitement, because she's being allowed a Saturday visit with her mum. The others follow close behind, with Cameron Gibbs the last to trail in. He pulls his Snapback up and gives me a nod. "All riiiight?"

"Nice to see you, Cameron." I try to keep my voice even, stripping it of anything he could misconstrue. I count my efforts as successful when he just shrugs and walks to the back of the room. One of the few wise things my dad taught me, back when I was young enough for him to take an interest, was to celebrate the small victories. So inside I give a little jig.

In the end, they all decide to make get-well cards for Niall. I can't help but find this funny. What I wouldn't give to be a fly in the wall when he gets fifteen hand-made cards for an affliction he doesn't even have. I'm definitely going to get these cards to him, not just because I'm feeling passive aggressive right now, though in my nervy state that's motive enough. The reason I really want to send them to him is I want him to come back. I miss him. I want to see him.

I'm beginning to realise what it is I truly want.

Nine Years Earlier

"Let me see." I try to duck under Niall's outstretched arm so I can twist myself around his body, but he's too quick for me. Grabbing the shoulder of my t-shirt, he stops my progress.

"Wait. It's not finished."

I change tack and nuzzle my face into his neck. If swiftness doesn't work, maybe seduction will. "Please, please," I whisper into his throat. "Show me my picture."

We've been doing this for six nights now. Each night he comes to my room we either smoke a joint or pop an E. Then we have sex, followed by a furtive moonlit trip to the art building. He paints into the night, staring at me and then at the canvas, mixing colours frantically like they're going to disappear.

At first I liked the way he looked at me, with his eyes narrow, and his mouth slightly open. But then he started paying more attention to the canvas than me. A few times, I even fell asleep. When I woke I caught him leaning on the table, staring right down at my naked body, and it sent shivers down my spine. Then I realised he was studying me a little too intently, with pupils that failed to dilate. For a moment, I felt like an object.

"You can see it after exam week," he murmurs, cupping the back of my head. "It'll be ready by then."

Exam week. The words are enough to kill the mood—studying, revising, test practice. All things I've failed to do for the past few weeks. My face must fall because the next minute he's holding me in his arms, kissing me hard and promising I can see it soon.

I kiss him back, but for the first time I'm half-hearted because all I can think is that I'm going to fail. I'll have to go home and explain to my mum and dad why I've managed to royally fuck up my life in the space of a few weeks.

Seeing the painting doesn't seem half as exciting anymore.

Now

15

"Why do you think you have to choose?" Louise asks. I let my head fall back on my chair as I look around her consulting room. As always, it's perfectly tidy.

It's been three weeks since I kissed Niall. The relief I feel about finally voicing my doubts is palpable.

"That's what you do, isn't it? Torn between two lovers? I can't just string two men along, it isn't the done thing."

"It's interesting that you call Niall a lover yet you've only kissed him once. Why do you think that is?"

"I don't know." I frown and rub my eyes. "I think he wanted more." Or was it me? Am I just projecting my emotions onto Niall? What if all he wanted was a quick, uncomplicated fumble?

He sure chose the wrong girl for that.

"Do you think your shared history has anything to do with it?"

I've told Louise everything. Laid all my secrets out like a dysfunctional offering. Shared things with her that I've never told a soul, not even Lara. She listens and smiles and empathises with me. Her acceptance gives me a peace I haven't had before.

"Maybe I'm putting more emphasis on it than I should. But the way he looked at me when I left that night, and the fact he hasn't been back to the clinic for three weeks..." I let my voice trail off. For the past two Thursdays Niall has sent a stand-in. Michael is nice enough. Good with the children.

But he's no Niall.

"Okay, so let's assume he wants something more. It's still not a simple choice between two men. Can you think of a third option, maybe?"

"Being with them both?" I wrinkle my nose up.

Louise bursts out laughing. It's the first time I've seen her crack more than a smile. I wonder if that's part of their training, trying not to show violent emotion. Perhaps there's only space for one crack-up in the therapy room. "No, I wasn't going to suggest you choose polyamory, though I'm not knocking it either. That sort of arrangement isn't something you go into lightly."

"Then what?"

She says nothing, another trick of hers. Louise uses silence the way a carpenter uses a saw. As if on cue, I hurriedly try to break it. "Choose neither?"

"Choose you," she corrects. "Concentrate on yourself. Get to know what you really want. Love yourself as much as others do."

I stare at her as though she's talking a foreign language. "That sounds selfish."

"Studies show that relationships are more likely to succeed if both partners have high self-esteem. It isn't selfish to take care of yourself. Think of it as laying strong foundations. So the question you have to ask yourself is *'what do I want?'*"

I sit there in stunned silence. I don't think anybody's ever really asked me that before.

* * *

It's strange how life goes on even as it's falling apart. Sometimes I wonder how my grandmother coped during the war. Separated for six years from her husband, not knowing if he was dead or alive, yet still she had to sweep the floor, buy the groceries, and clean the toilets. I expect she ate cake with friends—when she had the rationing coupons—and thought about the most mundane things. Somehow, human beings have the ability to survive no matter what's thrown at them.

As I watch Daisy slowly bring her glass up to her lips, her hands shaking like an old man's, I marvel that even she has a survival instinct forcing her to go on. A few weeks after kissing Niall, my own survival instinct is a different matter. I smother it with concerns for other people.

"How was she?" Daisy asks. She's picking at the skin around her thumbnail. A tiny bead of blood glints in the sunlight before she wipes it away, a ruby smudge angling down her thumb.

"She misses you." I think Daisy needs to hear this. "She wants to come home to you. Did Grace tell you if it's on the cards?" I know Daisy's been meeting with her social worker weekly.

Daisy shrugs. "She won't say. We're on supervised visits only at the moment. Until I can prove I'm clean and Darren's not coming back they won't let her come and live with me." Her voice is drowned out by the roar of a motorbike engine. We both wait for it to pass by.

"He's not coming back is he?" I try to swallow down the rising bile. A memory of her lifeless body flashes through my mind.

"He said he wasn't." Her voice lowers to a whisper. "When he let them… you know."

It turns out it wasn't Darren who beat her up, not that it really matters. He was the one who virtually pimped her out to his mates. The one who stood and watched as they bashed her to within an inch of her life. He poisons everything he comes into contact with, and I don't blame Allegra's social worker for wanting to keep him away from her.

"Why do you go back to him every time?" Of all people, I shouldn't be the one asking her this. It's like asking an addict why they take drugs.

Or why I can't keep Niall Joseph out of my mind.

"I love him." Her reply's so simple it makes me want to cry. That isn't love. It's sick and evil. She was so neglected as a kid that any attention equates to love in her book.

"But what about Allegra? What if he ever let someone hurt her as he hurt you?"

Her face twists as I ask the question, her lips turning thin. "Are you telling me I don't love my kid?" A lock of her dirty-blonde hair falls in her eyes as she leans forward. "Don't you dare fucking say that."

I'm hasty in backtracking. "Of course not. I didn't mean it like that."

"It's so fucking easy for you to judge me, isn't it? With your rich husband and lovely house and no worries about anything in life. Maybe Darren was right about you."

My heart starts to race. I'm never good with confrontation. "What do you mean?"

"He reckons I'm your bit of rough. Your project. He thinks you don't give a shit about me and Allegra, that you only hang around us to make yourself feel better."

Her words are a slap in the face. I feel the injustice of them as if it's a physical thing. "That's not true. I love you and Allegra." I want to say more but my voice catches in my throat, scraping at the skin.

"Then why do you judge me? Just because you've got the perfect fucking life. You've never had to slum it."

"I didn't mean it to sound like that. I can't stand the thought of Darren ever hurting either of you. You deserve better."

"If you think I'd ever let anybody hurt my baby you know fuck all. I can't believe you even said it." She pulls out a cigarette and slides it between her dry lips. "If I hear you've said anything to the social workers I'll bloody whack you."

I don't think she means to be intimidating. It's the way she is—the way she has to be—in order to get by. Life has taught her it's either fight or flight, and she's chosen to punch her way through the bad times. Part of me is glad she's coming out with her fists held high, that she's not going to let things bring her down. But it's still scary in the firing line.

The cafe door bangs open as the waitress comes out with our food. A teacake for Daisy and a piece of toast for me. Daisy pulls out the raisins before she butters it, piling them on the side of her white plate until they resemble a mound of dead flies. I scrape the butter across my own toast even though I have no appetite. The sound of my knife against the crunchy bread is better than the silence.

"I wouldn't come between you and Allegra," I say, finishing the dregs of my lukewarm tea. "I know how much she wants to come home."

Daisy seems mollified, though I'm not sure if it's my words or food in her stomach that softens her up. "I want her home. I won't do anything to endanger that." When I look up she's staring at me through watery eyes. "Help me," Daisy begs. "Help me get my baby back."

"How?"

"Tell Grace I'm better now. Tell her I'm a fit mother. I just want her back. She hates it at the home."

"I know." My fingers flex instinctively at the memory of Allegra's fearful hand clutching mine. "I want her out of there as much as you do. But you're going to have to convince them you're clean for good."

"I am." Daisy's reply is vehement. "I wouldn't risk Allegra for a high."

I try not to think of all the occasions she's done exactly that. The times when Allegra has found her mother out cold on the floor, or the nights when Daisy disappeared for hours, leaving her kid alone in the dark. History teaches us life follows a pattern, that things repeat themselves over and over again. Yet human nature makes us hope against hope it isn't true. That this time will be different.

"You'll need to prove that Darren's gone for good." I almost flinch saying his name, expecting her to turn on me again.

"He wouldn't have me back, anyway," she says.

I notice that she's not denying she still has feelings, or that she'd go running if he clicked his fingers. She's assuming he won't be returning. From what I know of Darren, it's a dangerous assumption to make.

My promises sound weak, even to my own ears, but Daisy's face lights up as if I've just offered her the world. The uneasiness in the air is mine alone and though I try to bury it, still it lingers on.

16

The following week I head across town toward the white stucco building that houses our marriage counsellor. I'm halfway down Harley Street when my phone buzzes, but it's buried deep within my bag. By the time I've rifled through the napkins and leaflets, it's already rung off.

I don't recognise the number, although that doesn't stop my heart from beating a little faster as I press the button for my voicemail, wondering if Niall has finally decided to contact me.

But the voice is female, deep and smooth, telling me my husband is running late, that he won't be able to make the appointment tonight. No apologies, no excuses, and for some reason that bothers me. It feels like the last straw. You can't swim against the tide when you're not even kicking your legs. We're both drifting, clinging onto the detritus of our marriage, when perhaps we should just let go. Let the current sweep us up, even if it pulls us apart.

In the past month, Simon has managed to attend exactly two counselling appointments. He missed the first one due to a late-running court case. His apologies sounded trite, even to me, and I began to wonder just how committed he was to the whole process. Even at home he's been quiet, holing up in his office, head bent over papers and depositions, only emerging for a coffee or a glass of whisky. While he managed to make the second appointment, he was noticeably silent at the third; contemplative even. He listened to what I had to say but didn't add anything to it.

It's almost as though he's deliberately withdrawing. As if he's given up before we've even started. That puzzles me too, because I feel as though I'm the one making all the effort.

If he was in love with me, wouldn't he make more time for us? And if I was in love with him, wouldn't I care more?

Because I still fall asleep every night with Niall's voice in my mind. With the memory of his lips on mine. If there was something worth saving, I'd be able to block him out. Forget about him.

"Kiss me, Beth."

The fact is, I'm obsessing about him more than ever. His silence has done nothing more than let me build everything up in my mind, until I'm not even sure how I'm supposed to feel.

One thing I do know is I'm sick of the whole situation. Simon's silence, the counselling, our marriage.

The thought is freeing. A breath of relief. It allows me to think what I've been trying to avoid. The one thing I've been too afraid to articulate.

Because deep down inside, I'm not sure I want to save our marriage.

The thought has been floating around in my mind for weeks. Each time I've tried to ignore it, it's come back stronger. A child that won't be overlooked. It taps at my brain, sticking its tongue out at me. Reminding me that happily ever after isn't an option here.

From the way he hasn't bothered turning up yet again at our counselling session, I'm starting to think that maybe Simon doesn't want to save it, either.

* * *

I wait for three hours, sitting on our brown leather sofa, barely looking at the magazine that's open on my legs. Three cups of coffee have kept me awake, the bitter taste lingering in my mouth, along with a headache that throbs at the base of my skull.

It's almost eleven when I hear his key turn in the door. There's a pause before wood bangs against plaster.

"Hello." He pops his head around the door to the living room. "I didn't expect you to be up."

I've been going to bed early. Mostly so I can pretend to be asleep by the time he crawls under the covers, but also because I'm knee deep in organising the clinic's annual gala. Both things are exhausting.

"I waited up for you."

He winces. "Are you very angry? Because I can explain…"

"I'm not angry at all." In spite of my emotions earlier this evening, I'm the calmest I've felt in a while.

Simon steps inside, his dress shoes clipping against the wooden floor. When he's sat down, he leans forward, clasping his hands together. "Aren't you going to ask me where I've been?"

"It doesn't matter."

He carries on as if I haven't said anything. "I was with Elise."

"Is everything okay?" Simon's daughter and I may not be bosom buddies, but I still care.

"Not really. It seems her accountant's made a mess of her tax return, and it's sparked an investigation. We're going to have to get someone else to look at the books."

"I'm sorry to hear that," I murmur. "I hope she isn't too upset."

He shrugs. "We'll sort it out. She still wants to take a table at the gala."

That's good. With only four weeks to go, it would be a pain to have to find another donor.

"I wanted to talk to you about something," I say. My heart starts to speed up; it's one thing to think about doing something, but the execution is something quite different. Tears spring to my eyes before I can even say the words.

"I don't think the marriage counselling is working."

Shock freezes Simon's face. It takes him some moments to collect himself enough to respond. "You said you weren't angry..."

"I'm not angry." I scoot forward, trying to cut down the distance between us. "I'm not saying this out of anger, or because I'm being a bitch. I'm not saying it because I want to hurt you or upset you—"

"Then what is it, Beth? You know how busy I am. I'm doing my best here to keep things together. What more do you want?" For the first time, he sounds passionate.

"I just think that if our marriage was your first priority, then you'd come to counselling, regardless."

"I have a job. A daughter. Do you want me to ignore them? Just look after little Beth and pretend nothing else matters?"

I drop my head into my hands. "No, that's not what I mean. Of course those things are important. But we're not moving forward here. Only backward." When I look up, he's staring angrily at me. I try not to cower away.

"Then tell me what to do. What will make you happy?"

I open my mouth but no words come out. Instead I'm remembering Louise's suggestion. That I should choose me, work on my own self-esteem. I can't remember the last time anybody asked me what would make me happy.

What would?

I try to imagine myself staying in this marriage. Waking up with Simon every day. Choosing a life of contentment, of companionship, letting him take care of me the way he takes care of his clients and his daughter. And there's nothing wrong with that life—it's one I longed for when I was at my lowest.

But will it make me happy?

"I don't know." It feels as if it's a confession. "I don't know what will make me happy."

"Then maybe you'd better find out," Simon suggests. "I love you, you know that. You're the best thing that happened to me in years. But I can't fight for you if I don't know what I'm fighting against. We can go to all the counsellors in the world, but until you decide what the bloody hell it is you want, we're just talking into thin air."

17

When Niall doesn't turn up to class for the fifth week running, I feel my patience starting to run thin. For the past month I've done nothing except analyse what I'm supposed to be feeling, what I'm supposed to be doing, and he just seems to have disappeared. It's as if he's set fire to a touch paper and then run away so he doesn't have to watch the explosion.

More than that, though, *I miss him*. When I look around the classroom I feel a sense of despondency, even though the kids seem happy enough that Michael is paying them some attention. As nice as the stand-in is, he isn't Niall, and I'm beginning to realise he's the one thing missing from my life.

What will make you happy?

I've been stuck on that question for over a week. Thinking through Simon's words every night when I close my eyes, trying to see a way through. And every time my thoughts drift toward Niall, to that kiss, to the way he touched me until my body felt as though it was on fire.

He made me feel alive. Something I'm not sure I've felt for a long time.

During my sessions with Louise, we've been talking through my choices. She's pointed out that I never really got over Digby's death or my role in it. That I was afraid to let myself feel vulnerable again. Maybe choosing to marry Simon was my way of protecting myself from pain, insulating myself from the world, and by wrapping myself in his protection, I've managed to numb myself for too long.

Now I'm exposed for the first time in forever. Letting myself feel emotions I'd forgotten about.

Passion. Fear. Vulnerability.

"It will hurt at first," she tells me. "Like when you pull a scab off a fresh wound. It might sting, it might get infected, but eventually it will heal again."

"What if I'd rather feel numb?"

"That's your choice. But if you honestly feel that way, what are you doing here? Why aren't you just going back to your old life, to your marriage? The fact you're coming to counselling tells me there's something you're not happy with."

She's right. She always is. Louise seems to have this ability to make me see myself more clearly. To cut through the bullshit and say it as it is.

I'm still thinking about it when Michael clears away the last of the paint bottles and says goodbye. I remember the other things Louise has suggested, that I should decide what I want, and not rely on everybody else to make decisions for me.

But what will make me happy? Not staying like I am, because at the moment it's making me feel miserable. When I rule that out, I know that the only option is to change things, to either transform my marriage or walk away.

We've tried to mend it. Both of us. For the past five weeks we've talked about making things better, but all we've done is talk. Neither of us has actually made any difference. Things are still the same as they were.

I don't want this any longer.

I'm tired of fighting for something I don't want anymore.

It doesn't feel as though there's even a decision to make.

* * *

We've been talking for an hour; going in circles, walking the painful perimeter of our marriage. Simon's sitting in his usual chair, his elbows on his thighs as he leans forward. I've noticed that Martin, our counsellor, has gone silent. He says nothing, watching us with interested eyes.

"I'm not happy," I tell Simon. "Neither of us are. And it feels as though we've done everything we can to make this work. What else is there to do?"

He says nothing for a moment. Just stares at me. His face looks drawn, old, and I keenly feel the difference between our ages.

"Christ." He rubs his face with open palms. "I don't know. It just feels like you're giving up too soon. I made you happy before, I know I did."

I nod, trying not to let my eyes fill with tears. "You did."

"So let me do it again. Stop fighting me all the time. Stop questioning me. Just let me take care of you the way I want to."

It doesn't work like that. He makes me sound as if I'm some sort of pet waiting to be groomed. Not somebody with my own feelings, emotions. My own needs.

"That's not what I want."

"What about what I want?"

"I don't think you want me like this." My laugh is mirthless. We both know he was looking for companionship and love, not a messed-up wife who is clearly unhappy. I feel a flash of sadness that I can't be who he wants me to be; beautiful, friendly. A trophy wife.

"So what do we do?"

I take a deep breath, trying to summon some courage. We can dance around this all day—God knows we have been—but eventually one of us is going to have to say it. Even as I open my mouth I hesitate, my heart full, my throat hurting, because as soon as I say the words I know nothing will be the same again.

I still need to say them, though.

"I think we should separate."

Slowly, he stands up and walks over, kneeling in front of me. Tears spill over my cheeks. He lays his head down in my lap, as if in supplication, and I find myself stroking his thin hair as he breathes into my thighs. We stay there for minutes, his tears soaking my jeans, my own still pouring down my face. Eventually he looks up, his eyes red, his hair mussed from my caresses.

"Stay," he whispers, taking both of my hands in his. "Stay with me."

I look for Martin, but he's left the room. We're on our own. It feels as though we always have been.

"I can't."

"Yes you can. I'll try harder, we both will. We'll make this work." There's a determined slant to his lips. He's a winner in life, he always has been. It's in his nature to fight.

"We've tried, Simon, and neither of us is happy. We'll be better off apart."

"And how are you going to afford to live without me?" he demands. "Your income from the clinic isn't going to get you very far."

"It isn't about the money." I know I'm not going to be able to find much. A bedsit at the most, or a grotty room in a shared flat. "Do you really want me to stay with you for your money?"

His laugh is harsh and humourless. "Yes."

Reaching out, I cup his face with my hands. His skin is cold and damp. "That's not true. You wouldn't want me to be a gold digger any more than I'd want you to be my sugar daddy. That's no way to have a relationship. We got married because we loved each other, because we wanted to be together." My voice cracks. "Because we worked."

"We can still work. Give it time, we can find another counsellor. We can go twice a week if we have to. Just tell me what to do and I'll do it."

"How many times are we going to try?" I ask. "Tell me, when was the last time you felt truly happy?"

He pauses for a moment, enough to wipe his eyes with a crisp, white handkerchief. "I don't know."

"I don't either, and that's not right. You deserve to be happy, we both do." I lean forward until our foreheads touch. It's an intimate gesture but not sensual.

"I know we'll both be happier in the long run."

Nine Years Earlier

Fifty-two percent. It's not a fail, but it's only a cat's whisker away. I read the number again, and wonder whether I should be pleased or appalled. Part of me is delighted I passed, despite my worst fears. I won't have to repeat a year or come back in the summer for retakes. I won't have to go crawling cap in hand to my parents and ask them to fund a fourth year at university.

But *fifty-two percent*. Just three marks less and I'd be in a world of trouble. It should be a wakeup call, a reminder of why I'm here. A second chance to make things right.

When I walk into the studio Niall isn't there. Instead I find Digby leaning over some clay-type monstrosity, his face screwed up with concentration.

"Is Niall around?" I ask.

Digby looks up from the table. "I haven't seen him for a while."

"I wonder where he is."

"I'm not sure." He stares back down at his clay and starts to mould what looks like an arm. "He said something about getting some supplies."

I try to hide my disappointment, but he sees it anyway. I've been spending a lot of time with Digby since we smoked white widow together at his house. He takes me for coffee and listens to me go on about Niall for hours. Even joins in sometimes.

I'm beginning to suspect he's got as big a crush on Niall as I have. For some reason it doesn't make me feel jealous. Having somebody who knows exactly how I feel is reassuring. Like I'm not going totally mad.

"Are you going to the party later?" he asks. There's a big rave going down at one of the racier halls. DJs and dancing. A whole lot of drugs. I've been looking forward to it for weeks.

"Yeah, wouldn't miss it for the world." I'm going to enjoy the hedonism while I can. It's only a week before I have to go home for the summer. Back to Mum and Dad, to overcast Essex. Back to pretending to be a good girl.

I'm dreading it.

"Save me a dance?" He gives me a suitably cute look. I'm going to miss his funny expressions over the summer.

"Of course. I'll only ever Macarena with you."

But we don't dance together that night.

Or ever again.

Now

18

Simon and I talk about moving my things into the spare room. I don't tell him I've tried that once already. This time I follow through. We've spoken more in the past few days than we have in months. With the spectre of our dying marriage finally put out of its misery, we're able to find some middle ground.

It gives me hope we can eventually discover that holy grail of separated couples: friendship. I can't imagine a life where Simon no longer exists. I hope I don't have to.

On Monday we part ways amicably. He heads for his office while I take a cab to the grey concrete building which houses the social services department. Daisy waits for me outside, frantically puffing at a stub of a cigarette. Her black skirt is a little too short, and her sweater a bit too tight. I just hope they realise what an effort she's made to clean herself up and look respectable.

She spots me and throws the butt to the floor, smashing it under the sole of her black boot. I incline my head to the metal ashtray affixed to the wall, and she quickly picks it up and stashes it in there.

"Are you ready?" I ask. We're due to meet with Grace O'Dell in ten minutes, but it doesn't hurt to be early. Daisy nods frantically before changing her mind and shaking her head.

"I puked my guts up this morning," she confides. "What if they never let her come home?"

I put my arm around her and we walk into the building.

We sign in at the desk, and the security guard gives us temporary passes that we loop around our necks. There's a bank of chairs on one side of the room and he directs us over. Daisy walks up to the cooler that's letting out a low-level buzz in the corner, her lips quirking up as she pours some water into a paper cup. "I've never seen one of these in real life before. It's cool."

She drains the cup and pours herself a second before finally coming to sit next to me. Her legs jiggle constantly, her eyes scanning the room in a nervous fashion, and I put my hand on her shoulder to calm her down.

"It's okay."

Though she nods her head, the scared expression remains. "I just want her back."

"I know."

Daisy gets increasingly nervous as the minutes tick by. Her movements become manic and her questions breathless. When Grace finally walks through the security door, I'm not sure which of us is more relieved.

"I'm sorry I'm late, everything's gone belly up in the office this morning. My last meeting overran by half an hour." She gives us a tight smile. "Still, we're all here now. Would you like to follow me?"

Before we even stand up, Daisy gives me a nervous glance. "Where are we going?"

"Just to a meeting room. A couple of my co-workers are there, and your case notes. Nothing to be alarmed about."

This reassurance does nothing to calm Daisy. Her nervousness is palpable. I can almost feel it vibrating in the air.

I reach for her hand as we walk through the security door, squeezing her cold fingers just to show I'm here,

"Please take a seat." Grace points at two empty chairs.

The room is small, barely fitting a table and five chairs inside. We squeeze past the two people already at the table—Grace's co-workers, I assume—and take the two vacant seats on the far side. As soon as she sits down, Daisy starts to rock on the two back legs. The movement makes the rubber feet squeak against the tiled floor. I grab on to the back of her chair to stop it, but then quickly pull my hand away.

She isn't a kid, so why am I treating her like one?

"Okay, I think we're ready to start." Grace shuffles through some papers as she talks. "How are you doing, Daisy?"

"I want my kid back."

Unflustered, Grace flashes her a smile. "Well, that's what we're here to discuss. Perhaps we can start with some introductions?"

We find out the man sitting opposite Daisy is a care worker from the group home where Allegra is staying, and the older woman is a representative from the council. Grace begins by outlining the main issues regarding Allegra's case, and explains about Daisy's hospitalisation.

Hearing the specifics from somebody else's mouth is harrowing. I feel myself choke up as they describe the specific occasions when Allegra's been neglected, left at home, and generally ignored. If I didn't know Daisy myself, I'd look at her and come to the conclusion she's a terrible mother. But she isn't. When Allegra has her full attention, Daisy can be great. It's her inconsistency that's so worrying.

As Grace refers to some reports, Daisy starts to rock on her chair again. She stares out of the window, her eyes glassed over as if she's not really here. I try to pay extra-close attention, knowing I'll probably have to explain everything all over again when we leave.

"And you've cut off all relations with your former boyfriend?"

I have to nudge Daisy, who does a double take. "What?"

"You've cut off any ties with..." The council officer rummages through her notes. "Mr Darren Tebbit?"

"We broke up."

The woman nods and makes some notes on her pad. I watch as her biro loops and swirls across the page, trying to make out what she's writing. I catch a few words, but nothing that tells me how the meeting is going.

As Grace details every interaction Allegra has had with social services, anger floods through my veins. There are the situations I know about; the time when Daisy disappeared with Darren for a whole week, the overdose that left her unconscious on the walkway outside their flat. But there're a million other little incidents I'm unaware of, too. Visits to A&E for a broken finger and lacerations, reports from her school about bruising on Allegra's arms. All of them occurring during the periods that Darren had been staying with Daisy.

The myriad of indicators stand out so boldly I'm no longer worried Allegra won't be going back home.

I'm more worried that *she will*.

Next, the group home representative gives us a run-down of his findings. He confirms what we already know—that Allegra is a very private little girl. She's found it extremely difficult to settle there. When he explains the highlight of her week has been our trips out on Saturdays it brings fresh tears to my eyes.

Thank God I never listened to Simon.

When we finally arrive at the conclusion, Daisy is still staring out of the window; it's as if she's not really with us. Grace has to say her name three times before her head snaps around.

"We've come up with a series of recommendations we feel will best serve your daughter's safety and security," Grace explains. "For the next two weekends we are recommending weekend visitation rights. You will be able to pick Allegra up at 5:00 p.m. on a Friday and return her to the home at 4:00 p.m. on a Sunday."

Finally, Daisy pays attention. "I only get her on weekends?"

"For the first two weeks. Thereafter, if the weekend visitations go well, we will return Allegra into your full custody."

"I'm getting her back?" A beaming smile breaks across Daisy's lips. "For real?"

"She'll remain on the At Risk Register for a period of six months, and then we will have a case review." Grace starts to outline the multi-agency action plan they've developed, which includes close monitoring, home visits and the requirement for Daisy to attend the clinic on a weekly basis. For her part, Daisy just nods, agreeing to everything without really paying attention.

"Did you hear that, Beth?" she asks. "I'm getting my baby back."

I nod at her, barely able to meet her stare. "I heard."

Grace starts passing over some papers for Daisy to look at, and though I lean forward I can't even focus on them. I'm still thinking about the lacerations and the bruises and the broken finger. How did I miss all that? I've been seeing Allegra regularly for the last two years, and I never noticed a single scratch.

What kind of friend does that make me? I'm an adult, I should have known, I could have protected her. A sick feeling lodges inside me, nestling in as if it's here to stay, and I start to think about all the times I've defended Daisy, and explained that although she's an addict, she's a good mum who really loves her daughter.

What kind of mother allows her boyfriend to abuse her child? I don't care if it's just a scratch or a fracture, *Darren hurt Allegra.*

When Grace calls the meeting to a close, Daisy and I walk back to the lobby, handing in our temporary passes. I'm in a daze when we finally emerge into the bright morning air, my mind full of bruises and hospitals. I can't look at Daisy when we say goodbye. Instead I rifle through my bag as if I've lost something, smiling tightly at her thanks. Watching as she heads to the Tube station, punching the air as if in victory.

I hail a cab in an altogether more sombre mood. Sliding into the backseat, I make Allegra a silent promise that no matter what happens, no matter what I end up having to do, Darren Tebbit will never, ever, touch her again.

I mean it, too.

19

There's one more thing I need to do. Even in the midst of everything else, all I can think of is Niall Joseph. For almost six weeks I've heard nothing from him except the occasional excuse via Michael. It's beginning to feel as if he was a figment of my imagination.

Christ, I miss him.

What will make you happy, Beth?

I want to mend my fences with Niall. I hate the way we left things, so frantic and up in the air. If I'm really going to take back control of my life, the way Louise has urged me to, then I don't want to regret anything else.

And I regret hurting him so very much.

In the end, I send him a text. Simple, but effective. A few words to see if he bites, if he'll actually speak to me again.

I know you're not sick.

Of course, he doesn't reply. I'm not sure I was even expecting him to. I just wanted to let him know I'm not stupid, that I'm thinking of him. He needs to know I won't give up that easily.

The following day I send another text, this time a little stronger; a question, rather than a statement.

Why won't you talk to me?

Another day of radio silence. I don't take his lack of response to heart, though. In fact, I'm beginning to look forward to it, sending these texts, letting him know I'm still around. On the third day, I try a direct approach.

I miss you.
I regret that one as soon as I send it. It's a bit too forthright. I decide that will be my final attempt—the last thing I want to do is come across as a stalker. But then, a few minutes later, my phone starts to ring. I'm shaking as I lift it up, seeing his name on the caller display, my throat constricted with nauseous anticipation.

"Hi," I whisper. The silence that follows makes me think he hasn't heard me. Just as I'm about to repeat the word, Niall starts to speak.

"Beth, are you there?"

I clear my throat. "I'm here."

"Christ, why can't you leave me alone? You're the one who walked out, the one who pushed me away. Do you want to torture me, is that it?" He has a natural break in his voice, but it sounds stronger than normal. I try not to flinch at his vehemence.

"I'm sorry, Niall, I..." Is this what I wanted? To feel guilty and miserable all at once? My father once told me I'm my own worst enemy, and I'm starting to believe he was right. "I didn't mean to hurt you. I thought we were friends."

"You definitely seemed friendly." Sarcasm drips through his words. "What do you want from me, Beth?"

"I want us to go back to the way things were before."

There's silence on the other end. I wait for a response, my whole body on edge.

"Niall, did you hear me?"

"I heard you." His voice is low, and I have to concentrate to hear him. "I just don't understand why you're telling me now."

"Because I miss you." The words tumble out of my mouth like they're in a rush to be heard. "The kids miss you, too. It just isn't the same without you in art class."

"What do you want me to say? That I'll be back tomorrow pretending like nothing happened? That we can laugh and joke and take the piss out of each other like that kiss was just my imagination?"

Is that what I really want? To forget that beautiful, sensual, amazing kiss? To obliterate the words his mum whispered to me? Forget about everything except our friendship?

"Cameron Gibbs made you a card. *Cameron bloody Gibbs.* The same kid who steals from art galleries and faces down coppers actually painted on a card to tell you he missed you. Doesn't that mean anything?"

"Of course it does," he replies, his voice thick. "You don't think I miss them too?"

Do you miss me, though?

"Then come back. I promise not to do anything else to upset you. I don't want to make you feel bad..."

"You think this is your fault?"

"Isn't it? I'm the one who kissed you then ran away. I'm the married one. Of course it's my fault."

"You know nothing. From the moment I met you at the door, I knew I was going to kiss you. I didn't care that you were married, in fact I still don't give a shit. All I could think about was how you looked and the way I knew you'd feel in my arms."

I hold my breath listening to him talk. I can almost feel the firmness of his biceps touching my sides. I remember the way he looked at me before he pressed his lips to mine. As if I was the eighth wonder.

"I kissed you back." My voice is small. Between the two of us, I hold the most culpability here. "I shouldn't have..."

"Jesus, Beth, don't you get it? I wanted you to kiss me back. I still want you to. That's why I can't see you again."

"You could do that?" I ask. "You could walk away and forget that anything happened?"

"I *have* walked away. I'm not the kind of guy that chases married women. I don't see a thrill in pursuing something that's not mine." He sighs deeply. "I won't be the one who ruins everything for you."

"You're too nice." My voice breaks.

"I know."

The pressure in my chest builds. "You're not the one who ruined everything, it was me."

"You're too hard on yourself." His tone softens. "You take the blame where it's not needed. Sometimes life is crap, it isn't anybody's fault, it just happens. I hit on a married woman; that's not your fault. You staying with Simon isn't your fault either. As much as it kills me to say it."

I don't try to correct him. I don't want him thinking I'm only calling him because I've split with Simon. That's the furthest thing from the truth. I'm calling because I want to be happy; because I want my friend back. Even if that's all we can ever be.

"Please think about coming back to class, if only for the kids' sakes. I'll even get Cameron to make you another card."

For the first time his laughter sounds almost genuine. "I'll think about it."

We're both silent for a moment. Not because there's nothing to say—at least not on my part. It's because there's everything to say, but I know I can't do it. I can't tell him how much my life is changing. There are some things you can only tell somebody face to face, when you can see their reaction, understand their emotions. So I force myself to maintain my equilibrium, when all I want to do is let everything out.

"I suppose I should go," I say, trying to keep my voice even. "Maybe we'll see you soon?"

"Maybe." His voice is soft. "I really do miss those guys, too."

And me, I want to ask again. *Do you miss me?* Of course, I don't. I bite my tongue and try to breathe, reminding myself this is just a start.

"Okay then, I'll keep my fingers crossed."

"You do that." A pause. "And what about you? Are you okay?"

When I answer him, I can feel myself smile. "You know what, Niall? I really think I'm going to be."

20

Niall comes back to the clinic the following week. I'm sitting at the little desk in the corner of the classroom, making seating plans for the gala. Between the catering, auctions and entertainment, I'm not getting a whole lot of sleep. Maybe that's why I don't notice him at first. I'm too busy scratching off the O'Donahues and moving them to an empty table nearer the stage.

"Hi." His voice is soft, but there's a swagger to his gait as he walks into the room. It doesn't seem like the walk of shame.

"You should have called," I say. "I would have prepared a fatted calf."

He glances down and smirks harder. "I've always thought you had slim legs."

I'm taken aback, not only by his sudden reappearance, but also by his relaxed banter. His sudden volte-face is confusing. I shake my head, looking down so he can't see my grin, and slowly write the O'Donahues' name on their new table.

Play it cool, I tell myself.

"So what were you planning to do today?" I'm still staring at the table, but my smile hasn't left. When I finally look up at him, he's perched on the table, looking at the paper.

"What's that?" he asks, ignoring my question.

"Plans for the clinic's gala. I'm trying to work out the best placement. The poor Smithsons have been moved three times already."

He laughs and pulls the paper toward him. "Where have you put me?"

"You're coming?"

"Yeah, Elise invited me." He notices my raised brow and quickly adds, "There're a few of us from the gallery going. She's asked me to donate a painting for the auction as well. I was going to talk to you about that."

"About what?" I'm still shocked he's even here. Let alone talking to me.

"The sort of painting I should donate. Whether there's anything in particular you're looking for."

"I don't know. I..."

"Hey, I've got an idea, why don't you come and take a look at the studio. I can show you what I've been working on and a few of my old sketches. You can help me choose which one to donate." He looks at me expectantly.

"What?" A few days ago he was telling me he couldn't bear to see me again. Now here he is, sitting on my table, a sexy smile playing at his lips. I know I should prefer cocky Niall to the broken one I glimpsed before—and I do—but I still can't work out what has caused such a transformation. "I don't know if I have time."

He leans forward until his face is inches from mine, so close I can feel his breath warming my cheek. "Make time," he whispers, and it takes every ounce of strength I have not to shiver. He hasn't lost any of his potency in the few weeks I haven't seen him.

I think about all the things I still have to do: visits to the hotel where we're holding the gala, meetings with musicians and organising the printing. I'll barely have a spare minute to myself in the next two weeks.

Damn it, I'll make time. Of course I will. "Okay."

I can only describe his resulting grin as "shit-eating". I try to ignore the effect it has on me. Try to forget the last time we were in a studio together, when he pushed me back on a table and wrapped my legs around his hips. Repressing those memories is easier said than done.

I'm almost relieved when he pushes himself off the table, and walks over to the door to grab a box of supplies. I catch myself following him with wide eyes, watching the way the seat of his jeans tightens as he bends down, willing his t-shirt to rise up enough so I can get a look at his skin.

"I thought we'd study some Klimt," he shouts, his voice almost absorbed by the cardboard. It's enough for me to pull myself together and remember where we are.

"They'll love the colours," I say. "Not sure the boys will like the hairstyles, though."

Twenty minutes later the kids arrive. At first, their attention is taken up by Niall's sudden reappearance, their responses ranging from delighted to muted, depending on their age and perceived level of coolness. Cameron gives him a nod, which is pretty much the Oscar of cool-kid recognition, and I'm reminded of something I've wanted to ask him since last week.

"Cameron," I say when I reach his desk. "Can I ask you a favour?"

With a dramatic flourish, he raises a single eyebrow and winks with the other eye. "You only have to say the word."

"Not that kind of favour, Cameron," I sigh. "You live on Allegra's estate, right?"

He immediately looks suspicious. "Yeah."

"Do you think you could keep an eye on her? Let me know if anything happens, or if you see anything strange going on."

"You want me to spy on her?"

"No," I reply, although that's exactly what I want him to do. "I only want you to look after her and tell me if you see any men going into her mum's flat."

He narrows his eyes. "Why should I do that?"

"Because you owe me?" I suggest. "Because I'm worried about her and want to know she's okay?"

He rubs his chin with his thumb and forefinger, as if he's considering my request. "What's in it for me?"

"Oh I don't know, maybe the knowledge you're doing something nice for somebody? Or if you prefer, you can think of it as payback for me sitting with you for hours in a London nick when I could have been at a dinner party."

"Oh la-di-dah. I'm so sorry I ruined your night, your majesty."

"You're forgiven. Or you will be if you do this for me."

He gives an exaggerated sigh. "All right, all right. I'll be your spy if you insist. Can I call you Miss Moneypenny?"

I try not to laugh. "No."

A mock-pout. "Drive an Aston Martin?"

"Don't even think about it." I start to walk away.

"Can I shag loads of women and have a speedboat chase?" he calls after me. This time I choose to ignore him, but it's almost impossible to hide my smile. Cameron may be a cheeky little git, yet I can't help liking him.

When class ends, the kids pile out noisily, shouting and pushing in an effort to be the first out of the door. Cameron sends me an exaggerated wink, and Allegra runs over and throws her arms around my waist. "Did you hear?" she asks breathlessly. "I'm going to stay at my mum's this weekend. She says I'll be living with her soon." She looks up at me, her face glowing and her eyes bright. I feel the slightest twinge of shame at the way I cajoled Cameron into spying on them.

"I heard, are you excited?" I try to echo her enthusiasm but it sounds fake to my jaded ears. That nagging feeling in my gut just won't disappear.

"I can't wait. Mum says we can decorate my room and buy a new bed cover."

See? I tell myself. No mention of Darren. I'm not heartless enough to put a dampener on her enthusiasm by sharing my concerns.

"Wow, what kind are you going to buy?"

She shrugs. "I don't know, definitely something pink. I love pink."

Her stating of the obvious makes me smile. I'm about to reply when her support worker pops his head around the door and looks at Allegra. "Are you ready? I've got a cab waiting outside."

"Sorry. I kept her back." I flash him a smile and grab a piece of scrap paper from my desk, hastily scribbling my mobile phone number on it, passing it to Allegra. "Here, make sure you keep this number with you in case you need anything," I say, trying to keep my voice light. "You could always call me and tell me what bedding you choose."

She stuffs it in her pocket and runs off, and I make a bet with myself that it will end up in the washing machine by nightfall, the ink bleeding into the water as it spins round and round. I'd give her a phone if I could get away with it, one with my number pre-programmed in, but that would look a bit weird. A lot weird.

"You okay?" Niall stops next to me, his arms full of paint pots. "You look miles away."

Only about ten miles, I think. In a crumbling concrete tower block where people can be beaten up and almost die and even their neighbours don't notice. Where kids wear bruises like armbands and nobody blinks an eyelid.

I take a deep breath. "I'm okay. There's just so much to do in the next couple of weeks. I'm not sure how I'm going to fit it all in."

"Can I help with something?"

"How are you at seating plans?"

"Pretty shite?" he offers. I try not to laugh.

"Dealing with hotel managers, fussy eaters, musicians, printers?" I start to reel off my list of woes. "Creating auction catalogues..."

"Now that I can help with. I've worked on enough exhibitions to know how to catalogue."

I look him square in the eye. "Who are you and what have you done with Niall Joseph? You know, that mean, moody asshole who wouldn't return my texts?"

"I'm trying to be your friend," he admits. "I said I would, and I failed miserably, so I'm giving it a second go, *friend*."

We stand there for a moment, staring at each other. I feel stupid, because I can't think of anything to say in response, so instead I stand there looking dumb and trying not to grin.

"Can I walk you out?" he asks. For a moment I think of Victorian gentlemen courting chaperoned ladies.

"No... I... um... have to finish up here. I'll be another couple of hours at least."

"No worries. I'll finish clearing up and then be out of your hair. Are you free on Monday to come to the studio? We can pick out a painting and talk catalogues."

I smirk before I reply. "Would you believe it if I told you that's the best offer I've had in weeks?"

* * *

After an hour of staring at names on the seating chart I realise I'm now just gazing into space. My eyes are stinging and I'm starving hungry, not to mention the fact I need a caffeine injection. So I head for the tiny kitchen on the first floor, hoping against hope that somebody hasn't eaten all the Bourbon biscuits before I get a chance to snaffle a few.

I don't spend a lot of time in the clinic outside of core hours. It's different when there are no clients in the building—

lifeless and sterile. If my life were a horror movie, this would be the part where the zombies break in.

I almost laugh when I find Lara in the kitchen. Though she isn't the walking dead, she does look like crap. There are dark shadows under her eyes, and her lips are dry and cracked. She looks as if she hasn't had any liquid for weeks.

"Hey, are you okay? You look terrible." Of course, I immediately regret my verbal diarrhoea.

Her face crumples. "I'm pregnant."

For a moment, my breath catches in my throat.

"Congratulations! Oh my God, I can't believe it." I go to hug her but she leans over the sink and heaves into it. I pull her hair away from her face as spasms wrack her stomach. Even though nothing comes out, I can't help but gag in sympathy.

"You poor thing," I murmur. "How long has this been going on?"

"A week," she says between heaves. "It's so bloody awful. Nobody tells you how bad it makes you feel."

"But you're having a baby! That's so wonderful." I stroke her hair as she wipes her mouth. There's not even a flash of jealousy in me about her pregnant state. Just excitement and anticipation and a whole lot of sympathy. She really does look bad.

"I know. I should be excited and running around but I just feel terrible all the time. Whoever called this morning sickness was either an idiot or a liar."

"Is there anything you can take for it?"

She shakes her head. "The doctor says it's normal. In fact, he went as far as to tell me it's a good sign, because studies show women suffering from morning sickness are less likely to miscarry."

I try not to laugh at the expression on her face. A mixture of horror and anger, with a dash of anxiety. "If men had periods and babies, imagine how underpopulated the world would be."

"You're not wrong." She takes a sip of water, rolling her neck as if to iron out the crinkles. "Anyway, what are you doing here so late?"

I wrinkle my nose. "Gala stuff."

"Ugh, poor you. It puts morning sickness into perspective." She almost smiles. "Still, at least you know it will be over in a couple of weeks."

"I've just had an offer of help."

"Who from?"

"Niall. He seemed really... weird, actually. Nothing like the guy who shouted down the phone at me last week. He was cheeky, almost cocky." I screw my face up, trying to find the right descriptor. "It felt as though he was flirting with me."

Lara becomes distracted by the fanlight window, staring up at it like it's the ceiling of the Sistine Chapel.

"Lara?"

She looks at me. Her expression is almost guilty.

"Alex might have told him about you and Simon splitting up," she confesses.

Oh.

I guess that would explain it. His light-heartedness. The way he grinned at me and called me *'friend'*.

"I hope he didn't get the wrong idea," I say. Lara knows I'm not up for anything—or anyone—else, not right now when I'm still under Simon's roof. We're trying to keep things amicable. To move on so quickly would be wrong.

She shakes her head, and I note a little colour has returned to her cheeks. "He wouldn't try anything. He knows you're vulnerable, and I don't think he's that much of an asshole. He feels really guilty about kissing you then blanking you."

"I don't want him to feel guilty. I just..." What do I want? I'm not sure anymore. All I know is that returning to our easy friendship today was like finding a lighthouse in a storm. He grounds me and lifts me up at the same time. Seeing him has made me feel happier than I've felt in weeks. If we can be friends, I'm all for it. "I don't want to lead him on, I guess."

"You aren't. You won't." She sounds so sure, and I love the belief she has in me. I only wish I had her certainty.

Nine Years Earlier

The air is thick with excitement and hormones, rising up from the bodies of three hundred dancing students. Drunk, high, in search of a good time. We're almost desperate in our need to celebrate, to feel young and free. We want to steal the night and take it as ours, because over the next few days we will be leaving, packing up our things and going home.

So we dance and we drink and we swallow and we do everything we know we shouldn't.

A makeshift stage has been set up in the grounds. The music pumping out of the big black speakers takes on a life of its own. Snaking around our bodies and soaking into our skins. Pulsing through our veins until we become an organic, sweaty mass. Jumping on the soft grass, our hair swinging, we scream out the words until our throats protest and our lungs threaten to explode.

Niall's arms are locked around my waist, his palms resting on my stomach. They feel sweaty and warm but I don't push them away. Instead, I lean against him and let him pull me with the crowd, until we are part of a huge wave of bodies that ebb and flow with the music.

We're rolling, and it feels so good it makes my skin tingle. The way we dance and move is sensuous; an orgy without the sex. Beads of perspiration soak my hairline before pouring down my cheeks. I wipe them away, too busy dancing to even care what I look like.

To my left, I notice Digby has stopped jumping with the music. His face is almost bloated, but his lips are pale and blue. Though he isn't dancing anymore, his body is still moving, being pushed to and fro by the crowd like a piece of flotsam on the tide.

"Are you okay?" I have to shout it twice. I lean in to him and touch his arm. It feels like fire.

"Yeah, I just need to take a break." He's still swaying. "I'm going to get a drink."

I open my mouth to offer to go with him, but the music changes and Niall's arms tighten around my waist. I turn to look at him, and he's smiling down at me, and for a moment it bleaches the thoughts right out of my brain. All I can focus on is his mouth. I press my own lips against it, closing my eyes, feeling the fire light up inside my belly.

When I open them, Digby is gone. I tell myself he'll be fine, that he'll get a drink and come back and we will all be dancing again, celebrating the final hours of our hedonistic freedom. There's no point in looking for him, he could be anywhere, doing anything, and he'll be back in a few minutes.

Of course, he isn't.

Now

21

I spend most of the weekend working. In a strange parody of what used to be our marriage, Simon and I sit at the dining-room table, staring at our respective laptops, occasionally breaking away to make each other a cup of tea. He tells me about his current case—some decade-old dispute about boundary lines—and I regale him with stories about the food orders I've had to negotiate. It's easy and light, a contrast to the tension of the last few months.

Not once does this new entente make me regret my decision. If anything it reinforces that it was the right one. We've renegotiated our positions, found new ones that make us comfortable in each other's company. If we were teenagers, I'd say we've entered the friend zone.

On Monday I fight through the morning rush hour to meet Niall. He surprised me by suggesting we meet at nine, offering to have coffee and pastries. I agreed readily, even though I always thought he would be the type to lie in.

His studio is based in an old warehouse, converted into a collective of small yet useable rooms, most of which have been populated by arty types. There are potters and basket weavers, painters and sculptors. When I see the light pouring in through the tall Victorian windows, I realise exactly why they've all clustered here; the brightness of the sun whitewashes the brown bricks of the warehouse. It illuminates, making everything appear so clear. Beautiful.

I walk along the first-floor balcony, heading for the little garret on the corner of the building that houses Niall Joseph, Artist. Though I'm carrying a huge bag full of notes and catalogues, the thing that's really weighing me down is this sense of desperation. The need to see him again pulls at my soul. The closer I get, the more my heart starts to speed, my breath shortening as his door comes into view. I have to remind myself that we are friends, this is a business meeting. It's nine o'clock on a Monday morning, for God's sake, but I can't get this inane grin off my face.

It's the smell of coffee that hits me first. The aroma of roasted beans escapes through the cracks surrounding his metallic door, overpowering the earthy smell of paint and the sharpness of turpentine, beckoning me over until I'm knocking at his door.

"Hi." He sounds breathless when he opens it, but it's his smile that steals mine away. The light floods in from the window behind him, casting a hazy glow behind his body.

"Hi yourself. Do I smell coffee?"

He shakes his head. "Nah, that's the bitter aroma of my lost dreams."

He takes my bag without asking and I follow him into his tiny enclave, looking around to get myself acquainted. One of the walls is lined with shelves full of paints and brushes and everything else he might need. The one opposite has sketches tacked to it—all at various stages of completion, from light etching to thicker pencil strokes. The third wall has a whole load of canvasses stacked against it, and it's these that draw my eye. I remember how impressed I was with his works when I first saw them at Elise's gallery. The ones in here are just as amazing.

When I look over at Niall he has his back to me, fiddling with the coffee machine.

"How do you like it?" he asks without looking round.

"Your studio?"

"No, Beth, how would you like your coffee?" He turns to look at me, amusement lighting up his eyes.

"Lots of milk and two sugars, please."

He does as I've asked, muttering something about sacrilege.

"What?"

"Coffee isn't ice cream. It's supposed to be strong and bitter." He hands me a mug, his fingers touching mine for the briefest of moments. "I bet you love a nice latte."

"And I bet you only drink espresso." I take a sip; it's warm and delicious. "You're a coffee snob."

When he laughs, the corners of his eyes crinkle up. "I take coffee very seriously."

I can see that. He has a corner of his studio dedicated to it. A grinder, a pot of beans, a coffee machine and mugs are all lined up like a shrine to caffeine. There's something so very *Niall* about it. I like these little nuances in his personality, the small insights into what kind of man he is. A good one, I think.

"What are you working on?" I walk over to the wall where he's tacked his sketches, studying the lines of his pencil, wanting to trace them with my fingers. When he stands behind me, his arm brushes against my shoulder, and I hear his soft breathing as he stares along with me.

"A bank in Dublin has commissioned ten paintings for their new office. I'm working on a few proposals for them."

"That's exciting." I turn to look at him, but he just shrugs.

"Local boy done good. It tells a good story, explains why they're spending so much money on useless stuff."

"Not just any local boy," I point out. "They chose you. That has to mean something."

He's too modest to reply. I finish my coffee and rinse my mug out in the sink, then smile at him. "Show me your paintings?" I ask.

He starts to laugh. "What, no small talk first, no discussion of techniques or your favourite artists? Just a blunt 'get 'em out'?"

I tip my head to the side. "You want art foreplay?" A little alarm bell starts ringing in my brain. I ignore it, concentrating instead on the way he smiles.

"An artist likes to be wooed. Pretty words, little compliments..."

I want to step forward and curl my fingers around his neck, to pull his head down until his lips are connected to mine. Want him to sweep everything off his old wooden table with a simple brush of his arm, and lay me down on it until we are both gasping.

That's why I take a step back.

"In that case, please could you show me your pictures because you're an amazingly talented artist and I so want to see them?" Sarcasm. My sword and my shield.

He catches my change in tone and responds accordingly. "I was just joking. I'm like a man carrying around pictures of his kids. You only have to mention them and I'm waving them under your eye, waiting for you to tell me what beautiful paintings I make." He inclines his head to the far wall. "I'll show you what I've been working on."

He tells me about the show he's planning for a few months' time, loosely entitled "Bodies of Art". I stare at the paintings he's done so far as he explains the concept, marvelling at how he manages to pick out the right shade of colour, uses the right texture to bring his paintings to life. He tells me about the model he's found with seventy-degree burns, and the psoriasis sufferer whose skin is practically peeling off. He talks of muscle density and bone structure, and I hang on his every word as if I'm some sort of art groupie.

"Did I show you this? It's the design for Alex's CD cover." He pulls out a small, square canvas and holds it up for me to see. The white background is covered with brushes of colour, each blending into the next. The hues mix together to form a shape in the centre. "It's a bird," he says, smiling wryly. "The album is called *Fear of Flying*."

"The same as their band? It's pretty." In fact it's beautiful, but I feel as if I've gushed enough. Like always, the way he layers the colours makes me want to reach out and touch them. As if by feeling them, I'll be connecting with him.

I wonder if the urge to touch him will ever go away.

"They seem to like it. It's going to be on their tour t-shirts." He catches my eye. "I'm going to be famous."

This time we both laugh.

An old canvas in the corner—one we haven't looked at—catches my eye. "What's that one?"

He puts the painting he's holding down and hurriedly responds, "Nothing."

Of course, his vague reply makes me want to see it more. I step forward, folding my hands around the wooden frame, pulling it back from the wall. The first thing I see is creamy flesh, then a slender neck, curving down into delicate shoulders.

A nude. I don't know why this affects me. Maybe because it's so realistic, I know it had to be painted from a model. A pang of jealousy hits me as I realise the picture shows pretty much everything except her face.

Niall almost runs to snatch it out of my hands. His cheeks burn as brightly as mine. "I can explain..."

"You don't owe me anything."

He carries on as if I hadn't said a word. "I finished it that summer. It was probably the only thing that kept me sane after Digby died. I did sketch after sketch from memory, and somehow it finally came together." When he glances up, he looks shamefaced. "I've never shown it to anybody."

It takes me a while to register what his garbled sentences mean. I lift the canvas gently from his hands and study it. My eyes follow the curve of my breasts, and the softness of my thighs. I want to cry because it's beautiful. The girl I was, before everything went wrong, is captured forever on oil and canvas. Unblemished skin, unbroken dreams, they're all there to see.

"You kept it." My voice thickens as I try not to sob.

"It was the one thing I did keep. The only good thing to come out of that time. Those last few weeks were senseless. We took too many drugs and did too many crazy things. But somewhere in there was a little kernel of something fucking amazing."

He looks so despondent, I reach out and take his hand. Immediately, his fingers wrap around mine. "There was," I agree.

We're silent for a moment. I'm hyper aware of the way he's holding me. The way he's looking at me. The thrum of my heartbeat is almost deafening.

"What about now? Is there something here still?" he asks.

My voice is a whisper. "I think so."

Gently, he takes the canvas and places it back, then runs his fingers across my cheek. I stare at his lips, taking in their colour, the way they tremble. I can't even breathe, so afraid I'm going to do something, or say something, to ruin the moment. Instead, I close my eyes, breathing him in as his forehead comes to rest on mine.

"I'll wait for as long as it takes," he tells me. "I'll be here; you only have to say the word."

He smells of coffee and mint, the two scents mingling as he slowly breathes in and out. I open my eyes to find him staring right at me. I have to swallow hard before I find the strength to speak. "You'll wait for me?" I ask. "Because I'm not ready, not now. With the separation and..." I trail off.

He cups my face with his rough hands and softly kisses my forehead. His lips remain there as he begins to speak. "As long as it takes."

22

The morning of the gala arrives with a fierce rainstorm. It rattles the windows and makes me wake with a panic, wondering if the hotel has enough umbrellas or if there's somewhere I can hire some. By six a.m. I'm in the kitchen, sipping at a mug of coffee and searching the web for rain canopies we can set up from the entrance to the road.

I've been growing increasingly edgy. My sang-froid of a week ago has boiled away, leaving behind a mixture of angst and anticipation that kills my appetite. Wisely, Simon's been spending most of his time at the office, avoiding the rather crazy, soon-to-be ex-wife who's haunting his townhouse.

When he pops his head around the kitchen door each night, announcing he's heading for bed, I silently promise him that as soon as this gala is out of the way, I'll be room hunting like nobody's business. He already has one twenty-something daughter. If I don't put some space between us, I'm in danger of becoming his second.

For the most part he's been lovely. Courteous when asking how it's going, sweet when inquiring if we should still be going together—to which the answer is, of course, yes. He paid for the table, after all, and it will be his friends filling the seats. I don't want to embarrass him by leaving an empty chair beside him. I know I'm making it sound easier than it actually is—after all, how comfortable can it be sharing a house with someone you no longer wish to be married to—but after the pain we've been through, this stage seems almost easy in comparison.

By the time he gets up on Saturday, I've already arranged for a rain canopy, checked in with the caterers and have showered and dressed ready to head to the hotel. My gown is hanging from the doorway in a garment bag, because I won't have time to come back and change. I watch as he slowly pours himself a coffee, a rolled *Times* clasped in his other hand. He turns to smile at me.

"Are you okay? I could hear you tossing and turning last night."

For some reason that makes me blush. His attention seems almost too intimate.

"Did I keep you awake? I'm sorry..."

"Not at all. I just want to make sure you're all right."

"Ask me at seven this evening. If I'm still alive, that is."

This time he smiles. "Do you want me to get there early?"

"No, it's fine. You don't want to see me pulling my hair out. Just get there after seven and I promise not to bite your head off."

Simon walks forward and ruffles my hair. It's a simple gesture, yet I find myself wanting to pull back, as if his touch is inappropriate. I don't know if he notices the discomfort on my face, but he steps away, going back to his coffee and his crossword.

I stand there for too long, while he fills in the tiny squares with his neat writing. When he takes a sip from his cup I feel a sense of nostalgia wash over me. Everything's changing. I won't be here for many more Saturday mornings. I won't watch him filling in the crossword or flinching when I add too much cream to my coffee. He'll be here and I'll be somewhere else and life will still go on. The thought makes me wistful.

"I guess I'd better go."

The day is spent in organised mayhem. I manage to miscount the number of guests, misplace two different auction items and lose my rag with the executive chef when he tells me there isn't enough chicken to go around. Each time I manage to solve one mini-crisis, the next one bares its teeth and laughs at my ineptitude. By the time I head up to a bedroom to shower and change, the only thing I'm confident about is that everything that can go wrong has gone wrong.

Lara arrives a few minutes after I get out of the shower, and the hairdresser half an hour after that. We're offered champagne but neither of us accepts—Lara because she can't and me because I daren't.

"When do you start house hunting?"

"Room hunting," I correct, because that's all I can afford. "Next week. I said I'd do it as soon as the gala was over."

"And you're still okay with that? It must be hard, leaving that beautiful house..."

We both know she isn't talking about bricks and mortar. "It isn't easy," I admit. "But it's right. I can't stay somewhere just because it's the easy thing to do."

An hour later, guests are starting to spill into the hotel. I'm vibrating with anxiety as I watch them check their coats in at the cloakroom and mingle around the bar area, where staff offer them glasses of champagne. I wander from group to group, shaking hands, smiling where required, though my laughter seems off even to me. By this point I should be relaxing, but there seems no end in sight for my frazzled nerves. The next time a waiter passes, I grab a champagne glass and guzzle it down, willing to do anything to stop the trembling in my hands.

Simon arrives with some old friends. Though they smile at me I can tell he's told them about our situation. It's in their eyes when they talk to me, the way their gazes wash down from my face to my dress, as if they're judging me for wearing clothes he's bought me.

Only when Elise enters do I realise the real source of my anxiety. Niall's standing next to her, wearing a black dinner jacket and tie. When he catches my eye my mouth suddenly turns dry, and I have to take another glass of champagne. I turn my head away, trying not to stare at the way Niall holds himself, or how his dinner suit makes him look. But even when I'm not looking, I can still feel his stare.

"This looks magnificent, darling," Simon whispers in my ear. His hand presses on the small of my back in a way that seems proprietorial. By this time I don't know if I'm reading into things that aren't there, or if he's making a point. My judgement seems so *off*.

"Thank you," I murmur. "It all came together in the end, thank God."

Why didn't I think about this before? The fact I was going to be in one room with these two men. Though they could both be classified as exes, my entanglements with them don't feel like that. It just feels awkward and cruel—to them, to me, to everybody. No wonder I've been so anxious; my subconscious must have been having a field day.

It's almost a relief when the chair of the clinic trust arrives and pulls me aside to discuss her speech. I switch back into work mode and discuss the agenda for the evening, highlighting our biggest donors and talking through the auction catalogue with her. The night gets even better when I run into Alex, propping up the bar. He's rocking a midnight-blue skinny tuxedo with a pencil-thin tie. His hair is slicked back with gel, his tattoos peeking past the collar and cuffs of his shirt.

Lara is to his left, talking to one of our more prestigious donors. She waves at me, then turns and gives a tinkling laugh. We're all on our best behaviour tonight.

"Hello, gorgeous." Alex pulls me in for a hug and I squeeze him back enthusiastically.

"You look amazing." I tug at his satin lapel. "Where did you find this?"

"It was my uncle's. I'm the only nephew thin enough to fit in it."

"Never put on any weight," I tell him. "This one's a keeper."

"How are you doing anyway? Lara told me about you and Simon."

She mouths a "sorry" and then turns away. I stifle a smile. She's so nosy sometimes.

"Bearing up." I'm offered another glass of champagne but shake my head at the waiter. I'm already buzzing. "It's better now we've agreed to separate."

Of course we both choose that moment to glance over at Simon, who's still with his group of friends. He's looking over at us, and for some reason the lack of expression on his face makes me want to shiver.

"When are you moving out?" Alex asks.

I can almost see Lara's ears flapping.

"I haven't had a chance to find anywhere yet. I've been too caught up with the gala arrangements. I'm going to start looking on Monday."

"Oh."

"What?"

Alex shrugs. "I dunno. It just sends out a weird message to a guy. *I'm leaving you but I'm still living with you.*"

Lara kicks his shin with her red patent shoe.

"Simon's fine with it. He knows why it's taking me so long. Hopefully it won't take forever for me to find somewhere. I'll be out of his hair soon."

"Of course he's fine with it." Alex laughs. "If he doesn't want you to leave."

"What do you mean?"

Lara gives up on her conversation and joins us. "Yeah, what *do* you mean?"

"For all his money, Simon's still a bloke and we're fairly simple creatures. You want to leave, you leave. You want to stay, you stay."

"You think he's happy because I'm still living with him?" The thought hadn't occurred to me.

"Of course he isn't," Lara says.

"All I'm saying is if he wants you to stay, then a bird in the hand is worth two in the bush. Maybe he has a false sense of hope." Alex shrugs, and drinks his beer.

"Oh God, you think I'm leading him on?"

"Alex, for God's sake," Lara huffs. She looks as anxious as I feel. "Not now, please."

Alex notices my white face and gently rubs my arm. "I'm not saying you're leading him on at all. I'm just saying he doesn't look like a man who's ready to let go. The sooner you move out, the faster you can both move on." He gives me a small smile. "You know, there's always the sofa at our place. I've missed seeing your ugly mug in the mornings."

"I bet she hasn't missed seeing yours," Lara jokes. I smile, trying not to feel too down.

"It won't come to that," I say. "I'm sure I'll find somewhere pretty soon."

When we sit down to dinner, I'm still thinking about Alex's comment. Everything Simon does is ripe for analysis, from the way he pulls my chair out before I sit, to his constant attention with the wine bottle. He's always been a gentleman—the type to stand when a lady does—but there's a fine line between kindness and flirtation. He's starting to step across it.

"More wine, sweetheart?" He brushes my hand with his finger.

"I'm fine." When I look over at Elise's table I see Niall staring at me. His eyes narrow as Simon leans across and whispers in my ear.

"Relax, it's all going so well."

After dinner has been cleared away, Millicent Clancy-Jones stands up to make her speech. I barely hear any of it, and don't even realise she's thanked me until I see everybody staring at me, clapping their hands wildly. Embarrassed, I give a small wave and a tight smile before looking down at the napkin laid across my lap. This evening is starting to resemble a nightmare.

The auction follows, and I sit back and allow myself to relax a little. Only a couple of hours to go and we'll be able to shut up shop for another year, claim the gala as a success and run the clinic outreach program on the proceeds. Everybody will go home happy, feeling they've given to a good cause, and I can start looking for somewhere else to live.

I take a moment to wonder where I'll be this time next year. Not sitting on Simon's table, I suppose. Will it feel weird to be just me again? I've become used to being part of 'Beth and Simon'. Yet there's a flash of excitement, too, when stepping into the unknown. It's that feeling I try to embrace when I think of everything that's ahead of me: moving out, splitting possessions, having to get used to a new space.

This is what I wanted, I remind myself.

Later, I'm on the dance floor with Simon, my hand clasped in his as he leads us across the floor. There's an awkwardness in our hold. I'm avoiding resting my cheek on his shoulder, not letting our torsos touch. It reminds me of the way children learn to ballroom dance, holding each other at arm's length. When Simon tries to pull me close I stumble over my toe, almost barrelling into him.

"Sorry." I laugh to hide my embarrassment. I can feel his hand pressing into the small of my back, pulling me closer still.

He laughs too. "My lucky day."

I'm reminded again of Alex's words. "I'm planning to start looking at rooms on Monday," I say. "I promise I'll be moving out soon."

"I wish you'd let me help you get a flat at least. I can't bear to think of you sharing a house with strangers."

"It's fine. I think I'd rather share." We've had this discussion before. He wants to buy me a place, offer it as part of any settlement. But if we go down that route he'll never let go. It isn't fair on either of us. I want to make this first step on my own, and let the lawyers sort out the rest. Anything else seems too personal.

As the band brings the song to a close, we slow our feet. I look up, expecting Simon to release me. Instead, his hand tightens over mine, and a serious expression washes across his face.

"Give me another chance." There's longing in his words, but I try to ignore it. I don't want to hurt him any more than I already have.

I struggle to find the right response. "I can't..."

"We were happy, weren't we? Until the last few months we got on so well. We can do it again. I'll call the counsellor, set up an appointment."

I don't want to tell him it's too late, because that sounds as though we waited too long to save this thing, and I don't think it was ever salvageable. We were always going to clash; we come from such different places. I can never be the person he needs me to be.

"Simon, it isn't going to work. I'm so sorry, but I'm leaving. I have to." It's even harder than the first time. Because this time, he realises I mean it.

His face twists with pain. "I love you."

I remain silent, because anything I say will only hurt him more. He pulls back, stepping away from me, and sends me a final, sad glance before he turns and walks away.

* * *

The night is almost over when I finally get a chance to speak with Niall. I've finished counting the donations and closed off everything with the hotel manager, and now I'm doing my final rounds. Thanking the donors and letting them know it looks as if we've made a record-breaking amount. I find him sitting in a dark corner with Alex and Lara. Just seeing them all is like rubbing a comfort blanket against my cheeks.

"Hey!" Lara stands up and hugs me. "Great menu choice. I even managed to keep most of it down."

"High praise indeed. I'll have to tell the chef." I hug her back tightly, and thank God I still have some friends. I don't know what I'd do without her.

"You did good, kid." Alex pulls me toward him and cuddles me so hard I end up squeaking like a mouse. When he lets go I turn to see Niall standing in front of me. It takes a moment to catch my breath.

"Hi." There's a gap between us that I want to close so badly. "Thank you so much for the painting. I'm glad to see it went for so much."

He smiles. "Me too. It's a really good cause." When I look down I can see him clenching and unclenching his fingers. "You did a great job."

"Tell me more. I can listen to flattery all night."

"You want me to tell you how beautiful you look? Or that I couldn't take my eyes off you the whole night?" His voice is low, but I glance around anxiously anyway. Luckily, Alex and Lara have moved back to the table. "Or I can tell you how much it hurt every time I saw you with him, even though I know how wrong that is."

I feel the need to reassure him, even though there's nothing between us, not yet. "We were here as friends. Nothing more."

"I know. Doesn't mean I have to like it, though."

We stare silently at each other, and there's something in his eyes that both reassures and exhilarates me. I could lose myself in their intensity.

"I suppose I should go." I sound regretful. There's nothing I want to do more than sit with him, to laugh and chat with Alex and Lara. "I need to finish thanking everybody."

"Okay." He says it slowly. "I'll see you on Thursday, though, right?"

"Of course."

"And the Thursday after that?"

I laugh. "For sure." I like this knowledge that I'll be seeing him regularly. We have a reason to interact outside everything crazy that's happened.

The impulse to be crazier washes over me.

"Niall?"

"Yeah?"

"You know you said you'd wait for me?"

He looks serious. "Yes."

"Well, I wanted to say...to tell you how much I appreciate it. I don't plan on making you wait too long, if you see what I mean?"

He breaks into a big smile. It makes me want to kiss him, which isn't a good thing right now.

"I just hope I'm worth it. The wait, I mean."

His grin doesn't waver as he takes my hand in his. He squeezes it tightly. "You are."

Nine Years Earlier

He's dead. That's all I can think of when I'm sitting in the police interview room. The only thing on my mind when the university investigator takes my statement. When a reporter tries to catch me on my way back to the halls of residence, all I can see is Digby's red face and thin lips as he tells me over and over how hot he is, how poorly he feels.

Sitting on the bare mattress in my bedroom—among the boxes and cases packed a few days before—I cover my face with my hands, feeling the tears wetting my palms.

But all this is a mere prelude to when my father arrives. He's dressed in his best suit, wearing a tie he reserves for weddings and christenings. I can tell by the way he pulls at the collar that the neck size is too tight for him, and the fabric is scratching at his throat. His constant fidgeting is distracting as he sits beside me, listening to the ethics officer's questions. His watery eyes turn on me every time he expects me to answer.

"The investigation will continue into the summer," the officer explains. "We'll also need to wait on any police investigation before a final decision is made. What I can tell you is that in the case of drug use, the university normally allows students to return to their studies if they commit to a course of therapy."

Of course, this all happens before Digby's parents get involved and manage to whip the media into a frenzy. Throughout the summer, headlines about *"Hedonism"* and *"Students in Turmoil"* scream out from the tabloids, marking our family's shame in smudged newspaper ink. I cry so much that my eyes are permanently swollen, the skin around them red and shiny. Tears roll down my cheeks when I think about Digby.

And the way I blanked Niall the last time I saw him.

Though I denied knowing him, I'm the one who feels crucified.

By August the university has been demonised enough. They take the decision to expel me, and I assume they do the same to Niall. The news comes in the form of a typewritten letter, folded into a small brown envelope that's pushed through our letterbox at 8:33 a.m. In the space of a few months I've gone from an academic golden girl to drug-addicted dropout. My parents can barely bring themselves to look at me.

I miss him, I miss him, I miss him. The thought curls around my chest, squeezing it until it's all I can do to breathe. When I close my eyes, it's his voice I hear.

Just whispers on the wind.

The only thing that gets me out of bed is the fact I can't stand to be alone with my thoughts. If I could escape myself, I would. I want to soar above the trees, far away from my body, my mind empty except for the feeling of freedom. For the first time I understand why people cut themselves. The urge to get rid of a bit of myself, to let it bleed out of me, is so overwhelming I can barely ignore it. Only the fear of my parents catching me in the act prevents me from trying.

September arrives, and I'm still a caged animal. Stuck in a routine of sleeping, eating and stagnating. With the occasional visit to a local group that labels me a sinner and urges me to give myself over to the Lord. I coast through my days as though I'm overdosing on downers, my emotions muffled by the depression that weighs down on my shoulders like an iron shawl.

I don't cry anymore. I don't feel anything. I hardly know if I exist.

The trees in our back garden fade into golds and oranges, curling and drying before they flutter to the ground. The air turns cold, coating windscreens and pavements with glistening frost, sparkling like diamonds under the autumn sun.

As the seasons move, I stand still. A statue amongst the blur of change. My parents go back to their normal routine: work and housekeeping, evenings at the club. Saturdays spent on the green or at the nineteenth hole. As the months pass, I gain a little more freedom, the ability to click online, visits to the library to borrow books I can't afford to buy. Slowly, slowly, I come to the realisation that I can't go on like this. If I don't make the change, nobody will. It's all up to me.

Maybe it always has been.

Now

23

Two weeks later I move into a shared flat, carrying my belongings up endless staircases to a small room that overlooks an internal yard. Complete with dustbins, abandoned bicycles and a resident cat, it has all the elements to guarantee a sleepless night. Yet it isn't rattling bin lids or screeching kittens that keep me awake, but a strange mattress and the lack of body heat. Not to mention an overactive thought process that just won't shut up. I lie in the darkness and make plans. Determined this is a stopgap; I can't live like a perpetual student forever.

The next week is spent doing all the crappy things you never think about before a move: changing my address with the world and his wife, setting up contracts, and finding the strength to telephone my parents and break the news to them. When I finally get around to it, I end up having to lean out of my window to get some reception.

"Bethany, how lovely to hear from you." My mother has that 'we have company' tone to her voice. She's overdoing the gushing. "How are you, darling?"

I can almost picture what she's wearing: some variation on the skirt suits she always chooses when she hosts dinner. She'll have been to the hairdressers in the afternoon to have a wash and set, possibly while the steaks marinated in the fridge. Dessert will be bought from the local delicatessen, because by the time they get to it, none of her guests will notice it's not homemade. Even if they do, they'll be too sozzled from my dad's elderberry wine to care.

"I'm fine. Listen, Mum—"

"And Simon, how is Simon?" She's always been a fan of his.

"That's what I'm calling to talk about."

"Is he all right? What's happened?" An edge of alarm coats her words.

"Nothing like that. We've decided to separate. I wanted to give you my new address." *You know, in case you ever want to visit,* I add silently. *Fat chance.*

A long, heavy silence, followed by a deep sigh. "Oh, Bethany. What have you done?"

If I live to be eighty, I'll still feel like a small child who never lived up to her parents' expectations. I sit down heavily on my bed. Why does everything have to be my fault? No mention of Simon's role in any of this.

"It was a mutual decision. We both agreed it was for the best."

There's a pause for a moment, as if she's trying to absorb my words. "I suppose you'll want to come home like the prodigal daughter," she says crossly. "I'll have to move all of my scrapbooking. We've only just got rid of your bed."

"I don't want to move home," I sigh. "You don't need to move anything. I've found somewhere temporary to live and I'm looking for something permanent." I rub my head, trying to soothe away the sharp, stabbing pain behind my brow.

"Well, I'm sure you and Simon will sort it out." She lowers her voice. "Just wear a short skirt and appeal to his baser instincts. That's what I always do with your fath—"

"Mum!" I don't know what's more appalling. The fact she's trying to pimp out her own daughter, or the sudden vision I have of her dancing around my dad. "Anyway, I'd better let you get back to your guests. Have a lovely evening."

"How did you...oh, yes. But we need to talk about you and Simon..."

I hang up before she can impart any more wisdom. My duty is done; she won't be calling up Simon's house and getting a nasty shock. I mentally tick that particular chore off my ever-growing list with a mental flourish, breathing in deeply to calm myself down.

* * *

I come to life whenever Niall's close. Like one of those stop-motion videos, where you see a flower blooming in sped-up time. Even when the children run into the classroom with their excited chatter and loud footsteps I still feel his pull.

Niall is at the front of the room, talking about Van Gogh's starry night. There's an intensity to his eyes when he mentions the yellowness of the stars and the inky blueness of the sky. He urges the kids to go out and look at the heavens tonight, and remember it's the same one that Vincent saw all those years ago. I look around the room, amazed at how the children are hanging on his every word.

All except one.

Cameron Gibbs catches my eye and stares at me, giving me an exaggerated wink. It takes a minute for me to realise he wants to tell me something. Even longer to work out he wants to talk to me in private. I get a sinking feeling when I realise he can only have one thing to talk about.

Niall is still explaining how Van Gogh painted while he was a patient at an asylum—a fact that the kids barely bat an eyelash at—and I realise there's only one thing for it.

"Cameron, can you help me get a couple of things out of the supply cupboard?" I ask.

Niall breaks off his speech to look at me. "I can help."

Any other time I'd have jumped at his offer, but I'm anxious to hear what Cameron has to say. "It's all right, you carry on. This'll only take a minute."

When we walk to the cupboard I leave the door open so I don't arouse suspicion. This means we have to speak in lowered voices, but it's worth it just to find out his news. There's a smug expression on Cameron's face, as if he knows he holds all the cards.

"What's up?"

"I've found some stuff out."

What I thought was smugness is actually pride. It melts my heart a little. "About Allegra? What's happened?"

"I've seen that bloke hanging round. The one with the slicked-back hair and leather jacket. Face that looks like papier mâché."

My stomach drops. It sounds just like Darren. He must've had bad acne as a kid, because his face is pocked with tiny craters.

"Where did you see him?" My tone is urgent. I need to know if Allegra is in danger. "Do you know if he went into their flat?"

Cameron screws up his nose and thinks. "Nah, I seen him hanging 'round the park. Doing some deals, smoking with his mates." His face lights up as if he's just thought of a brilliant idea. "I could follow him next time, like one of those detectives. I'm stealthy; he won't notice a thing."

Fear chills me to the core. "No," I whisper-shout, my eyes widening. "He's dangerous. If he even knew you were watching him he'd go mad." How stupid I was, involving a kid in something so foolish. "Don't go anywhere near him."

He stares at me as if I'm crazy. "I wouldn't let him see me."

"Cam." I reach out and squeeze his shoulder. "Thank you so much for looking out for Allegra. You're a good kid. But I don't need you to keep an eye out anymore. It's fine."

"Are you sure? I don't mind." He almost looks disappointed. He thinks this is a game. Something to do when he gets bored of kicking a ball around with his mates. If I tell him how dangerous Darren can be, he'll see the whole thing as a challenge.

"Nah, I reckon you've repaid me twice over. I don't want to end up owing *you*." I make an expression of mock-horror, hoping he can't see right through me.

"I suppose not." He shrugs. "Have it your way then. As long as we're even?"

"We are." I nod. "Definitely even."

I send him out with some old boxes of magazines that need recycling, directing him to the big bin at the back of the clinic. When I walk back to the front of the room, Niall catches my eye and inclines his head. "Okay?" he mouths.

Even though I'm far from okay, I give him a brief smile before I nod. I'm not ready to share this yet, not until I think through the implications. My eyes gravitate toward Allegra, who is dabbing gold paint on the black paper Niall has given them, creating her own version of the Starry Night. Her sleeves are rolled up, enough for me to see her pale forearms, unblemished by red marks or bruises. I check the rest of her exposed skin: face, neck, and skinny legs, but there's nothing to give me alarm.

She looks like a normal eight-year-old kid. As normal as she'll ever be.

Of course, there could be all sorts of horrors hiding underneath her clothes, or even worse, beneath her skin. I walk over and stand behind her, admiring her work, and Allegra turns to smile up at me.

"Do you like it?"

"It's beautiful. I bet your mum will love it. Does she put your paintings up in her kitchen?" I try to picture their dingy flat, hoping the mess in there has long since been cleared up.

"Maybe." Her face lights up as if I've suggested something world-changing. "I'll ask her. We could tack it to the wall."

"Or put it up in your new bedroom?" I suggest.

Her expression darkens. "We haven't painted it yet. Mum says we'll do it soon."

"I expect you've been too busy to do much decorating. Is it nice to be home?"

Allegra nods. "Mum lets me stay up late and watch TV."

I swallow hard. "And have you caught up with your friends? I expect they were glad to see you."

"Yeah, it's nice to play at the park with them."

The park is on the far corner of the estate. It's the same place that Darren has been hanging around, dealing to kids. "Do you go to the park often?"

She shrugs. "If the weather's good. Otherwise we go to Shona's house and play on her Xbox."

"What about your mum? Does she see much of her friends?"

A blank look. Allegra turns and adds some more paint to her stars. "Dunno." I chastise myself for being so obvious. She must think I'm crazy, shooting so many questions at her.

"Well, maybe we can all go out and do something nice soon. Go out to the cinema or something?"

Allegra stops painting again and looks up with a smile. "I'd like that," she says.

So would I. I don't say it, but she knows. I'm already thinking how I can bring up the whole subject of Darren with Daisy without making her defensive. The last time I saw her was outside social services, celebrating the return of her child. Would she really give it all up, put everything in danger for the sake of a scumbag like him?

For the rest of the afternoon I let Niall take the lead, while I sit at the desk and try to think things through. My mind feels full of cotton wool—soft and mushy. Trying to find clarity is almost impossible. Every so often, Niall glances over at me, and I guess there must be something in my expression that worries him. More than once his look turns into a stare that seems to see right through me.

I don't have the slightest idea what to do. My first instinct is to run over to the estate, grab Darren Tebbit by his collar and beat the shit out of him. But it's never going to happen—I'll end up lying at the bottom of a ditch somewhere. I could go and see Grace the social worker and tell her about the sightings, but as soon as she starts questioning me and discovers I'm relying on the word of a thirteen-year-old kid who's recently been arrested, she'll probably laugh me out of her office. If I mention I've actually asked this same boy to keep his eye out for a criminal—and I still can't believe I did that—she'll probably blow her top with me. No matter what I do, I can't see a good resolution to this situation.

"A penny for 'em?"

"I don't want to fleece you. They're not worth that much."

Niall raises his eyebrows. "You've been miles away all afternoon. You missed an amusingly gruesome re-enactment of Van Gogh's ear being chopped off."

"Kids love a bit of gore. Maybe we should make it a prerequisite that all artists chop a body part off." I catch his eye. "Present company excluded, of course."

He smiles, though it doesn't quite reach his eyes. He's too busy looking at me with concern. "Did Cameron Gibbs say something to you?"

Niall's more perceptive than I give him credit for. Damn him.

"It wasn't like that. He wasn't being a pain or anything. I just asked him to keep an eye on Allegra and he was reporting back."

He looks more confused than ever. "Keep an eye on her? Why?"

The temptation to let everything spill out is overwhelming. I'm desperate to share this information with somebody, but half of it is probably confidential, while the other half paints me in a terrible light.

"I don't even know where to start." When I look up, Allegra's walking over to us, holding her painting out for me to see. It effectively silences any conversation we can have about her, still I don't feel the relief I expect to. Instead, I experience a pang of regret. I want to hear what he has to say, because his opinion matters to me.

So when Niall turns and mouths "Later" to me, I find myself nodding in agreement.

24

An hour later, the classroom is empty of children. The white-painted walls no longer echo with their excited chatter, though the paint-splattered floor is evidence they were here. We share the cleaning as usual, with Niall pegging their starry paintings on the drying line we've strung across the ceiling, twelve pieces of paper swaying in a gentle breeze. We seem to have fallen back into the old rhythm of washing, stacking and making the occasional comment. It's as if we both know we will be talking later. For now, we can just be.

Although it's hard to simply *be* when Niall brushes past me. The second time he does it, I wonder if it's on purpose. He's very good at being surreptitious. By the time I think to comment, he's on the other side of the room, and I'm opening and closing my mouth like a demented fish.

The feelings I have for him are confusing. A mixture of nostalgia and desire, maybe, but there's something more, too. An ache to be with him, to know what he thinks on every subject. I want to get to know him all over again.

I want him to know me. *The real me.* The one I've been trying to suppress ever since Digby's death. The one I thought I'd left behind. It turns out she was here all along, waiting for me to find her for real.

And I think I like her.

"We done?"

Niall smiles at me. There's a smudge of black paint along his jawline and without thinking I reach out to wipe it. Like a reflex response, his hand circles my wrist, keeping my fingers resting on his jaw.

Neither of us breathes.

"You have paint," I finally say. "On your face. Black paint." Am I making sense? I'm not even sure.

He unclenches his fingers from my wrist and moves his hand up to cover mine. "Have I?" Not once does he move his eyes away from me.

My palm presses harder on his rough skin. His beard is starting to emerge. It's scratchy, but somehow I like the way it feels. As I stand there, my thoughts drift back to that night in his flat, remembering how his jaw felt against my neck, my chest, my cheek. It burned in such a sensual way.

Reluctantly, I pull my hand away and let it rest on my hip. "I guess it's time to go back to my glamorous bedsit."

"Are you liking it there?" Though his voice is even, his eyes are still dilated. I like the way I affect him.

"It was a bit weird at first, getting used to just living in one room. It's nice to have somewhere I can call mine, though."

"What do you do in the evening? Do you share the cooking with your housemates?"

I laugh, thinking of the takeaway cartons scattered around our tiny kitchen. "No, I hardly see them to be honest. I think they prefer kebabs to nouvelle cuisine."

"You don't sit and watch telly with them?"

"We don't have a living room." It was strange at first, realising there was no communal space. I guess the landlord wanted to squeeze every penny he could out of his real estate. What used to be the living room is now a third bedroom. "The only time I see them is when I'm making a cup of tea. It isn't so bad."

His nose screws up. "What does Simon think? Won't he pay for something better for you?"

"I don't want him to. It isn't his choice I moved out. I don't want to look as if I'm sponging off him."

It would feel so wrong. Everything Simon has, he owned before we got married. Even at our lowest, the last thing I thought about was taking him for all he had. It's his money, not mine. I'd like it to stay that way.

"It seems unfair that he has everything and you're living in a dingy room. You know the offer of my spare room still stands."

It would be so easy, moving into his place, drifting into a relationship; maybe never leaving, but if Niall and I are ever going to be together it won't be by default. This time I want any relationship to be on an equal footing.

"It's fine. Just somewhere to stay while I work everything out. They don't make too much noise, don't have crazy parties. They just keep to themselves."

Diane and Peter. It even took me a few days to remember their names. These are people I'm sharing a bathroom with.

"Well, any time you need to escape, you know where I am." He doesn't say any more, just walks over and grabs his jacket from a hook at the back of the room. "Do you want a lift home?"

I try not to laugh. My flat's in completely the opposite direction of his place and he knows it. I'm about to refuse when an idea pops into my head. "Actually, do you have enough time to take a detour? I just want to check on something."

* * *

His car still stinks like a tepid pond. It doesn't appear to have been cleaned since I was last in it, and I find myself kicking an empty water bottle, wondering if it's been in the foot well all this time. He climbs in on the driver's side and stretches his long legs out to press the clutch down, and I try not to watch as his thigh muscles push against his jeans.

"So, where are we going?"

"Do you know the Whitegate Estate?"

He turns and catches my eye. "Only by reputation." His voice is low. "Why do you want to go there?"

I take a deep breath and let my head fall back on the headrest. "Allegra MacArthur lives there with her mum."

"Okay…"

"I want to check she's all right." I look at him again, and he's waiting patiently for me to expand. For a moment, I sit and try to work out the right words. "Her mum has this on-again off-again boyfriend and I think he might have hurt her in the past. I want to go over and see if he's back hanging around there."

"He left?"

Another deep breath. "After he landed Daisy in hospital with multiple injuries. Now I hear he might be back."

"Why not call somebody? The police or social services?"

It's a good question, though not one I'm particularly delighted about answering. "Because I did a stupid thing," I admit. "I asked Cameron Gibbs to keep an eye on her and let me know if Darren came back."

"Darren's the boyfriend?" Niall clarifies. He gives up trying to start the car and turns to face me. "The one who beats them?"

"Yes. I know it's stupid, but I can't call up social services just to tell them he's been hanging around the estate. It's only hearsay; they'd laugh at me. If I could just see for myself, then at least I'd have something to tell them."

"And if he isn't there?"

"Then I can go home knowing Allegra's safe."

He reaches out and runs his finger along my cheekbone. The intimacy of the gesture is almost painful.

"Okay, let's go. But if you get out of the car I'm coming with you."

It takes a while to get there. The evening rush hour halts our progress every few blocks, and we idle in long queues while motorbikes and couriers flash by, weaving in and out of the vehicles. Neither of us says very much, because I'm too busy worrying about Allegra, and Niall's too busy concentrating on the road.

Eventually, he leans forward and switches on the radio, and the drive-time D.J. introduces the all-request hour. The Fray comes on, and our eyes meet. This song was in the charts the year Digby died. As the bittersweet melody fills the interior of the car, I wonder if Niall listened to it as much as I did.

"I hate this song." Niall flicks off the radio. *How to Save a Life* fades away.

"It was everywhere that summer… I couldn't escape it. And every time I listened to it, I felt as if I was being judged."

"You're not the one who deserved judgement. You didn't do anything wrong."

The silence is so heavy it actually hurts. I can feel his pain dissolve into my own. "We were just kids, Niall. It wasn't your fault."

"I gave him that tab. Whose fault was it?"

We come to another stop behind some temporary traffic lights. Somebody beeps their horn.

"You gave me one, too, and I'm still alive," I say firmly. "It was one of those things. The blame doesn't lie on you."

"It doesn't lie on you either. When are you going to realise that?"

When I close my eyes I can picture Digby palming the tablet as Niall passes it to him. All three of us swallowing tiny white pills. Looking for ecstasy and finding only death.

"I should have listened to him. When he said he felt ill."

Niall's fingers tap against the steering wheel in a silent rhythm. "The poor guy never stood a chance. He was diagnosed with a congenital heart defect in the post-mortem. Did you know that?"

I shake my head, feeling the nausea rise in my stomach the way it always does when I think about him and about those days.

"I read it in the papers. It came out in the inquest."

That would make sense. I stopped reading anything after the first two days. Seeing myself vilified in print was more than I could bear. "He still wouldn't have died if it wasn't for the E."

"True. But none of us knew what would happen, including him." He tips his head to the side, and looks at me with a curious expression on his face. "Do you still think about it a lot?"

"Yes," I reply. "For a long time I couldn't think of anything else. It's taken me forever to forgive myself for not following him that night."

Niall's voice is thin. "He would have died anyway. You know that, don't you? It wasn't our fault."

"But he wouldn't have died alone." That's the worst thing. Knowing he was suffering without anybody looking after him.

"True." The cars ahead of us start to move, and Niall follows them, inching his Fiesta along the tarmac. "But it is what it is. Do you know what I mean? Eventually you just have to accept that it happened and try to move on. That's what I've been attempting to do."

"I know." He's right. I know he is.

"Is that why you work at the clinic? To atone for his death?"

I give him a small smile. "At first, I think. Now I work there because I love the kids. They're the victims in this, and the potential addicts of the future. If I can make a difference, it's all worth it."

"You do make a difference. I can promise you that."

When we pull onto the Whitegate Estate my heart speeds up. The streets are empty save for piles of trash littering the pavements and a burnt-out, abandoned car haphazardly parked on the side of the road. I direct Niall toward the park, thankful his car is dilapidated enough not to stand out.

We stop short of the playground, where a cluster of kids are hanging off a spinning roundabout, hair fanning out in the breeze. The swings have been commandeered by teenagers who use them as benches. A few of them smoke from half-used cigarettes as they try to look achingly cool.

Eventually, I spot Allegra crouched under the slide, playing some sort of game with another girl—a white-haired, pretty little thing who looks about the same age.

"You okay?" Niall asks. I don't know whether it's from genuine concern for my well-being, or just something to cut through the silence. Either way I answer him.

"Yeah, I'm just looking for Darren. Cameron said he was hanging around here the other day."

"Only kids here now."

"Yep." I wonder if Darren takes a break when the children arrive. I can't believe he does; after all, the teenagers are probably his best customers. I still can't get rid of that nasty taste in my mouth. If I were a psychic I'd say I could feel him. There's just something a little off about this whole situation.

"You want to get out? Take a look around?"

I crane my head to look at the tower blocks surrounding the green space. Standing like sentinels, they're identical in design, all constructed from the same dull concrete. Something about them makes me shiver.

"Can we drive to that building?" I point to the block where Daisy lives, trying not to think about the last time I came here. It feels like a lifetime ago. "I want to pop in and see Daisy."

Even I'm surprised at my words. They come out before I really get a chance to think them through, but as soon as they do I'm sure it's the right thing. Go up and see her, maybe say something about Allegra forgetting something. Reassure myself that Darren isn't back.

"Are you sure? Will she mind if you drop in on her unannounced?" Niall starts the car up anyway.

"I won't be long. Just in and out."

As we climb the stairs I get a sense of déjà vu. My heart races with a mixture of exertion and anxiety, and I find myself clinging on to Niall's hand for reassurance. When he stops to look at a piece of intricately designed graffiti on the stairwell I get to catch my breath for a moment, admiring his face.

"Do you like graffiti?" I ask.

"They're the wall paintings of our time. Social realism in art form. I think they're fascinating."

I can see what he means. "Have you ever done any?"

He laughs. "Hasn't everybody?"

I shake my head and laugh lightly. "Not me. I'm a good girl, remember?"

His voice is soft. Low. "I remember."

We step out onto the familiar walkway that leads to Daisy's flat. Nothing has changed in the months since I was here. There's still broken glass on the floor. Flat 403 still has boarded windows. There's a twitch in the yellowed net curtains as I pass 408, and I assume a nosy neighbour is keeping an eye out.

"Do you mind waiting here?" I ask Niall before we turn the corner to Daisy's row of flats. "I don't want to turn up unannounced with a stranger. I won't be long, I promise."

He grabs my hand before I can leave. "If there's anything wrong in there you scream, okay? I'll be in there like a shot." He drops his forehead until it's resting on mine. "Take care of yourself. That's an order."

I nod and it moves both our heads. "You're lovely."

"I know." He grins and it makes me want to hug him. Linking my arms around his neck, I pull him in tight. A second later he tugs me closer, his hands resting on my lower back, palms warm through my t-shirt. That's where I want to stay. Safe in his arms, warm and cosy and perfectly content.

But I can't, not until I've seen for myself that Darren Tebbit hasn't made a sudden reappearance.

As soon as I pull away, Niall wanders back to lean against a wall, and I walk over to knock at Daisy's door. Trying not to think about the last time I did this.

It takes her less than a minute to answer. She yanks the door open, lifting a cigarette to her dry lips. Brow furrowing as she realises who it is.

"What are you doing here?"

"I was just wondering how you were doing. I haven't had a chance to catch up with you."

Daisy stands aside and I walk in, relief enveloping me when I realise she's in here alone.

"I do have a phone you know," she grumbles. "I'm in the middle of making tea."

"I won't stay long then. Is everything okay? Allegra settling in all right?"

"She's fine." Daisy's eyes narrow. "Haven't you just seen her? She's been at class, right?"

Shit. Fuck.

"Um, yeah, we didn't get a chance to talk."

The microwave pings and we both ignore it.

"Why are you really here?"

There are times when I wish Daisy was stupid, that I wasn't so dumb. She knows I live nowhere near this estate. There's no reason for me being here. It must be obvious I'm checking up on her. "I heard Darren was back."

She stubs her cigarette out in a pale green ashtray then swings to face me. "So you thought you'd run in here and be Miss Nosy Bitch, did you? Come checking up on the poor people? Want to sneer down your nose at us?"

"I wanted to make sure he hasn't been bothering you. Not after everything you've been through." I'm lying and she knows it. I can tell by the way she frowns. She folds her arms tightly across her chest.

"Well, he's not here, is he?"

"I can see that." I try to say it lightly, but I come across as a fool. "Everything's okay, then?"

I'm eyeing the door, already wishing myself out of here. Why on earth did I ever come up? It seemed so simple: pop in, say hello, then walk right out, knowing Darren wasn't anywhere near either Daisy or Allegra. Now all I've done is put Daisy's back up again, and I know it's going to backfire somehow.

"I'm about to call Allegra in for tea, so you need to go." Daisy grabs her phone.

That's when I see it. Hanging casually on the back of a chair. A black leather jacket—too big to be Daisy's. Too roomy to belong to anybody but a man. I step toward it, reaching out to touch, then I'm yanked back, my spine jarring at the sudden change in direction.

"Get out of here." Daisy's voice is low. A warning. She releases my shoulder and I step back.

"Is that Darren's?"

"None of your fucking business. Now get out of here." Her face is twisted and angry. She steps toward me and I can feel the menace.

"It *is* my business. Is he back? He shouldn't be around Allegra. Not after what he did last time." My breath comes faster, the adrenaline kicking in. "I can't believe you let him come back."

"He's not back, now fuck off and don't come back." She pushes me and I stumble, grabbing onto the doorjamb for support. "I don't want you near Allegra, you interfering little bitch. Keep away from us both."

She's so angry, the room vibrates with her fury. I make a grab for the door handle and yank at it. The door swings open, crashing against the wall.

"That's right, piss off. And don't come back," Daisy shouts after me. "If I hear you've been anywhere near her I'll deck you."

A loud bang tells me she's shut the door, but my heart is still racing when I reach Niall. Breathing fast, I run straight into his arms, needing his comfort more than ever. My mind is buzzing with thoughts of Darren and Allegra, and what I should do to try and sort this whole mess out.

When we walk toward the stairwell he slides his hand on top of mine and holds me tightly, not once letting go.

It's only when we're halfway down the stairs that I feel as though I can breathe again.

25

Neither of us speak as Niall navigates the potholed roads of the estate. The car bounces every time he hits a dip too wide to avoid. It doesn't feel like an oppressive silence, though. I'm too busy thinking, and I suppose he is, too. We barely notice our surroundings as we make our way north east. The blur of chicken takeaways and kebab shops are only a blip on my radar.

When we're a few roads away from my flat I finally find my voice. "How do you know where I live?"

Niall makes a neat little manoeuvre, sliding the Fiesta into the tightest of spaces. Either he's an excellent parker or he doesn't give a damn if he dings his car. "Alex told me."

Alex has a lot to answer for. Most of it good.

Niall climbs out of the car, squeezing himself between the bumper and the car in front. When we reach my building I find myself hesitating.

I've not invited anybody up before, unless you count Alex and Lara when they helped move my stuff. It's strange, I realise, because I've never had my own place until now, never had the freedom to invite somebody in without checking. For the first time, I'm in charge. The thought doesn't scare me as I thought it would.

I show Niall the kitchen when we pass it. We climb the stairs to my room, squeezing in between the easy chair and the bed, until he's standing in the middle of the carpet. I watch his face as he scans his surroundings, noting the furrow between his eyes, the way the corner of his lip pulls down.

"So this is it. Chez moi. Small and bijou but all mine." I sound like my mum, lapsing into franglais. It's only when he stares at my poorly made bed that I realise where we are.

Niall Joseph is in my bedroom.

The last time we were in a bedroom together I was nineteen years old, heady with infatuation, dizzy that he'd noticed me. Now... I don't know. I feel like a seasoned gambler at a high-stakes table. Calm on the surface, but underneath there's so much going on. I'm not sure where to start.

"Cup of tea?"

He shakes his head and sits down on the easy chair. A second later he fidgets and puts his hand under the cushion, pulling out a hairbrush. I try not to laugh when he raises his eyebrows.

"I still haven't unpacked properly. Anyway, you can hardly talk; have you seen the inside of your car?"

He has the good grace to laugh. "I wasn't commenting on your storage options, it just surprised me when I felt the spikes on my arse."

Of course my eyes automatically go *there*. They can't help it. When I look up I notice he's smirking, and there's something about it that makes me overheat. "I apologise for your discomfort." I don't mean it, not a word. I hope he feels as uncomfortable as I do.

"I've had worse."

My phone vibrates then and I lift it up, seeing my mum's name flash up on the screen. Pressing a button to send it to voicemail, I find myself grimacing. Much to Niall's amusement.

"My mum," I tell him, as if that explains everything. "I've only just told her about the split."

He licks his lips slowly and inclines his head. "You two don't get on?"

"I let her down." There's no need to say why. His eyes soften with understanding.

"Alex told me what you went through at home. I'm sorry."

I look up. "Did you have it any easier?"

"You've met my mam, right?" He smiles in a disturbingly sexy way. All crinkles and lifted cheeks. "When she found out about the drugs I thought she was going to kill me. But later on, she was pretty cool, listening to me talking about Digby, and about you."

"You talked about me?"

"All the time. She probably got sick of it."

"I thought you'd forget about me."

"How could I forget you? I spent most of the time either painting you or thinking about you."

"But you never called."

"Nor did you." He says it simply, guilelessly, but I still feel it sharply. There's no answer, because he's right. I was too caught up in my own misery to think about dealing with anything else. Why would it be any different for him?

He stares at my lips. I feel self-conscious enough to pull my gaze from him and look away. "What did you do after that?"

"I moved to California for a few years. My uncle lives over there and managed to get me enrolled in an art program. It was his personal mission to clean me up."

"Did he succeed?" This is the answer I need to know. If Niall is still using—even the tiniest amount—it will be a deal breaker. After the devastation I've witnessed, I couldn't cope with that as well.

He sits stock-still, his face masked in seriousness. "Are you asking me if I still take drugs?"

I take a deep breath. "I am."

He stands up and walks over to where I'm perched on the end of my bed, dropping to his knees so his face is in line with mine. For a moment I forget to breathe as he takes my hand in his, raising it up to cup his jaw. "I haven't taken anything for eight years, Beth. I had a few false starts, but I got there. Beer and the occasional cigarette are my worst habits now."

There's an intensity to him that draws me in and I lean forward until we are only inches away. I inhale and notice his cologne and a faint trace of soap. Why does he always smell so good? There's barely time to think about it before he's clearing the final distance, and the next moment I feel his warm lips meet mine. Soft yet insistent.

He takes his time, moving slowly, tilting my head with his hands. I kiss him back, surrendering to his warmth, and the need that's pushing at my chest. I find myself wanting to laugh and cry all at once, but settle for looping my arms around his neck, pulling him closer still, sighing loudly when his tongue slides between my lips. Lights flash behind my closed eyes as he presses his body to mine. Hard enough to make me fall back on the mattress. I bounce until he steadies me with his hands. Hovering over me, he cages me in with his arms, staring right into my eyes.

"Come here." I put my hands on his shoulders and try to pull him closer. The muscles beneath his t-shirt flex, but he doesn't move an inch.

"Is this okay? Kissing you, I mean."

I nod quickly. We might have talked about waiting and being ready but lying underneath him I'm certain it's right. "More than okay."

He kisses me again. This time I wrap my legs around him, lifting my hips until I can feel him *there*. His moan vibrates through my lips and into my mouth, so I do it again, moving against him until we are both caught up in a fog of need.

I don't know how long it goes on for. At one point he pushes my sweater up to my neck, stroking my stomach with his fingers, then his lips, soft enough to drive me crazy. If I was nineteen I'd be shimmying out of my jeans and he'd be tearing my knickers off without thinking twice. Instead we stick to caresses, gentle touches and hard strokes. His muscled thigh pushes between mine and I clench around him, still kissing him hard and fast. I need more. I could climb inside his skin and even that wouldn't be close enough.

When we pull apart we're both breathless, filling the room with loud sighs. Niall rolls off me and onto his back, flinging his arm over his head. My lips feel raw and bee stung. I trace them with my finger. Their tenderness surprises me.

He smiles when he catches my eye. It's tentative, almost embarrassed and I want to laugh out loud. It's as if nine years have disappeared and we are Niall and Beth making out after lectures. Except this time there's nothing chemical involved.

For that reason, it tastes so much sweeter.

"I guess that's what they call heavy petting." Niall grins harder and pulls me into his crook. I snuggle in, feeling warm and protected. "The Christian Brothers always warned us about that."

"Did they tell you about eternal damnation?" I ask, tracing his jaw with my finger.

"Yeah, but they forgot to say it would all be worth it."

I close my eyes and press my face into his chest, enjoying the warmth radiating through his t-shirt. Part of me wants to ask him what this means, what this thing between us is, but I hold my tongue for fear of the answer. I'm too tired to talk anyway. The emotions of the day are weighing too heavily on my soul. So I let him hold me and trace his fingers along my spine, pressing his face into my hair, whispering words I cannot hear.

Just for tonight I let myself be.

* * *

He leaves just after midnight and I kiss him all the way to the door, clutching at his shirt when he comes back for one final embrace. Our lips curl with laughter as we press them together. I don't want him to go but he can't stay. Not unless we're both ready for the next stage, and I don't think we are. Not yet. We knew it was time to stop making out when he spent more time adjusting himself than touching me, his face taking on a glaze of discomfort.

It didn't mean it was easy, though.

"I'll call you." He kisses me again and I run my fingers through his hair, tugging at it.

"First thing. Before you get up."

"All right, bossy girl." Another brush of his lips. "I'll be up with the dawn chorus."

There's something so easy about our interaction. It's gentle and light-hearted, a stark contrast to the heated passion of before. He leans forward for a final kiss before leaving, and I stand at the door, watching as he clambers down the stairs. When he turns a corner I run to the kitchen, spotting him as he heads toward his car. He's just a shadow in the street light but I'd know that walk anywhere. The same almost-swagger I remember from when we were young.

I barely sleep all night. When I'm not thinking about Niall I'm fretting about Allegra and praying she's safe tonight. I left a message for Grace that I want to meet with her tomorrow, not knowing what else I can do. I can hardly call the police and tell them I've seen a suspicious leather jacket loitering around the house. They'd laugh me off the phone then arrest me for wasting their time. The only thing to do is wait until tomorrow and pray nothing happens in the meantime.

* * *

The next morning my phone rings at half past six and I talk to Niall. His voice is heavy with sleep; hearing it makes me feel giddy. He tells me about his day—meetings about shows and commissions—and he asks me not to go anywhere near the estate without him.

It isn't an ultimatum or a demand, just a heartfelt plea. I find myself agreeing.

I'm at the clinic when Grace calls. She's on a home visit but offers to drop into the clinic at two. As it's a Friday there's no class, and I agree readily, hopeful we can finally sort things out. With a few hours to kill and a quiet morning ahead, I clear out the art cupboard, a chore I normally avoid at the best of times. Today it's cathartic. Throwing away dried-up bottles and brushes that have turned stiff as boards takes my mind off the bigger things.

I'm still in there when I hear a small rap on the door, and I pop my head around to see Grace O'Dell.

"Oh, hi." I smooth back my hair, knowing I must look a state. "Is it that time already?"

"I'm early. My last appointment cancelled. Do you have time now?"

There's something in her manner—a certain tenseness—that puts me on my guard. I feel my forehead crease into a frown. "Sure, do you want to talk here?"

"As good a place as any."

We sit down on the orange plastic chairs. They're covered with dried paint but Grace doesn't appear to notice. In her job she's seen much worse.

"Do you want to start?" she asks.

For a moment I flash back to all those years ago. Another room, but the same sort of feeling. As if I'm losing from the beginning. I don't know why I get the impression that she's judging me before I get to say a single word.

"I think Darren Tebbit's back."

"What makes you think that?" Her words are clipped, almost dismissive.

"I saw his jacket in Daisy's flat. When I asked her about it she got all defensive, as though she was trying to hide something."

"So you saw a jacket. Anything else?"

I realise how lame I must sound. Without Cameron's information I'm just a paranoid fool, but I can't tell her that he's been spying. "No, but I know he's back."

Grace raises her eyebrows but keeps staring, like I'm the bad guy in this. "I saw Daisy this morning. She told me you went barging into her flat making all kinds of accusations."

"That's not true," I protest. "She was the one shouting."

Grace raises a finger as if to silence me. "Then I went to Allegra's school and asked her if Darren had been hanging around. She told me she hasn't seen him for months."

"But Daisy was so defensive. When I saw the jacket she practically pushed me out of the door..."

"See it from her point of view. She's trying so hard to make it work, putting her all into doing the right thing by Allegra. Then you swan in and make her feel like she's being judged."

"I didn't swan in. I just wanted to check everything was okay."

"Why?" she asks.

"What do you mean?"

"Why wouldn't everything be okay? It's as if you're expecting her to fail and it's not on. We've analysed all the risks and given her the chance to prove herself. Your spouting off accusations isn't helping anyone. Least of all Allegra."

Tears prick at my eyes, and my hands clench with frustration. It's not the fact she doesn't believe me which grates, it's the knowledge that Allegra could get hurt and there's nothing I can do to stop it. "You're not going to do anything?"

"Daisy assured me he isn't back. That jacket was something he'd left behind; she wore it to pop out to the shops."

Am I going crazy? I feel like I might be. It's as if I'm seeing the world through a different lens, insisting the sky is blue when everybody else sees green. "You believe her?"

"Would Allegra still be there if I didn't?" Grace's reply is terse. "There's no sign that he's back. Daisy looks healthy and clean; I don't think she's using. The flat was tidy and full of Daisy and Allegra's things. Not Darren's." She almost glares at me. I must look like a flake to her. The girl who cries wolf. "I think your going round there did more harm than good."

I instantly recoil as if I've been slapped in the face. "How do you mean?"

"Daisy thinks you've had it in for her ever since you heard our suspicions about Darren. She's got this idea in her head that you're going to take Allegra away." She pauses. Long enough for me to take it in. A moment later, she drops the bombshell. "For both their sakes I think you should stay away from them."

"Stay away?" I echo. "How long for?"

Grace shrugs. "Until Daisy feels comfortable with you being around. She isn't your biggest fan right now."

"But I'll still see Allegra here, right?"

Grace shifts awkwardly on her seat. "I don't think that's appropriate."

"I won't get to see her at all?" The last word comes out as a sob. I have to cover my mouth to stop it from developing into anything more.

"It's for the best." Grace's expression softens when she sees how horrified I am. Leaning forward, she reaches out to pat my free hand. Her gesture does nothing to ease the knot in my chest.

I remove my hand from my mouth. "It's not fair," I whisper. "I love that kid."

"You've broken the first rule," Grace tells me. "You've got too involved. You haven't got the distance you need."

Her words make me want to scream. I don't need distance or judgement or anything else she thinks I'm lacking. There's a little girl who can't protect herself against an evil bastard, and I'm not even allowed to help. The thought of him getting close enough to hurt her makes me want to throw up.

"What if I see her anyway?" I ask, grasping for straws where there's only air.

"Then Daisy has every right to call the police. She's Allegra's mum after all."

26

I spend the next week trying not to be a stalker, despite my urge to drive over to the Whitegate Estate and accost every muscled, weasel-faced guy I can find. Instead I spend the evenings at Niall's flat. We eat dinner together, watch whatever happens to be showing on the telly, and then somehow end up tangled in each other's arms, kissing the hell out of each other while our programme is forgotten.

On Wednesday night we kiss and grind for so long that I feel him freeze above me, his spine arched and his mouth tight as he makes a mess of his jeans. I laugh so hard I give myself a stomach ache. He vows revenge when I don't let him forget it.

Niall's plan to get me back comes good on Friday night, when we are on his bed, kissing hard and fast as I'm straddling his waist. He moves his lips down, dragging them softly against my neck, and presses his leg against me. His muscled thigh creates friction in an unbelievably sexy way. When I start to moan he flips me over and holds me in his arms. I shudder, gasp and melt inside. He kisses me hard and I can feel him smile against me, pleased with his victory.

We've regressed to being teenagers, and I love every moment of it. Our evenings are the only thing getting me through the day. When I see Allegra's empty table where she should be at art class it's all I can do to make it through without the rest of the kids seeing me cry.

By Saturday I'm such a mess of emotion—both good and bad—that Niall drags me to his studio and tells me to sit by the window that overlooks the Thames. He sketches my profile as I try not to think too hard. Staring out at the grey, choppy water, I follow the progress of a flotilla of boats that make their way upstream. Smaller rowboats bob in the wake of the pleasure cruisers. I wonder if they feel as lost as I am, unable to do anything but wait for the waves to stop crashing.

"What are you thinking about?" Niall asks softly. When I turn my head he's staring at me over his sketchpad. I get a sense of déjà vu; any minute now Digby could walk through that door and tell us to hurry up.

"I was watching the boats. You have an amazing view."

"I know."

From the way he smirks I know he's not talking about the river. He has this way of looking at me, his head tilted to the side, the corner of his mouth quirked up. It's an expression of intent that lights a fire deep inside. I cross my legs and try not to squirm, but my body has other ideas.

My discomfiture worsens when he places his sketchpad on the table and walks over. Putting his hands on my hips, he swings me round until he's standing right between my thighs. When he leans down his eyes are bright and fierce, as though he can read every dirty thought that's going through my mind.

"Do you have a thing for boats?"

"What? No!" I try to laugh but he's too close and the impulse dies in my throat. Instead I try to breathe.

"Then why are you looking at me like that?" He runs a finger up my bare arm and I shiver.

"Like what?"

"Like you want me inside you as much as I do."

Oh my God.

His words are enough to chase every thought out of my mind, as if there's only enough space for him. When he leans down to press his mouth against mine, I close my eyes and melt into him, clutching at the back of his t-shirt as if he's the only one who can save me. Kissing him back, our lips move slowly, our tongues sliding together as though we have no other choice.

But there's a choice and I've made it. I choose him.

He drags his lips down my neck and I wrap my legs around his waist, threading my fingers through his hair. His hands reach under me, palms digging into my behind as he pulls me closer to him, our bodies moving together in a rhythm that feels more natural than breathing. I arch my back and grab fistfuls of his shirt, desperate to feel him close.

When I slide down from the window he seems as surprised as I am. Even more so when I drop to my knees and run my finger down the front of his jeans. He stops breathing. When I look up at him from my position on the floor I can see his eyes reflecting sunlight as he stares down at me. His cheeks are flushed, his lips have fallen open. I try to hide my smile at his obvious shock. Taking my time, I unclasp his belt and button, slowly dragging the zipper down. Not once losing eye contact with him. He's as still as a statue.

"Are you sure?" His voice is low and thick.

I smile when I nod because there's something so perfect about his concern. Niall can be strong and determined when he wants to be, but here—in this room, towering above me—he's not afraid to be vulnerable. To make sure this is all okay.

He makes me feel safe and I love that about him.

God, I love everything about him. My chest is full of that knowledge. I'm not ready to say it yet, but it's in every glance I take, every touch of his skin. It's in the way I curl my fingers around him and try not to smile when he gasps short and low. And when I finally take him in my mouth it's in the way I stare up at him. I know he can feel it.

He gently cups my head, staring down through fevered eyes, and I feel it right back.

"Beth." His voice is little more than a breath.

I drag my tongue against his tip, watching as his jaw slackens, his head dropping forward. I glance at him through my lashes, meeting his gaze. Though his eyes are half-shut, I can still see the heat there.

I can taste it too. He hardens in my mouth, hips rocking involuntarily. When his breath starts to shorten, I take him deeper, feeling him drag against my lips. Then he stops moving and his breath catches as he tries to pull out, to move away. But I don't want to let him go. Instead I grasp his thighs and suck him deeper still, letting him take over all my senses. And when he comes, spilling inside my mouth, he whispers my name again.

It sounds a lot like love.

* * *

The following week I meet Simon inside a smart restaurant just off Upper Street. Arriving early—a sure-fire sign of my nervousness—I order a small gin and tonic. I sip it as I sit at the table and wait for him. Even on a Thursday night the restaurant business appears to be booming. The room is full of smart couples and businessmen, soft conversations and clinking glass. I feel lost amongst the gentility, like a child dressed up in her Sunday best. The tight black dress I'm wearing feels uncomfortably restricting, and I keep pulling at the neckline to give myself room to breathe.

Simon arrives a few minutes after seven. He has that 'straight from the office' look. His shirt is lightly crumpled and his sleeves rolled up. From the way his thin hair falls in disarray, I don't think he checked himself in the mirror before he left. Still, as soon as he sees me sitting at the table his expression softens and a genuine smile forms on his lips.

"You look beautiful." He presses his lips to my cheek. "How are you?"

"I'm good. How are you?" I sound polite and measured. This is how relationships die; one careful word at a time.

"I'm okay." He pauses and guilt unfurls its wings, fluttering in my belly. "Getting used to things."

Thankfully, the waiter chooses that moment to interrupt us and bring our menus over. Simon orders a whisky—stronger than his normal aperitif—and takes the wine list, asking if I'd prefer red or white. When we've ordered he removes his reading glasses, and I notice the bruise-like circles under his eyes.

"You look tired."

"I haven't been sleeping well. It's not the same without you there. I keep worrying about you."

The guilt-bird nesting in my stomach takes flight.

"I'm fine, honestly. The room is nice and my flatmates seem friendly enough."

I don't tell him I haven't been spending much time there. I'm not cruel, plus there's a big difference between honesty and rubbing his nose in it. Still, I owe it to him to be truthful, and that's a big reason why I'm here tonight. Things are getting serious between Niall and me, and I don't want Simon hearing that from anybody else.

When the waiter brings the wine over we stop talking. Simon tastes the red, pausing to sample it before nodding at the waiter. It's achingly familiar, as if we're part of a play repeating itself night after night. The script would have us finish our food and go home, where I would take off my makeup and crawl into bed, while Simon puts on his reading glasses and picks up the latest Lee Child. Instead we are winging it, ad-libbing where the script requires strict adherence. I can't help thinking I'm happier with our new situation than he is.

"How's the clinic?" His question takes me by surprise, not least because I don't know how to answer it. Do I tell him these past weeks have been difficult, that I've been crying more, scared for the fate of a little girl who doesn't belong to me?

"It's good. Especially now the gala's over." I give him a small smile. "At least until I need to organise next year's event."

"You did a good job. You always do."

Silence falls again and I wonder how things became so awkward between us. Part of it is me. I'm hiding something and my lack of candour is colouring our conversation. My chest tightens when our first course arrives and I realise I need to say something soon. But I look at him—the man I married, the one who saved me when I thought I was unsalvageable—and it just seems so cruel. As though I'm breaking his heart all over again.

Putting his knife down, he looks right at me. "When are you coming home?"

"What?" My brows knit together.

"You've made your point. I get it. I neglected you, I should have paid you more attention. There's no need to string it out, you can come back home now."

This isn't the first time he's asked me to come back to him. Yet every time I tell him it's over, it doesn't seem to sink in. He's still talking to me as if I'm a child. The prodigal daughter, waiting to return.

"Simon..." I'm not good at this. How many times can you break somebody's heart? My own feels as though it's cracked in two.

"You know I can take care of you. We work best when I'm making the decisions. Stop fighting me."

He's talking about a Beth I've left behind. I don't want her back, I like being me, and the way I can make my own decisions. I don't want to be the little wife anymore.

Sometimes, you have to be cruel to be kind.

"I'm seeing somebody." I blurt it out in my usual cack-handed way. "I wanted to tell you face to face."

I watch as emotion clouds his expression. Confusion morphing into surprise. "As in seeing a boyfriend?"

I nod. "It's early days. I just thought you should know."

Simon stares at me silently. I look down at the chorizo and scallops congealing on my plate. Any appetite I had has long since been stolen by my words.

"Do I know him?" he asks.

My hands start to shake. "You know of him. He's an artist. Niall Joseph."

His eyes narrow and he drops his head. "The one you've been working with?" When he opens his mouth to say more, my phone rings, and I shuffle through my bag to find it, embarrassed that I'm subjecting the whole restaurant to the sound of chiming bells. I'm about to switch it off when I notice the caller. My hand freezes in the air, shock stilling any momentum it might have had.

It's Daisy MacArthur.

"I need to take this call." I look up, but Simon's staring at his plate. Maybe a few minutes to let him collect himself is a good thing. "I'll be back in a moment." My chair scrapes across the polished wooden floor when I stand up and walk to the front door. Pressing accept, I put the phone to my ear and walk out into the cool, evening air.

"Daisy, is everything okay?" In the silence that follows I find myself wondering whether she's dialled me by mistake, or is merely working up to giving me another earful. "Daisy, are you there?"

The sound is so quiet I can barely hear it at first. I press the phone closer to my ear, trying to drown out the cacophony of traffic and conversation reverberating through the street. Then it gets louder until I realise she's crying, and the drawn-out sobs chill me to the bone.

"Daisy?"

"I can't wake her up."

I stop breathing. It's not Daisy's, but Allegra's voice I can hear through the phone.

"I keep shaking her but she won't open her eyes."

"Allegra? What's happened? How long's she been asleep?"

"I don't know... I was at Shona's... her mum cooked us... some tea. When I came back... I found Mum... on the floor... like this." Between the crying and the sobs it takes her a while to get the words out.

"Is she hurt? Are there any bruises?" Of course, my first thought is Darren. If he's beaten her up again and Allegra's seen it...

"She's been sick, and there's blood on her nose. Can you help me wake her up? Please help me."

I feel myself start to choke, but I need to hold it together. "I'll be right over. In the meantime I need to call an ambulance, okay?" Please God, let Daisy be all right.

"Don't hang up. I'm scared." She starts to wail louder. "Please don't leave me."

"I won't leave you. Not ever." Suddenly, I couldn't give a damn about the posh restaurant and any sense of decorum they may require. I run back inside and grab Simon's arm, demanding he dial 999. A hush falls over the room as everybody listens in to our conversation and my garbled explanation. Even the waiters freeze on the spot. Moments later I have two phones in my hand, and am relaying instructions across to Allegra as she listens and cries.

Simon throws a pile of cash on the table and we leave, hailing a taxi with one hand while he holds me with the other. When a black cab pulls up he yanks open the door and we climb inside, Simon's expression a mixture of horror and concern. He says nothing as we pull away, just reaches out to wipe the tears that are pouring down my face as I keep talking to Allegra, telling her I won't be long. And though I don't say it, from every response she gives to my questions, I know that Daisy is in deep trouble.

27

My mind works overtime as the cab winds its way through the dusky London streets. I can almost hear it whirring as I try to work out the distance between us and the estate, leaning forward to check the cab's milometer to get an estimated time of arrival. I whisper reassuring words down the phone in an attempt to keep Allegra sane, trying not to wince at her shuddering breaths echoing down the earpiece. Since the initial shock has worn off, I've found myself becoming calmer.

Allegra deserves to have somebody be strong for her. It's a role I find myself stepping into without question. I take on the mantle of white knight gladly. If anybody needs a champion on a steed, it's her.

When the cab pulls into the estate I jump out, leaving Simon in my wake. He's about to follow me toward the tower block when I lay a hand on his shoulder, halting his movements.

He looks shell-shocked. Old. A flash of pity washes over me.

"Can you stay in the cab and wait for the ambulance?" I ask. I don't tell him he'll be a liability if he follows me up the stairs. "When it gets here, tell them the flat is on the fourth floor, on the second corner. I'll have the door open for them."

Simon hesitates and I take it as a submission. He stays seated.

"Don't let the cab leave without you, okay? I'll stay with Allegra and call you when we get to the hospital." I feel as if I'm talking to an elderly gent, but he's such a fish out of water here I'm scared he's an easy target. Even the cab driver seems jittery, and I hear the clunk of the car doors locking as soon as I walk away.

I'm nearly at the tower block when Simon winds the window down and shouts out. "You can't go up there alone."

I don't have time to quell his fears. I still have Allegra on the phone, her wailing replaced by a more ominous silence. There's no doubt she's my number one priority right now.

"Yes I can."

Making my way across the littered square and into the stairwell, my high heels bang against the hard concrete. Though I consider taking off my shoes to speed my ascent, the thought of broken glass makes me rethink. Instead, I put my weight on the balls of my feet, eschewing my heels altogether. I pull the hem of my dress down in order to look halfway decent.

It's fairly quiet when I get to the fourth floor. I make my way to Daisy's flat, all the while speaking softly down the phone. "I'm nearly there, sweetheart. Just another minute, okay? Keep breathing." By this point Allegra's unable to talk. The only sounds I hear are soft sobs and the occasional gasp. I want to hold her and tell her everything is okay. But it isn't; it hasn't been for a long time. We've let her down, every single one of us. Made this eight-year-old child grow up so quickly.

"I'm outside the door, can you open it?" Taking a deep mouthful of air, I steel myself for what's inside. There's a rattling, followed by the complaining creak of a hinge, and the door swings open. Allegra launches herself at me, her head slamming into my chest. Her loud wails cut through the silence and it takes me a minute to realise she's actually trying to say something. Chant it, really. I have to stoop down to make out the words.

"I'm sorry, I'm sorry, I'm sorry, I'm sorry." Like a litany, she says it over and over.

I stroke her hair, murmuring gentle words in an attempt to calm her. "It's okay, it's not your fault."

"It is, it's all my fault. I lied, I said he wasn't here. I told them she wasn't taking drugs. Please don't hate me."

"I don't hate you, I love you." I hug her close, trying to show how much I mean it. Allegra's cries become louder, almost hysterical. I bury my face in her hair. "I need to go inside and check on your mum. Do you want to wait out here?"

"Don't leave me." Her small hands make fists against my chest, clinging onto my dress as if she's trying to hold me back. For the first time I hesitate, torn between an unconscious woman and her distraught child. When I see Daisy's neighbour poking her moon-face around her door, I almost want to smile.

"Hey, can you come and help?" I look directly at her.

A flash of recognition passes over her face. She must remember me from our conversation a few months ago. The last time I found Daisy in her flat.

"What's up?" She leans on her door jamb and crosses her arms, looking down at Allegra. "Has that bastard hurt her again?"

"I don't know what's happened. All I know is Daisy's unconscious in there. Can you look after Allegra while I go inside?" When I say her name, Allegra clings on tighter. I have to unclasp her hands finger by finger. I go to move away and she starts to shake, her whole body wracked with shudders.

"Don't leave her. I'll go in and check. If that arsehole's in there I'll fucking cut him."

I don't know what it is about this woman, but I'm impressed by her. She's fierce, but if she has your back, you're golden. She doesn't wait for an answer, just pushes past us into Daisy's flat. The door swings behind her and Allegra grabs hold of me again, pressing her face against my shoulder as if she's avoiding looking inside.

We stand on the balcony, clinging onto each other, and listen to the faint wail of sirens in the distance. They're moving ever closer to the estate. In the moments that follow, bright blue lights flash as an ambulance speeds toward the building, flanked by two police cars. I'm not surprised to see the police are here; this place is too dangerous for the paramedics to come without backup. Only fools like me would make that kind of misjudgement.

* * *

The police make their way to the fourth floor. I notice they're armed, wearing thick bulletproof vests that remind me of a muscle suit. By this point Allegra has all but collapsed against me. I realise how heavy she is when I try to support all of her weight. Shock has strange effects on people, and with Allegra, it's sending her to sleep. As if it's the only way for her to maintain a semblance of sanity. I can empathise with that.

"Can you tell me what happened?" A policeman steps in front of me. He's an older guy, maybe in his early forties, with one of those faces you want to spill your secrets to. Open and honest.

I hug Allegra a little closer. "She found her mum unconscious on the floor. When she tried to wake her up there was no response. That's when she called me."

"She was alone?" His face says it all. The situation is appalling.

"Yes. It's just the two of them. She's only been back for a while. Was in care before that."

"So it's just her mum in there?"

"No. One of the neighbours has gone in to check on her. She's from four-ten." I point at the open door and he nods. It's interesting, the way he takes everything in. I get the impression he's noticing a lot more than he lets on. Perhaps he's weighing up the risks, assessing what the next steps should be. I just wish he would hurry up and get Daisy some help.

"Anything else I should know?"

"She has a boyfriend. He's a dealer." I can't bring myself to say his name. "He went away for a while but I've heard he's back. I don't know if he's involved but he isn't here at the moment."

It isn't even worth lowering my voice. Trying to shield Allegra from the cruelty of life is futile. She's seen everything, heard it all, and been knocked down by reality before she's even learned to stand.

When the paramedics are given the all-clear, they enter Daisy's flat, carrying bags and equipment, conferring with the policemen who accompany them inside. I'm immediately struck by the lack of action. There's no shouting, no running in and out. Such a difference from when I found Daisy beaten up on her bed. That time there was a lot of noise, loud attempts to stabilise her condition, before moving her down to the ambulance and rushing her to hospital.

This time, however, their silence seems ominous, almost unbearable. My heart drops when Daisy's neighbour finally emerges from the flat, her lips turned down and her eyes barely meeting mine. When I do catch her gaze, she shakes her head slowly and I know for sure what I've suspected all along.

Daisy's gone.

That's why they aren't hurrying or shouting, and that's why there's no frantic dash to the ambulance as a paramedic covers her mouth with an oxygen mask. There's no urgency when she's already left us. Time can run a little slower for the dead.

Instinctively, I pull Allegra closer. Then the kind-faced policeman walks out, his cap held in his gloved hands. There's a pale tinge to his face when he comes to a stop in front of us. "Can I have a word?"

I gesture helplessly at Allegra and his expression softens. He seems like the kind of guy who has his own kids. Knows exactly why I'm hesitant. "Maybe Dee can look after the little one?"

I must look confused because he points at Daisy's neighbour. It takes me a moment to realise she must have a name. *Dee.* So average and normal for somebody in such a messed-up situation. The banality of her name somehow makes everything feel worse, as though the world is off kilter. I try to shake the feeling off as I pass Allegra to her. She's barely aware anymore, her consciousness shut down like an overheated computer.

The policeman waits patiently. When I'm free he places his hand on my shoulder, leading me out of Allegra's earshot.

"Are you a relative?"

"Of Daisy's? No, we're friends. Or at least we were." I frown, recalling the last few weeks. "I work at a drug clinic where she's being treated."

Not anymore, the little voice in my head says. I feel myself choke up.

"Do you know of any relatives at all? Any who live nearby?" He's still softly spoken. Non-judgemental.

"She doesn't talk to her mum. Hasn't seen her for years…" I trail off, trying hard to think. "I don't remember her mentioning any other relations." I'm not including Darren. He's not a relative, he's a parasite.

"In that case I'm going to need your help." He looks over at Allegra. Dee is leading her into her flat next door. Her arm is wrapped protectively around her. "I'm so sorry to have to tell you that CPR hasn't worked. They tried to revive your friend for the last ten minutes, but there's no sign of life."

"You mean she's dead?" Even though I'm expecting this, I'm still taken aback. It's the thought of somebody larger than life just disappearing that gets to me. She seemed invincible.

Every time life beat her down she managed to rise up better than ever, like a messed-up phoenix. "Are you sure?"

"She's a-systolic." He says it as if it should mean something, and it does. Memories from nine years ago assail me—another night, another death. "The paramedics declared her dead a few minutes ago." He rubs my arm and it feels vaguely comforting.

"How... how did she...?" I break off. I can't even say the word. If I say it, I'll make it real.

How the hell is Allegra going to get over this?

"There are all the symptoms of a heroin overdose. We can't confirm it until after the post-mortem, but there doesn't appear to be any foul play."

Heroin? What an awful way to die. Horror and disgust wash over me, tinged with an edge of anger. Even if Darren didn't hurt her, and even if he wasn't the one doing the injecting, he's still the man responsible for her death.

Not that Daisy doesn't bear blame, too. But with her body lying on the floor of a run-down tower-block flat, I can hardly bring myself to think it. They're all victims here. Her daughter most of all.

"Darren Tebbit." I say his name with a low voice. "Her boyfriend is called Darren Tebbit. He hangs around the rec dealing to kids in the afternoons. Feel free to chop his dick off." I walk away, fury boiling in my veins because I have to go and break a little girl's heart.

28

When I see Niall's name flash across the screen of my phone, I have to bite my lips so I don't cry. Three simple words turn me inside out.

How's it going?

He's asking about my dinner with Simon.

My reply is just as brief—brutal, even—but I don't have the energy to sugar-coat things. Daisy's dead.

Allegra stirs in my arms, murmuring unintelligible words before she drifts back into unconsciousness. Her head rests against my chest, all tear-stained and red. Even in her sleep she sobs—tiny gasps that come every three breaths—and I stroke her hair, hoping somehow she knows I am here.

We're sitting on a beige faux-leather sofa in Dee's tiny flat. It's very clean and tidy in here. Even her cat seems well-trained and under control. When she gives me a mug of hot, sweet tea and strokes my forehead with her plump hand I try to reward her with a smile. It turns out twisted but she doesn't seem to mind. She may be taciturn, but she's a star. I don't know what we'd have done without her.

My phone vibrates and I know it's him. The thought somehow grounds me.

"Hi." I speak softly down the mouthpiece, trying not to disturb Allegra.

Niall doesn't seem to have received the memo, though. His voice is loud and thick with Irish. It makes me flinch. "What the hell happened? Are you okay, did you get hurt? Jesus, babe, I'm freaking out here."

"Hush, Allegra's asleep." There's some kind of irony going on here. I'm the calmer of the two of us. "Daisy overdosed and Allegra found her. She called me at the restaurant and I came right over. The police are here now and we're waiting for social services." I can tell him all this without getting emotional because they're just facts. If he asks me how I am, I know I'll end up wailing like a baby.

"Is Simon with you?"

"No. I told him to go home. There's nothing he can do here and he looked really uncomfortable." I don't tell him that Simon looked like an old man, shaking softly as he stared at the poverty surrounding him. He was shocked, that much I could tell. As if he couldn't believe a world like this could exist in the centre of London.

"Are you still at the Whitegate Estate?" He doesn't wait for an answer. "I'm on my way."

"It's okay. You don't need to come over. We're just waiting for the social worker to arrive." I don't tell him there's no way I'm letting them absorb Allegra back into the system. I'll fight them tooth and nail if I have to.

"I didn't ask for your permission. I'll see you in half an hour." He sounds pissed off but it warms me inside. I like that edge to him; the protective side that doesn't take no for an answer. It's the reason he waited for hours in the rain while I sat in a police station. He wants to take care of me. I can live with that.

As long as he lets me take care of him, too. Equals in everything.

Allegra and I are still sitting in the same position when Niall arrives about thirty minutes later. Dee has turned on the TV and some inane late-night detective show is flickering across the screen. Allegra is still out for the count, her dark hair tangled across her face. If it wasn't for the fact there's a whole phalanx of police outside, I'd steal her away before the social worker gets here. I want to tuck her up in bed and hold her until morning.

I hear his voice before I see him. It's distinctive—deep and slightly gravelled, his accent adding a cadence you don't find in a native Londoner. Having him close feels as if somebody has placed a warm blanket across my shoulders. He's there, standing in the doorway, his hair messy and wet as if he's just stepped out of the shower.

"How is she?" When he comes closer I can smell the clean scent of his soap and the soft fragrance of his shampoo. He reaches out to stroke Allegra's matted hair, his expression full of compassion. "Poor kid."

"She's been out for a while. It all got too much. The shock, her mum..."

He sits down beside us, lifting her legs onto his lap. The gesture makes me want to cry. Instead I look at him and he stares right back and it feels as if he can see right inside my soul.

"I want to take the two of you home and board up the door. Not let anybody inside." When he strokes my cheek I have to close my eyes for fear I'm going to lose it.

"I think we might like that. At least for a while."

He reaches out to squeeze my hand, and a single tear escapes from the corner of my eye, trailing down my cheek. I wipe it away almost angrily. I want to be strong. For Allegra. For me. But Niall's having none of it.

"It's okay." He brushes my cheek. "You can cry, she won't notice. Even if she wakes it doesn't matter. You should cry, it's worth crying about."

The need to sob thickens my voice. "If I start I don't think I can stop." I can't be the one to break down. When Digby died I barely surfaced for months. This time, though, Allegra needs me. Desperately. There's no way I can wallow in useless self-pity.

"You know, my ma has all these stupid sayings and I can't even come up with one right now. But I do know that crying isn't weak. There's a strength in showing your emotions. In taking control and letting them out. So don't hold back on my account."

My bottom lip starts to tremble. I try to still it with my teeth, but all that does is make my eyes water harder. I go to wipe them with my hand, but he holds on, not letting me pull away. When the tears start to fall he shuffles closer. Allegra's prone body lies across us both, and he curls his arm around me. My head rests on his shoulder, and he strokes my hair when I start to sob. I cry for Daisy, for the futile pain of her death. I cry for Allegra, Niall holding me until I'm all out of tears.

Even then my shoulders shake with dry sobs.

* * *

We're still huddled together when the duty social worker arrives. I don't recognise this one, and from her relative youth and maximum unease I get the sense she's newly qualified. In this case it's a bad thing, because she's trying to stick too tightly to the rules.

"I need to take her to the group home and we can assess the case in the morning," she says when I ask if I can take Allegra home with me. "I can't allow you to bring her to an unknown house. It's against our guidelines."

"Would you say the same if Beth was her aunt?" Niall asks. "This kid has just seen her mother die in front of her eyes and you want to take her away from the one person she knows? What kind of fucked-up guidelines are these anyway?" He can be scary when he's angry. The social worker cowers away. I reach out to calm him.

"I'm CRB checked and known to social services. I'm even known to the staff at the home. Can't you let me take her home for one night?"

She shakes her head and I hear Niall mutter, "Fucking jobsworth." In another minute I think he might actually explode. I'm so much calmer than him, icy even, because I'm absolutely certain I'm not going to let them separate Allegra from me. Even if I have to handcuff the two of us together, the only person she's going to be waking up to is me.

"I'll go with her to the home." I don't pose it as a question. "If it will help you sleep tonight I'll stay there and in the morning we can talk custody. But I'm not leaving her tonight."

The social worker flails a little, but then nods her head, relieved not to have to fight anymore. Niall bristles next to me, staring at her with a sullen expression. I want to stay here, in our little bubble of three because no matter how tortured and painful Allegra's sleep is, it's nothing compared to the pain she'll face when she wakes up.

When she remembers her mum is dead.

In the end we get to the group home just after three in the morning. The night worker shuffles to the front door, opening it to reveal her Winnie the Pooh onesie tight against her body. Yawning, she shows us to an empty room. Niall walks in behind us, carrying Allegra in his arms, a tender expression on his face. He lays her down on the made-up single bed and pulls me into an embrace.

"Call me in the morning, okay? Let me know how she's doing." On the way over here we made hushed plans in the back seat, and agreed that I'd take the lead. Trying to present ourselves as some kind of viable couple when we've only just reconnected would be crazy.

Not to mention the fact I'm still married.

"I will." My voice wobbles. No matter how determined I am, the future seems daunting. He cups my face with warm hands. I'm barely breathing when he brushes his lips against mine. I cling to the back of his shirt for a moment too long because I'm so scared this may be the last time we are together.

"If you need me I'll be here. Remember that." Another peck and he pulls away.

When he walks out of the door, the only thing stopping me from running after him is Allegra. Her tiny body is curled up on the bed, her *One Direction* t-shirt twisted around her waist. She sleeps fitfully, her body occasionally shuddering at some invisible monster haunting her dreams. I walk over to the ramshackle armchair in the corner of the room and pull it toward her bed as if I'm visiting her in hospital. Though it's late at night there's no possibility of me falling asleep. There's so much to think about.

This morning I was a woman on the way to divorce, trying to juggle a burgeoning relationship with a desperately fading one. Living in a single bedroom in an insalubrious part of town. But now... now everything changes. It's as if the world is twisting on its axis, shifting to the left until all I can do is cling on with weak fingernails, my legs flailing behind me as I try to find a footing.

As for Niall, I don't even know where he fits in to all this. It was complicated enough as it was, with our shared history and our rocky start. That's nothing compared to this new addition. I don't even know how he feels about kids, let alone whether he would want to be involved in Allegra's life. It's not the sort of conversation I considered having with him in between kisses and dry humps.

As Alex would say, "Shit's just got serious."

There's another problem, though. Even if I could work out how Niall and Allegra fit into my life, there's the small matter of somewhere to live. There's no way I'll ever be allowed custody if I'm living in a shared house. I don't even have a bedroom to put her in. On my limited wage I can hardly afford to live in a bedsit, let alone a two-bedroom flat.

Which brings me to Simon. I know he's the obvious solution here. He's offered to buy me a flat and I've turned him down. I don't want his money, I want to be able to move on without it, but that doesn't help with the current housing situation.

I rub my face with the heels of my hands, as if the answers to all my problems are in there somewhere. I press them against my eyes so hard I can see tiny stars swirling in the darkness, but no miraculous solution appears.

Daylight sneaks through the curtains like a naughty child, stealing its way across the pale green carpet until sunlight washes across Allegra's face. Her mouth twitches and she moans a little, rolling over to escape the brightness. Her body has reacted a moment too late, because the morning has chased away the comfort of sleep, leaving her blinking and confused as she slowly sits up. She frowns when she sees me sitting next to her.

Her lip wobbles and her breathing turns ragged as realisation dawns. Memories return like a cruel dagger, and if I live to be a hundred I never want to see such pain in her face again. It hits me in the chest, hard enough for me to gasp, and as soon as she starts to cry, I feel my own tears well up.

"My mum..."

I shake my head. "I'm so sorry." When I reach out for her she snatches her arm away, hands tightening into fists. She looks angry, as if I'm the one responsible.

"No! She isn't dead. She's just poorly, like last time. She told me you'd take me away from her. She said I should stay away from you."

I can't lie, the rejection hurts. It's natural, though, and I can't blame her. Instead I let my hand rest on the side of the bed, ready for her if she needs it.

"She didn't make it," I whisper. My voice sounds hoarse with emotion. "They tried to save her, they really did, but it was too late. She'd already gone."

Allegra opens her mouth as if she's going to talk but no words come out. Then I realise she isn't speaking at all. She's silently screaming. It's all I can do not to join in. I ache to hold her, to comfort her, but I can't, not until she's ready, and it's killing me to wait. She starts to rock back and forth, wrapping her arms around her waist, her breathing still stilted and harsh.

And still I wait, because that's the only thing I can do.

It takes five minutes for her to calm down enough to speak, though it feels so much longer. She turns to me with wide eyes and asks, "Where will I go?"

How terrible not to know where you belong. I understand that feeling all too well. I tried to escape it by getting married, but even then it haunted me.

"You can come with me, if you'll have me. It might take a few days, and you'll have to stay here and be very brave, but I promise you I'll sort things out as quickly as I can.

She inches a little closer to me. Her movement's barely perceptible but it's *there*.

"I have to find us somewhere to live, and I need to talk with your social worker about some grown-up stuff." I lean closer, hoping she can feel how serious I am. "But I'm going to sort things out as fast as I can, because I want you with me."

Her bottom lip trembles. "But Mum said I shouldn't talk to you."

Oh God, how to discuss this without shadowing her memory of Daisy? "I think... I think she'd want you to be with me. I know she was angry with me, but we would have made up. Like when you have a spat with your friends. Eventually you get over it, right?"

Allegra nods slowly.

"Well it was a bit like that. We argued about something stupid, but I still loved her. And you. We just had a difference of opinion."

"What did you argue about?" Her voice is quiet, almost contemplative.

"About Darren." I try to keep it as basic as possible. "I don't like him very much but I upset your mum when I told her."

She's silent. I watch as she picks at the bobbles in her blanket, pulling off fibres and letting them fall gently onto the sheet. When she looks up at me, there's something resembling understanding in her eyes.

"I don't like him very much either." She whispers it, as if he's close enough to hear. There's so much to deal with, not only her mum's death, but the way Darren treated her. It's going to take more than a few weeks to mend her broken heart.

29

When Niall arrives later that afternoon I all but throw myself into his arms. Unlike me, he's showered and dressed and is wearing a button-down shirt and navy trousers. He's kind enough to ignore my dishevelled state. He holds me tightly, kissing my face with soft lips. I sort of melt into him, trying to absorb him by osmosis. I want his strength, his determination. In return I give him my paralysing fear.

"They won't let me take her." Three hours of meetings and about a hundred forms later, they told me it could take weeks for any application to go through. "Until I have a stable home they're keeping her here."

He tilts his head. Though his expression is sympathetic it isn't shocked. I guess I got my hopes up and thought being on the inside would help me. All it did was land me with a hot cup of disappointment.

"We should get a lawyer," he says. My eyebrows rise up when I hear him say "we". "Do you know any good ones?"

For the first time in days I feel the urge to laugh, because I know a whole bloody chamber full of them, not that it's any good to me now. "Apart from Simon?"

Niall stares at me for a minute. His next sentence is completely unexpected. "You should call him."

One minute he's kissing me, the next he's telling me to call my husband. I don't know what to make of it.

"Really?"

"What? You think I'm gonna get all macho and ban you from seeing him?" His lips twitch as if he's trying to suppress a laugh. "That's not me, you know that."

Running his fingers through my ratty hair, he smooths it away from my face. I can't stop staring at him. Does he know how right he makes me feel? Like I'm not that ditzy girl who broke down for years after Digby's death. He looks at me as if I'm strong. Capable of anything.

"I love you." I say it because I can't think of anything else. Because it feels as though my chest will explode if I keep it in any longer.

This time he has the good grace to look surprised. "Because I told you to call your ex?"

"Because you're you. I wanted to tell you before, when we were at your studio but..."

He starts to laugh. "You had your mouth full at the time?"

I hit him on the arm but the grin doesn't slide from his lips. So I lean forward to kiss it away, brushing my mouth against his. He kisses me back and I feel the curve of his lips as his smile widens.

"I love you, too. So fucking much. And that's why we're going to sort this out. You, me and a whole army of ex-husbands. Whatever it takes."

When I call Simon the first thing he does is offer me his house. Of course I decline, telling him I couldn't afford to run it. The truth is I can't even picture us there. It's Simon's house and always will be.

He sounds relieved when I say no, then starts telling me about a friend of a friend who has a tiny cottage to rent in Brighton. For a minute I think he's making inane conversation and I feel myself start to bristle. Only then do I realise he's offering it to me.

"Brighton?" I sound sceptical. "You think I should move there?"

Niall looks from his phone, his expression unreadable. His eyes stay on me as I listen to Simon.

"It's just an option," Simon continues. "The cost of living is cheaper than London and children love the sea."

For a minute I can picture Allegra on the pebbled beach, wind lifting her hair and pinking her cheeks. In my imagination she looks happy and that makes me start to wonder.

"Brighton..." I say again. Niall smiles and looks back down at his phone. "What's the rent like?"

We talk for a while longer. Simon promises to email some more details of the cottage, and then tells me he's going to speak with the family law section to find out what I can do. He doesn't mention last night, or his pleas for me to return.

Maybe he really has accepted it this time.

When we say goodbye I feel almost hopeful, enough to smile at Niall when he stands up and walks toward me.

"What's that for?"

"What?"

"That smile?"

"You mean this one?" I bare my teeth at him, grinning like a loon. "I'm smiling because you're lovely. And not at all macho."

He looks affronted, though I think it's a ruse. "I'm macho." When he pulls me into his arms and lifts me off my feet I start to giggle. "And later, when you're ready, I'll show you just how macho I can be."

* * *

Later that evening I'm standing in Niall's shower, letting the powerful spray wash away the stress of the day. It took some persuasion to take me away from the home, but the support workers promised I could come back after dinner and spend the night with Allegra again.

After I rinse the conditioner from my hair, I step out and wrap a towel around my body, shivering slightly in spite of the summer heat. It's not the first time I've been in Niall's bedroom, but it's the first time I've been in here alone. I can't help but be a little bit nosy as I wander around his space.

Glancing in his wardrobe, I see he's just as messy at home as he is in his car. The floor is covered with a myriad of different trainers and shoes. A couple of t-shirts lie on top of them, having fallen from their hangers. The disorder isn't limited to his clothes, however. The rest of his room is filled with canvasses and paints, propped against walls and stacked in corners. I have to give it to him: he's managed to use every available space.

On the dresser next to his wardrobe is a photograph of his family. His arm is slung around his mum. Next to him are two men that look so alike they must be his brothers. They share the same inky-black hair and piercing blue eyes. I remember from our first time together that they are younger than him, but for the life of me I can't remember their names.

There's still so much to learn.

Sitting down on the edge of his mattress, I use a second towel to dry my hair. At some point he's taken his watch off and has laid it on his bedside table, and I lean over to check the time.

That's when I feel the urge to look in his drawers. I'm not sure what I'm expecting to see, other than a lot of boxer shorts and socks, but it takes everything I have not to pull at the handle, even though my fingers are lingering there.

"What are you doing?" Niall walks in, holding a spatula in his hand. He looks amused rather than affronted, grinning as he stares at my guilty expression.

"Nothing." Quickly, I pull my hand back. "Just drying my hair."

"Did you need my boxers to help you do that?"

"I wasn't looking in there," I say. "I was just… resting for a little while." What a stupid explanation. But it's true, I haven't looked at his pants.

Yet.

"What did you expect to see?" His voice softens as he steps toward me, placing the spatula next to his family photo, on his chest of drawers.

My eyes widen. "I don't know. Pants, socks… condoms." I start to babble, trying to think what the hell men actually keep in their bedside drawers. Mine is always stuffed full of books and chocolate, but Niall doesn't need to know that.

"Condoms?" His voice is as amused as his expression. My throat goes dry as he comes to a stop in front of me. His height makes me feel tiny in comparison, and I shiver again, but this time not because of the cold.

"And pants," I say.

"You've got a strange obsession with my pants and condoms." He drops to his knees in front of me, wiping my wet hair out of my face. "Should we investigate this further?"

I swallow hard, but my throat remains parched. When he's this close I find it hard to think. The sensation of his rough hand against my cheek makes me sigh.

My skin is still damp from the shower when he runs a finger down my neck, trailing it across my chest. He unhooks my towel with a flick, so it falls open, crumpling onto the bed.

His eyes are dark and narrow as he looks at me. I reach out to him, running my fingers through his hair. Then his lips are on mine, hard and frantic, moving desperately as we kiss.

"Is this okay?" He pushes me back onto the bed, and my wet hair fans out behind me.

"Yes."

He drags his lips across my throat. "I know you've had a hard day."

"I have." I'm still answering in monosyllables. It's hard to think of anything except the way he feels, how good he smells. Then his hands are cupping my breasts, fingers brushing against my nipples, and any sentient thought is chased away.

His lips capture one of my nipples, his teeth pulling softly at my aroused skin. It's all I can do not to rub myself against him.

All I can do to breathe.

"We could make it a bit harder," he murmurs into my chest. Then shows me what he means, pressing his erection against my thigh, and I push back, desperate to feel him, needing to give as good as I get.

We're a mess of wet towels and dry clothes. My fingers shake as I unbutton his shirt and pull down the zipper on his jeans. A minute later we're both naked and needy, our skin hot, our breaths fast. I marvel at how he feels as good as I remember.

Sinewy and smooth, all hard muscles and soft skin. I can feel the definition of his chest as he presses it against mine, and the tautness of his stomach as I run my hand down it. When I wrap my fingers around him, it's his turn to sigh, and he closes his eyes, his mouth falling open as I start to move my hand up and down. His hips move to the rhythm I've created, undulating softly as I drag my palm over him.

I'm so consumed that the sensation of his finger dragging against me is a shock. I open my eyes to see him staring right at me as he caresses softly, gently. Enough to make me moan.

"Is this okay?" he asks again.

"Yes, yes." I can barely keep a breath. Looking down I see his hand pressing against me, his tanned skin a contrast to my pink flesh. I watch the tendons and knuckles flex and contract, and I feel the sensation shoot straight through me, my toes curling every time he passes over my clit.

Then he's on top of me, body sliding on top of mine. We are wet and hard and nothing but sensation. My head falls back on the bed as I rock my hips up, and he's a moment away from slipping inside.

It feels so different yet it feels like home. Because we have changed, Niall and I, and yet we've come full circle, back together. When he thrusts against me, his tip touching my aching flesh, I have to bite down on his neck to stop myself from screaming out.

"God," he sighs, squeezing his eyes closed. "Oh God."

"Please." I don't even recognise the voice as mine. It's needy. Desperate.

"Beth, I just…"

"What?" My breath is coming fast. I can feel my muscles contract even though he's not inside yet. I rock again and the way he slides against my hot flesh almost makes me come.

"Condom. Top drawer." He barks it out. There's a look of concentration on his face, and his whole body tenses against mine.

Though it takes a minute to locate the condom and roll it on, I'm still trembling when he finally lines up with me. I can feel his pressure, hot and thick. My thighs wrap around his hips, afraid to let him go.

Before he's even inside I'm on the cusp, my breath captive in my throat as he slips easily through my slick flesh. Then he's filling me, surging into me in the most delicious way. I start to tighten against him, my whole body stiffening, waiting… waiting for that moment to explode.

I let out a whimper as the pleasure takes over, flames licking at me from the inside out. I'm pulsing and crying and scraping my nails against his flesh as Niall lets out a low-pitched growl.

And it's his turn to freeze, as he pushes inside me one last time, breath catching in his throat. I cradle him in my arms, and he presses his whole weight against me, kissing me with soft, desperate lips.

"Beth…"

He buries his face against my shoulder, breathing rapidly. I can feel his heart hammering in his chest as it pushes into mine.

"Is that what you were looking for?"

I close my eyes and let the smile pull at my lips. He kisses me one more time and I nod.

"I think it was."

30

It takes three days for a case conference to be arranged. Three days that I spend at the group home, sitting with Allegra, holding her when she cries, teasing her when she's ready to smile. I take my cues from hers, watching her expression with a wary eye. Waiting to see what she'll do next.

We meet outside the social services building: Lara, me and the family lawyer that Simon has recommended. Rafiya—the lawyer—advised that it would be better if Niall wasn't present for the first meeting. She's ruthlessly efficient, and explains she doesn't want to complicate matters with explanations of my love life.

We're called into a meeting room just after eleven. I sit in another hard, plastic chair, my hand firmly folded in Lara's, and listen to the discussions as if I'm not really involved. Rafiya goes through a list of events that show I'm part of Allegra's support network—the classes, the trips out, my involvement with Daisy. She explains about the move to Brighton, telling them why a new start would be so much better in the long term. And I marvel that all these people who don't know Allegra or me get to make decisions about the rest of our lives.

This isn't the only time we'll be subject to this kind of scrutiny. In time, I plan to adopt her, and the rigorous investigations that it will require make this look like a walk in the park. I've already had to listen to Rafiya explaining all the pitfalls, and now I'm being lectured all over again.

This is right, I tell myself. We're talking about a child's future here. No amount of scrutiny could be too great.

"It's very important that Allegra receive counselling." Grace addresses me directly, ignoring Rafiya altogether. "Have you investigated provision in Brighton?"

My lips twitch because Grace knows I have. We had an hour-long telephone discussion about it last night. I wanted to make sure I'd covered every base.

"Yes, I spoke to a child counsellor this week. We've made a provisional appointment to see if a relationship can be built. I've also spoken to the local school and explained the situation. They've confirmed there's a place available for Allegra."

Lara squeezes my hand and I manage to breathe a little easier.

The meeting continues with talk of my suitability as a foster carer. Rafiya presents them with a report from my doctor and three testimonials from friends. The room is quiet as everybody thumbs through the documents, and I find myself scrutinising their expressions, trying to see if I'm standing a chance. When Grace catches my eye she gives me the smallest smile. Even though we've had our differences we both want what's best for Allegra. I can live with that.

Toward the end of the meeting I'm asked if I want to add anything. I clear my throat, shuffling through my papers to find the statement that Rafiya helped me to prepare. But then I have second thoughts, knowing how cold and clinical reading words out loud would make me sound. Instead I look around the room, catching the eye of everybody sitting opposite me.

I want to be heard.

"I know we're all here for the same reason: because a little girl has lost her mother. The mother she saw die in front of her eyes. I understand you have to make sure that wherever she goes she will be cared for. I don't want to leave any of you in doubt about my feelings for Allegra. I love her. It's that pure and simple. You may want to tell me that love isn't enough, and I couldn't agree more. In the clinic where I work we see children who suffer every day, regardless of how much their parents love them. So I can also promise I'll dedicate myself to bringing her up well, to providing her with a stable home. One where she doesn't have to wonder whether she'll get any dinner that night. One where she can feel safe enough to feel sad, feel happy, feel whatever she needs to. Where she can push the boundaries and be pulled back from them." I take a deep breath, trying to loosen the tightness in my chest. "I want to give her back the right to be a child again."

When I look at Lara she's beaming at me, even though her eyes are glistening. There's silence in the room, and I wait for a response, looking down at the speech I never made. Finally, somebody clears their throat. Grace smiles softly and looks at the rest of the panel.

"Do you have any more questions?"

There are murmurings of no, accompanied by the frantic shaking of heads. I breathe a sigh of relief. It has to be good news, I hope, if they don't want to question me further.

"Very well, we shall end it there. I believe you're having a visit from Brighton and Hove children's services tomorrow?"

"That's correct." Rafiya answers for me. Perhaps she's decided I've talked too much.

"Barring any issues arising from that, I can confirm we will be supporting the application for kinship foster placement."

It takes a moment for it to sink in. Then I realise all eyes are on me, and I glance up to see five expectant faces. But relief turns me mute; I'm unable to say anything that approaches coherence. Instead I nod and concentrate on trying not to cry.

Allegra's coming home with me. To *our home*, where I can take care of her and watch her grow. A place where we can go to the beach and breathe in the fresh air and pretend we can see

France. Somewhere that Darren Tebbit and guys like him can't touch her.

She's coming home.

The next few minutes are a blur. Rafiya talks in hushed tones with Grace, while Lara hugs me and tells me how proud she is. I nod in the right places, holding her close as I try not to get hysterical. When we leave the office Rafiya shakes my hand, explaining she'll be sending over some paperwork before the visit to Brighton tomorrow. Then she's gone and it's just me and Lara, two giddy women unable to complete a sentence.

"Oh my God, I'm so happy…"

"Thank you so much for being here. I couldn't have done it…"

We both laugh and try to calm down. Lara takes a deep breath and starts again. "I can't believe we're both going to be mums." I glance down at her stomach and see the small bump rising softly from her belly. "And I can't believe you're leaving me. Brighton is so far away."

"It's an hour by train," I say. "You can come and visit as much as you like." I try not to show it, but that thought is the only disappointment. I'm so used to seeing Lara every day at the clinic, even if it's only a few minutes, and now our interactions will be by telephone and email. "I promise I'll be there for the birth."

"You'd better be. Alex is scared by the sight of blood. I'm half expecting him to run out screaming when the first contraction starts."

I laugh at the image this conjures up. Alex always seems so cocky and in control. Maybe the baby will soften him a little. "I'll be there."

We walk out of the building and a fine mist of rain covers our hair, leaving water clinging to the strands like dew on a cobweb. Lara hugs me for a final time and heads for the Tube, while I lean against the wall and pull my phone out. I need to call Niall, to let him know how it went, before I head back to the home to spend time with Allegra.

A movement to my left catches my eye, making me look up. That's when I see him. Dark hair turned black by the rain, pasted to his forehead. Droplets run down his cheeks, falling onto his shoulders. Even though he's soaking I run into his arms, letting him hold me as I tell him everything that's happened. Niall's hands tighten around my waist as I tell him she should be coming home in a couple of days.

He presses his face to my hair and breathes in. "You still smell of rain."

I smile as his words conjure up memories: our first kiss in the rain—drug fuelled, sweet and full of need. Though we are older now—and sober—that need still claws at me, demanding to be fed. So I slowly raise my face until my lips are millimetres away from his. "Do I taste of rain, too?"

His smile is devastating. He drops his head to lightly kiss me, and it feels as though the sun has blasted away the clouds. Because that's what he does to me. So I kiss him back, tongue sliding softly against his lips, my fists clutching the back of his jacket as if he's some kind of life raft.

I marvel that once we were so destructive it took me years to get over the cataclysmic results. Yet here we are, holding each other as if we're in a normal, functional relationship. Regardless of my separation and his unpredictable career and the fact I'm about to foster a child, somehow, for the first time, I actually feel grounded.

He breaks away, his face flushed and glistening with rain. When he pushes my wet hair off my face, his fingers are soft. Little more than a caress. Then he steps back, running his hands through his own soaked hair and says, "Let's go see our girl."

Nine Months Later

The tide is slowly creeping in, the water sneaking farther up the beach with every wave. It's cautious at first, flowing gently as if it's trying the new bit of sand out, before running back to join the rest of the sea. Allegra hops the wave as it breaks, letting it chase her up the beach, hair flying behind her as she runs. Any sound she makes is stolen by the springtime breeze, but I can tell by the shapes she forms with her mouth that she's laughing. It warms me to see her so carefree.

Picking up my thermal cup, I swallow the last of my coffee, before turning my attention to the papers resting on my knee. I have my first lot of exams next week. I'm so scared of failing them that I'm taking every chance I can to revise. Though the degree is only part time, it's a full-time job trying to fit studying in around my work at a local drop-in centre and looking after Allegra. At this rate it's going to take me six years to pick up the letters after my name. I don't mind. I'm just enjoying the learning.

"Can we get a dog?" She's breathless when she flops down beside me on the blanket. "A really big one, with loads of fur."

"No." I reach out and ruffle her hair. I'm getting better at saying the 'n' word. At first, after Daisy's death, I couldn't bring myself to deny Allegra anything. It's taken us nine months to get here; to the sort of relationship where I can refuse her and she doesn't cry. We're still a work-in-progress.

"A cat?" She doesn't give up.

"Maybe a rabbit or a guinea pig," I concede. "Something low maintenance."

"A hamster!" Her eyes light up. "Rebecca Grant has one of those and it's so cute. It does keep her up all night, though."

I smile and offer her a bottle of water. We'll work it out. Maybe take a trip to *Pets at Home* to see what the different animals are like. One step at a time, I remind myself. A year ago I was in a childless marriage. Now I'm a mum to a nine-year-old girl. I'm not perfect, but I'm trying my best. We both are.

"Can Rebecca come over to play after school next week?"

"Sure, I'll give her mum a call." I mentally flip through my calendar, another thing I've learned to do since fostering Allegra. We have to plan out our schedules with military precision. Between dance clubs and play dates, plus school, college and work we live a pretty busy life. I'm about to ask her what day she wants to do it on when my phone rings.

"It's Lara," I say, glancing at the screen. As I answer, Allegra runs off to collect more shells for her pile at home. She knows Lara and I talk for ages on the phone. Now that we're both mums—of sorts—it's nice to have that support network there.

"Hey," I say into the phone. "Is Max asleep?"

"I just put him down. I figure we have half an hour before he starts to squawk." Lara sounds exhausted, just like any parent of a three-month-old baby. "How're things in sunny Brighton?"

"Not sunny." I look up. "The sky's full of grey clouds."

"It's lovely here. The sun's out, the sky's blue and everybody's in bikinis. You should definitely move back to London."

I laugh at her blatant lie. Every time we talk she tries to persuade me. Whether it's the free museums, great restaurants or beautiful weather, she uses any excuse to encourage us to move back. There's a part of me that misses the hustle of the city, the excitement that seems laced in the air. But this move has been the best thing for Allegra. Better schools, open spaces and still only a short train journey from the big city.

"Or you could move down here," I counter.

She laughs. "Imagine Alex's face, he'd throw a fit."

"How is Alex?" I haven't seen him since he came to visit for the day with Lara and Max a couple of months ago. I bite down a smile as I remember him telling me that their sofa was big enough for me and Allegra. If we ever wanted to move back with them.

"Busy. There are a few managers sniffing around the band. He seems to think he's Mick bloody Jagger." I don't like the way her voice trembles. I get the impression there's more to it, but I'm not sure what to do. Maybe a trip to London is in order.

"He's always been a show-off."

"You're not wrong there." Her laugh is short, then she changes the subject. "Have you heard from Niall?"

"Pretty much every day." He's been in the US for the last three months, putting on an exhibition. It isn't only his constant texts and messages that make me smile—although they do—but the fact he sends Allegra postcards every few days. Blank ones that he draws zany pictures on. She's pinned them all up on her wall as a shrine to Niall Joseph, making me smile every time I walk into her room. "He's coming home next Thursday."

There's no need to tell her I can't wait. We've been taking things slowly, Niall and me. He still has his flat in London, but has been spending weekends with us in Brighton, getting to know Allegra. It may not have been the ideal way to start a relationship, but we've muddled through as best we can.

And when I watch him painting with her, seeing his kind patience as he talks softly and makes her giggle, I can't help but fall in love with him all over again.

"Has there been any news on the adoption?"

"The wheels are slowly turning." I'm momentarily distracted as I watch Allegra run too close to the sea. She screams and runs away again, the bottom of her jeans stained dark blue by the water. She waves at me and I wave back, my grin matching hers. "Rafiya says a few more months and we'll be there. I can't wait." I want that piece of paper, the one that says Allegra's mine. Until then I'll still be a little edgy.

"That's great. We'll have to start planning that party. Any excuse for a knees-up." I can hear the smile in her voice. "What are you guys doing this weekend?"

"We're off to Essex tomorrow to visit my parents for lunch." Another side effect of my fostering Allegra; a rapprochement of sorts with my mum and dad. They've fallen in love with her, seized the opportunity to be grandparents as if it's their only chance. "We're at the beach now. Allegra's chasing the waves."

"That sounds perfect."

"I forgot to tell you, I saw Simon last week. He drove down to Brighton for the day." I smile when I remember his visit. We had a few last things to hash out, but decided to take the paperwork to the beach. He drank tea from a thermos flask and we ate sandwiches wrapped in foil. He looked a bit out of place but I think he enjoyed it.

"Really? How is he?" Though Lara was never that close to Simon, she knows he's always been kind to me.

"He seems pretty good. He's bought a weekend place in Scotland, some kind of hunting lodge or something. Oh, and he's got a girlfriend." Saying the word makes me smile. Simon seems a little too staid to have a girlfriend, but that's what he called her. Apparently she runs the estate agency that managed his purchase, which explains why he's visiting Scotland nearly every weekend. He seems happy, content, and there's a light in his eyes I haven't seen for a while. That fact alone makes me like this new development very much.

"A girlfriend? Wow. I didn't expect that." I hear shuffling in the background, as if she's walking into another room. "I'd better go. Max is waking up. I'll call you back tonight."

"Okay, speak soon." I hang up and put my phone down. Most of our calls end this way. Either Max wakes up or Allegra needs help with something. We rarely get to say goodbye.

* * *

An hour later, the beach is getting busier with couples out for their afternoon walk, their dogs bounding across the pebbles, chasing waves and sticks. A group of teenagers pull open cans of drink and play music on their phones.

It's probably time to go home. I stand up to walk over to Allegra, but my legs refuse to move.

He's here.

He walks up the beach, sunglasses covering his beautiful, bright blue eyes. The seaside breeze wafts at his hair, pushing it back from his face. I want to run over and tear the glasses from him, to look deep inside and see what he's feeling. But I'm anchored to the spot.

Niall smiles as he approaches. I don't know if his gaze is on me or not, but mine doesn't waver.

"Hi." He comes to a stop a few feet away, and stuffs his hands into his pockets, rocking awkwardly back and forth. "I hope you don't mind, I thought I might find you here."

Mind? Is he crazy? A huge grin splits my mouth and I launch myself at him, hurling myself into his arms. He catches me, laughing, and the next moment his lips are on mine. I don't care that we're on the beach, or that everybody can see us, I just want to kiss him.

When we finally pull back, both of us breathless, there's still a smile on his face.

"How come you're back so early?"

"We finished up yesterday so I changed my ticket. They had me on standby. I didn't tell you in case it fell through." He pushes his hair out of his eyes and I notice how long it's grown. His jaw is dark with stubble, as though he hasn't shaved in a while. He looks like the artist he is.

"So, I have some news," I say.

He tips his head to the side, scrutinising me through narrowed eyes. "What kind of news?"

"My divorce came through."

In the end we agreed that Simon would file on the grounds of my adultery. It was either that or wait for two years, something neither of us wanted to do. A clean break was best for all of us—and less confusing for Allegra. Now Simon's found somebody else, hopefully it's good for him, too.

"Really?" Niall pulls me against him again and we both start to laugh. "I can't believe it, I thought it would take longer." His enthusiasm is infective and warming inside. "We should do something to celebrate. Champagne or something."

I look over at Allegra, who's staring out at the sea. She hasn't noticed him yet. If she had, he'd know about it.

"Allegra wants to buy a hamster."

"The perfect way to celebrate," he says. "Champagne, balloons and a hamster. All the Hollywood stars are doing it."

We grin at each other for a moment. The laughter lines around his eyes look deep and well used. I like that a lot.

He takes my face between his hands, his palms warm against my cheeks. It's as if he's going to kiss me, and I feel my breath catch in my throat. Instead, he leans forward until his forehead touches mine, and I'm staring into ocean-blue eyes.

It's more intimate than a kiss. More baring. Because he's staring at me as if he's searching for something, and I'm desperate for him to find it.

"Does that mean we can talk about us? Our future?"

I throw my arms around his neck and pull him close. We've held back from any big discussions, at least while Allegra was adjusting to all the changes. But now I'm no longer married to Simon, I know it's time to talk about us.

From the corner of my eye I spot Allegra watching the two of us with her back to the sea and her hands on her hips. Then she starts running, her hair flying out behind her, her skirt whipping around her knees. By the time she's made it across the pebbles she's out of breath, her cheeks pink from the wind and exertion. Like me, she runs at Niall, and he's holding his arms open ready to catch her.

I burn inside when I see him grab hold of her, burying his face in her hair as she clings to him.

"You're back, you're back!" She starts to babble. "You said you wouldn't be back 'til next week. I've got so much to tell you. I've got a new best friend and I'm going to be in a dance recital and I'm going to get a rabbit."

"A hamster," I correct her, my voice deadpan.

"And we're having fish and chips tonight and eating them on the sofa while we watch *Britain's Got Talent*. Beth says we can split a portion between us and we still won't manage it all." She pulls back from him and frowns. "I suppose we'll have to buy two now."

"It's okay, I'll buy them." He sounds very serious, and I love that. "Shall I get cakes as well, or is that too much?"

She looks up again and I shrug. Another thing the therapist said. Let her make some decisions. Give her a sense of security, make her feel she is in charge of her own life.

Within reason. Always within reason.

"Um, okay. I guess cakes will be nice."

"That's grand. I'll go out at six for cakes and chips all ready to get my ears blasted off." He looks up and smiles at me. "Is that okay with you?"

"It sounds perfect," I reply.

"Wait a minute," Allegra says. "How did you know we were on the beach? How did you manage to find us?"

He reaches forward and gently pushes her hair away from her eyes. She doesn't flinch. In fact his touch makes her smile. "I'll always find you, beautiful. If I have to knock on every single door in town I promise I'll find you. For as long as you want to be found."

His words are better than a thousand I-love-yous, as sweet as a hundred kisses. Allegra steals the words out of my mouth when she whispers her response.

"I definitely want to be found."

* * *

Allegra goes to bed after an evening of terrible singing and even worse impersonations, and I make sure she cleans her teeth well enough to make up for the sugared doughnuts we all devoured. She asks Niall to read her a story and I linger in the doorway, listening to his soft, lilting voice as he impersonates all the characters.

When he's finished she tells him about her dancing classes and asks him if he can come to her recital. He kisses the top of her head and promises he will.

I don't know if I've ever seen anything more beautiful than the two people I care about the most falling in love with each other. I'm so fiercely protective of Allegra, it's taken a lot for me to let him break through, but I'm so glad I did. Because standing here, watching the two of them, I can't think of anything I want more than for us to be a family.

Later, after we've put the dishes away and Niall's checked every lock he can find, we climb the narrow, steep stairs to my tiny bedroom, squeezing past the chest of drawers and the wardrobe to get to the bed. A sudden shyness overcomes me, as if the months he's been away have made everything awkward and new. I sit down on the mattress, fingers clutching at the coverlet.

Everything has been leading up to this point. I've been working so hard to settle Allegra down, and then there was my divorce and Niall's show. We've never really talked about what happens next, where we go from here. Never had the luxury to think about "us".

Right now it's all I *can* think about. As he stands at the window, staring out into the inky night, I find myself worrying whether he knows what he's letting himself in for. If he realises how hard it can be, especially when something reminds Allegra of Daisy and she retreats into a stubborn, angry shell.

"What can you see?" I ask him. The muscles beneath his t-shirt ripple as he twists to look at me.

"The moon. It's beautiful. Big and round like a dinner plate. All it needs is a cow jumping over it." He holds his hand out. "Come and look."

I walk to the window and he stands behind me, his arms wrapped around my waist, body pressed against my back. I feel warm and safe. Cocooned. A tiny sigh escapes my lips as I stare out at the night.

He's right, it's beautiful. The moon hangs low in the blue-black sky, a pale yellow disc surrounded by a peppering of stars. It's so pretty it could almost be a painting. I crane my head to look at Niall, about to tell him how perfect it is, but then I see the expression on his face, intense and hot.

His lips meet mine, tongue slip-sliding inside. I curve my body into his, needing to get closer. Threading my fingers in his dark hair, I pull gently, making him gasp. He trails kisses along my jaw, down my neck, nipping at the skin softly as he moves. When I close my eyes, I can feel the need tugging at my stomach as his hand brushes against my breasts, my head falling back onto the cold windowpane. Placing his hands on my hips, he pulls me up until my legs are wrapped around his waist. I have to hold on to his hard biceps, steadying myself as he continues to scrape his teeth across my skin.

It's so overwhelming, this need to be with him, to have this connection. He carries me to the bed—no more than a couple of steps—placing me gently down before climbing on top of me. That's when desperation takes over, urgent fingers fumbling with buttons, awkward hands yanking at shirts.

We're skin on skin, my breasts pressed to his chest, and I take a moment to marvel at how wonderful it feels. It's a sensation I want to keep forever, like a wrinkled and folded snapshot I can carry around in my wallet. When his mouth dips down, capturing a nipple between his soft lips, desire obliterates everything else.

Niall pushes inside me, kissing me soundly to swallow my cries. We take it slowly, hands exploring, lips moving together like we can't bear to be apart. I squeeze my eyes shut as pleasure radiates from me, my body tightening around him like I can't bear to let him go. Then I hear his breath catch in his throat. He freezes above me, and I open my lids to see his own eyes squeezed tightly shut as he tries not to cry out.

It's a moment filled with tiny perfections. The angle of his lip, the bulge of his arm muscles as he tries not to crush me, the ripples in his back as I cling onto him, and the soft curve of his bottom as I slide my hands down.

He drops his face to mine and I feel his breath, warm and fast on my cheek. I turn and we are kissing again, slower this time. The tenderness in his touch squeezes at my heart. As he rolls to his side, pulling me against him, his hand cradles my head to the hard planes of his chest. And I know for sure I'm exactly where I'm meant to be.

It isn't perfect. We aren't angels. But the three of us have something I've been searching for all of my life.

We're a family. And nothing will tear us apart.

The End

Also by Carrie Elks

Halfway Hidden
Fix You

Coming Soon

Breaking Through

About the Author

Carrie Elks lives near London, England and writes contemporary romance with a dash of intrigue. At the age of twenty-one she left college with a political degree, a healthy overdraft and a soon-to-be husband. She loves to travel and meet new people, and had lived in the USA and Switzerland as well as the UK.

An avid networker, she tried to limit her Facebook and Twitter time to stolen moments between writing chapters. When she isn't reading or writing, she can usually be found baking, drinking wine or working out how to combine the two.

www.CarrieElks.com
www.facebook.com/CarrieElksAuthor
www.twitter.com/carrieelks
carrie.elks@mail.com

Acknowledgements

They say writing can be a lonely experience, but I'm so lucky to be surrounded by lovely and talented friends, whose constant feedback and support have been invaluable. I couldn't do this without them.

Firstly, all my love and thanks go to Lucia Valcikova, Mary Whitney and Claire Robinson. You ladies never fail to make me smile, even with gentle criticism. You're a dream team!

To Meire Dias and Flavia Viotti Siquera, your unstinting support is amazing. I'm counting down the days until we can share another bottle of wine. Rio next?

Deb, your kindness in helping with my writing is very much appreciated. You make it look effortless, my friend.

Melanie, my friend, your support is amazing. Thank you for being there.

Caroline, thank you for telling me the difference between Guards and Garda. Not to mention the Christian Brothers!

To Kate, who is always there for the first lines. Thank you. You're my muse, my friend, my everything.

Gemma, I love reading your messages every morning. I'm so glad we're exploring this new world together. Now get back to writing.

To all my friends in *Carrie Elks' Corner*, thank you for your lovely posts, for sharing the word and reading ARCs of the book. I love our little space, and spending time with you.

Emily Nemchick edited and proofed the book, thank you for your kind words and careful reading.

To all my writer, reader and blogger friends, who put a smile on my face every day. Thank you for being there and for making this fun. That damn World Wide Web may be a time-eater, but it's also a life saver, because it allowed me to meet you.

Last, but not least, thank you to my family. The ones who put up with me while I'm squirreling away. You wait patiently for answers that never come, put up with an ever-growing pile of dirty laundry, and still manage to be my biggest supporters. I love you so much. Mum's back in action for a while, get your requests in while you can!